SYMPHONIC STORMS

Book 1: Peace Keepers

Ellyn E. Hugus

iUniverse, Inc.
Bloomington

Symphonic Storms
Book 1: Peace Keepers

Copyright © 2011 Ellyn E. Hugus

This is a work of fiction. All of the characters, names, incidents, organizations, and dialogue in this novel are either the products of the author's imagination or are used fictitiously.

iUniverse books may be ordered through booksellers or by contacting:

iUniverse
1663 Liberty Drive
Bloomington, IN 47403
www.iuniverse.com
1-800-Authors (1-800-288-4677)

Because of the dynamic nature of the Internet, any Web addresses or links contained in this book may have changed since publication and may no longer be valid. The views expressed in this work are solely those of the author and do not necessarily reflect the views of the publisher, and the publisher hereby disclaims any responsibility for them.

Any people depicted in stock imagery provided by Thinkstock are models, and such images are being used for illustrative purposes only.

Certain stock imagery © Thinkstock.

ISBN: 978-1-4620-3334-8 (sc)
ISBN: 978-1-4620-3333-1 (hc)
ISBN: 978-1-4620-3335-5 (e)

Library of Congress Control Number: 2011910679

Printed in the United States of America

iUniverse rev. date: 6/20/2011

For all who have believed in me and have helped me make this dream come true.

PART 1

Changes

Chapter 1 — A Beginning of Sorts

At first it was a voice, whispering softly in my mind as we sat in peaceful tranquility, mind blank. She spoke to us together rather than individually, so I heard her speak all of our names by way of greeting. "Thomas McCarthy, Katarina Contigas, and Lisbeth Moore. A son and two daughters; I am pleased you have found one other." Frozen at the sound, I refused to acknowledge the fear entangled with the overwhelming completeness the words brought. I felt her chuckle softly at our reactions. "I am glad that some things carry over through the ages; you do not know who I am my children, but you have ideas." She paused. "No Thomas you are not loosing your mind; Kaya, you too, are perfectly sane." She paused again.

It was during this pause that I had my first surge of memory. Not a present memory from my then 24 years of life, but memories of a previous lifetime.

"You know who I am child." It was not a question. She knew what I was remembering: my birth.

"Mother Earth?" I voiced mentally my uncertainty of the sensations that filled my mind.

"Yes my daughter. I am your true mother, your first mother: Mother Earth." I could feel her soft smile. "I have come to you at last in this new lifetime. I was worried I might be too late." Her emotion was tangible as she spoke those last words, but she offered no explanations and offered no chance for questions. I simply felt her take a deep breath and appear as a vision in my mind, painted on the black backs of my eyelids.

She embodied all of us. Her hair nearly reached her knees and had no specific shade, seeming rather to consist of every possible natural hair color. It was pinned back with small twigs and leaves were scattered throughout. Her body, like her hair, had no specific type being neither tall nor short, neither willowy nor curvy nor stout. She simply looked strong, like silken steel.

2

This was true of her face as well: eyes a swirling mix of browns, blues and greens, skin perfectly tanned. She wasn't beautiful, but neither was she plain. I realized, as I stared into her face, that I could see in her traces of people I knew - whether it was the nose, the eyes, the mouth, jaw or any other part of her - but I could never manage to pin-point one specific person: in some way or another she was all of them at once.

As this thought crossed my mind I both felt and saw a smile spread across her face. I could not tell if Tom or Kaya had remembered yet; I was unable to hear what they were thinking or remembering, despite being able to hear Mom simultaneously. We were separate from each other, connected only through her. She did not speak, simply smiled at me for a time far shorter than it felt. And so we sat, in our circle, deep in the meditation we began every morning with, feeling the sun on our faces as it shone tentatively through the window - the first weak rays of the dawn.

I didn't think anything of it when I saw her eyes close, a smile still on her face, but it didn't take any of us long to feel the result. At first it was simply a heightening of the senses: I could smell the coffee brewing in our neighbor's kitchen, hear the dog barking for his breakfast down the road, feel the caress of each ray of sunlight. Then I felt my spine become more erect and the base of my skull tingled as if from a sudden surge of electricity.

Something "woke up" inside of me then that I would come to recognize as my life source, or my core-like center of energy. I couldn't control it, couldn't rein it in as I felt it uncurl and lash out to the very tips of my limbs, weave its way into my skin and find its way to the ends of my hair. Subconsciously I knew I was glowing, not that soft angelic yellow light talked about in books and movies, but an earthier bronze-brown light. She opened her eyes, and I became aware that it came from her. My mother. We both smiled.

I opened my eyes a moment later to see Tom and Kaya's opening slowly as well; feeling slightly dazed feeling from what I'd just experienced. The bronze light was gone, though I never doubted its existence. She had left us to absorb her message in our own time. Somehow I knew that this was not the last time we would see or hear from her, and that she wasn't going to help us figure this out any quicker than we were able to. With a stretch after a longer meditation than usual, we began our day, a Saturday, thankfully, that we had succeeded in keeping free from work and other engagements so that we were able proceed at our own pace.

Despite an age difference of three years, Tom and I had been friends since a childhood spent in a small farming town of South-Eastern Wisconsin. Time had only made us closer; so when Tom made the decision to join the Chicago

Police Academy I chose to follow close on his heals to attend college in the city as well. Our hometown had forever questioned the friendship, but until now I hadn't found any reason to do so, let alone actually find it strange. The relationship I'd wondered about was with Kaya. Driven initially by an intense curiosity about the younger woman, whose mutual knack with animals had led to immediate and lengthy conversation, I'd soon introduced her to Tom. It was only a matter of course that we'd made arrangements to move, soon after, into our home in suburban Chicago: neatly designed with a fenced in backyard that had suited our needs perfectly.

Whatever I, or my roommates, felt about our friendships, we'd settled easily into our new neighborhood. Tom's gift with plants made his gardens the envy of the neighbors, who thankfully had appreciated my love of music and repeatedly requested lessons for their children in piano and violin. Then of course there was Kaya's unique style of cooking that made her dishes the talk of the neighborhood on the rare occasions we were invited to various neighborhood functions and parties.

In a word: we were happy. The gardens took shape under Tom's guiding hands; the house did so between Kaya's and my demanding tastes. I claimed a room for my vast collection of music and instruments; Kaya took over, and gave no quarter, in the kitchen. The three of us compromised on gradual decoration of the interior, but collaborated to organize the fitness center that replaced half of the unfinished basement. This morning slid the final puzzle piece into place.

Chapter 2 — Awakening

As I walked into the kitchen that afternoon, hair wet from my post-run shower, I found Kaya in the midst of preparing dinner. We took turns on kitchen duty, like any other family, and tonight it was her turn. We're having fajitas so she was making the tortillas, the vegetables and meat already sliced, diced and awaiting the frying pan in neat piles on the cutting board while she rolled tortilla dough into a round ball between her palms. I stood for a moment in the door, smiling to myself as I watched her work.

My sister Kaya is five-feet-two-inches and of mixed-Hispanic descent. Her hair and eyes are chocolate colored with touches of amber in them, and her body that of an athlete: strong while still appearing feminine. Her mother's family is Mexican and her father's is Chilean; both legally immigrated to the United States decades before, but, in spite of being third generation, she still spoke fluent Spanish. Her grandparents had made sure of that. Over the last year I had come to know that her heritage was one of the most important things to her. Both families were native descendents of their countries with almost no Spanish in their family tree, a point of pride for all of them.

I could hear Tom in the back garden going through and pulling out those weeds that stubbornly resisted the charm of his voice. Tom was Irish-Italian; his mother Italian and his father Irish. His looks seemed to be the perfect mix of the two: no distinguishing features characteristic of either. Everything about him is in the middle really: middle height at about five-feet-nine-inches, medium build with shoulders that weren't too broad, but muscular. He kept his light brown hair cropped short, setting off a slightly boyish face with deep blue-green eyes. Like Kaya he didn't stand out, a fact he liked as he preferred the quiet and his plants when he wasn't at work for the Chicago Police Department.

My curiosity piqued when the calm was suddenly disturbed by a violent string of curses coming from Tom in the backyard. Kaya and I both went to see what had set him off. I had barely reached the back door when I saw what had happened. Apparently the ivy liked what Mom had done during her morning visit. So much so in fact, that it had wrapped itself around Tom until it had left only his head visible. Hence the string of curses still issuing steadily from his as yet uncovered mouth.

Kaya and I struggled not to double over with laughter at the sight. A fact that hardly made Tom any happier.

"Would you mind giving me a hand here? Or are you going to stand there laughing until I'm strangled to death?" He growled at us.

"Well…" Kaya trailed off suggestively, glancing at me as she started to turn away. We both cracked up. Then he growled again, the ivy had started to cover his head, working its way into his short-cropped hair.

"Right! Well… what can we do exactly?" I was suddenly hit with the singularity of the situation. What were we supposed to do? Nothing like this had ever happened to us before. "Ummm…Kaya grab those shears. I don't know if it will listen to us like it usually does Tom." Neither of us had any distinct talent with plants. Kaya did with the herbs, spices, and the other plants she used in cooking, but left the garden to Tom.

Kaya gripped the shears and held them in a threatening position. I saw the ivy pause in covering Tom's face, but it didn't retreat. The shears didn't seem to frighten it much. Finally I took a deep breath and gave it a try. The first thing I could think to do was to beg, "Ivy, you need to leave Tom alone. Please. Go back to your wall."

"We realize you don't want to. That you'd rather stay wrapped around Tom, but we need him back." Kaya chimed in, following my lead. "If you don't let him go, who will take care of you? Certainly not us! We know nothing about you." This seemed to connect as I saw a visible loosening in the Ivy's hold on him, but still not letting go completely.

"Would you please go back to your wall?" I asked, as courteously as if I were speaking to the President, not garden ivy. Then I shifted tactics. "No one makes that wall of the house look as beautiful as you do. What will we do if you don't continue on it?"

"And what will the other plants do, too, if you don't let him go? I'm sure they want him just as much as you do!" There was a further loosening in the ivy, Tom's head was finally free. Kaya began to lower the shears, saying as she did, "We would never hurt you. We just want you to let Tom go, okay?" The ivy let go, dropping in a pool around Tom's feet. Apparently it had actually been afraid we were going to simply cut it to pieces.

Tom let out a huge sigh, finally able to breathe properly again, and looked down at the now sulking ivy. "Thank you. Now why don't I go and get you your favorite fertilizer while you work your way back onto the wall." With that he walked over to the shed in the middle of the wooden fence running along the back of the yard. The Ivy began its slow progress over and up the wall, and Kaya and I returned to the kitchen. This time I joined her in making the tortillas as I both puzzled over what had just happened.

A comfortable silence spread over the house. Each of us lost in our thoughts, puzzling over the events of the morning. Usually there was some music on, courtesy of my own obsession, but somehow the silence held more comfort than sound that evening.

An hour later I went in search of Tom and left Kaya to finish sautéing the meat and vegetables. The sun had begun set in the time since the incident in the garden, so I had to start turning lights on as I made my way through the house. A glance at my wristwatch told me it was 6 o'clock.

I found him right where I thought I would: sprawled on top of the quilt on his twin-size bed, eyes trained on the white ceiling as if he were lost in thought. I stood in the doorframe silently for a moment, not quite ready to bring him back to earth. He noticed me first.

"You going to stand there, or come in and sit down?" The look on his face told me he already knew why I was there.

"Well I was considering it." I joked as I moved into the room, claiming his rolling desk chair for my seat. We sat for a moment in silence; neither of us wanted to be the first to speak.

Finally he went first, "We always knew we were different. Now we know just how different." I had always appreciated the fact that Tom had never been one to talk around a subject.

"Yes. I just can't seem to understand. I feel so confused." I looked up and caught his gaze as I said this. Hoping to explain more with a look than I could with words. He seemed to understand.

"I know what you mean. She… I guess I should call her Mom … she didn't answer as much as create questions. The ivy… I've never had a plant react that way to me before." His gaze returned to the ceiling as he struggled to express himself, lips flapping like a guppy as he searched for the words. I empathized with his lack of words since I'd felt the same all afternoon. After a moment he continued, "It was like it was trying to feed off of me. Like it recognized something in me, and… I have absolutely no idea what that "thing" is. All that I know is that it's only there now because of her; it wasn't there before this morning. Or at least if it's been there it hasn't been this strong before." He looked back at me as he said this last, his expression pleading.

I smiled slightly in sympathy. "I know. I feel it in me, too. Its like she woke something up. Something that was dormant for my whole life, but has always been there." I stopped, still confused and we sat in silence again.

There wasn't a chance to continue the conversation; Kaya was suddenly all but screaming our names, wanting us to get downstairs fast. We didn't hesitate, flying out his bedroom door to see what could possibly be the matter. The answer to that question was seated, or perched rather, on one of the chairs in the backyard. Kaya stood, speechless now that we had answered her previous screams, staring at the red-tailed hawk. Its wing was broken.

We all stood in a trance, incapable of doing anything more than stare at the bird in front of us. Kaya had the door open, seemingly unaware of the fact that she did. I suddenly became aware that Kaya had moved. Shifting herself slowly so that she could step out onto the little brick patio the chairs stood on. Tom and I didn't dare to move, standing almost breathless as we watched our sister walk toward the injured bird.

I couldn't understand the look on her face. She seemed to be focused intently to something, or someone, but I couldn't tell what. She was looking intently at the hawk, which I then realized was perched quite calmly on the chair. Odd behavior for a bird of prey; they were supposed to avoid human contact, not seek it. Kaya crept slowly and steadily towards the hawk; her head cocked as if she were trying to catch something the bird had said, though I couldn't hear anything.

When she reached it she seemed at a loss as to what she should do, continuing to simply stare intently at the bird. The hawk let out a screech, and in the next instant Kaya's hands spread over the top of the outstretched broken wing. It was as if thunder had suddenly peeled through the air; I was suddenly deaf, but hadn't heard anything. The next thing I knew the supposedly injured hawk was flying swiftly away from the house, and Kaya had crumpled, falling as she fainted onto the brick patio.

That was all it took to snap me out of the trance I'd stood in. Tom and I threw ourselves out of the house, racing to reach Kaya where she lay, eerily lifeless. Her cheeks too pale for someone so naturally brown. The next moments were tense as we struggled to bring her back to consciousness.

The first words she spoke confirmed my thoughts. "He called me. I heard him all the way in the kitchen... I thought I was crazy... but then I saw him and..." She looked up at our faces. Tom insisted on carrying her into the living room since her color was returning. I followed in silence. It seemed our sister's talent was going to be healing.

Kaya sat up as soon as Tom set her down so I sat next to her while Tom went to get a glass of water. I looked at her after he'd left the room; searched her face for proof that she was really all right. She met my gaze immediately, her eyes glowing with knowledge. I could almost feel the elation that seemed to have made her speechless. It didn't last long; as soon as Tom walked back into the room she seemed to find her voice again.

"He spoke in my head." She accepted her glass of water. "He sensed my presence, he could feel I was here." She took a sip of water, again lost for words. Then she continued musingly, "He pulled it right out of me. I tried to tell him I didn't know what I could possibly do... then suddenly he was flying away and I blacked out." She looked up at us now with eyes wide and mouth slack as if in awe.

We sat there in silence after that. None of us had any answers, each as confused as the other. It was as Tom had said to me earlier, it was as if our new mother had only created questions and answered none. It had become clear, through what had happened in the last few hours, that she had awoken something within us during her morning visit. But we still had no idea of what that thing could be, or what it was capable of. In the case of Tom and Kaya, it seemed connected to plants and animals; I wondered what it had awoken in me. The one question it did seem to answer was why we had been so drawn to one other, and why we were meant to stay together.

Chapter 3 — Remembrances

We sat in comfortable silence, lost in thought. Kaya jumped up a moment later, exclaiming that she had left dinner on the stove, and rushed to rescue it. The hour or so that followed we spent in the usual bustle around the dinner table. Tom set the table while I got water glasses out of the cupboard and Kaya finished off the meat and vegetables before setting them on the table with the tortillas. We ate in silence; the usual questions about the day suppressed by the fact that the events of the day didn't beg to be discussed.

The after dinner routine went much like the one before dinner. The table was cleared, and Tom rinsed so that I could stack the dishwasher. Finally everything that could be cleaned had been, and we turned the lights off on a spotless kitchen. I caught the glow of the digital clock on the microwave: it read 8:31pm. It was like someone had hit a switch and we were suddenly exhausted; it was a unanimous decision to go to bed. We each took a different route to the stairs, catching lights as we went through the house and up the stairs to bed. It was an early night, even for us.

That night sleep came easier than I had expected. Asleep as soon as my head hit the pillow, I slept deeply and dreamed. The dreams were vivid; the scenes eerily familiar in a way that tugged gently at my subconscious.

They began in a time too long ago to seem real. Seated with several others around a fire in a cave, all could see through the caves entrance was the clean whiteness of snow and the swirls of a blizzard. I held something I couldn't recognize in my hands, but could feel the music it was intended for. The scene shifted: I played a flute in a field of wild horses. I could feel the softness of a doeskin dress against my skin and recognized the look of trust in the eyes of the horses that stood in a herd before me. The scene shifted again before I was able to completely recognize what it meant. This one was less peaceful: the faces of those who surrounded me devoid of hope. I was singing something, and, for all the marks of fear and sadness etched onto their faces, they began to hold more peaceful expressions as they listened.

My dreams continued in that strain: momentary clips, a preview, of what I instinctively knew was really a feature film. Just as I began to grasp this on some level, the dreams changed. This time I knew that I was watching someone who was really alone. It was a young woman, with long red hair and pale skin to match. She wore a simple deep blue dress, the style of which seemed more appropriate for the late nineteenth century than modern day. Then it hit me: it was me, or rather a form of me, in the nineteenth century.

I stood in the middle of a field as a powerful storm raged around me. The wind howled and the rain pelted my skin. Lightning flashed, dangerously close to where I stood, and thunder rolled on the heels of the fading light. I saw my lips move, face tilted into the rain, arms raised as in welcome. A pressure built in the air and I knew instinctively that it was guided by me.

I wasn't prepared for what happened next. On the end of yet another clap of thunder I heard a voice, my own I realized as it sang with the storm. Not simply into it, but with it. Just as I reached this realization I began to hear music, it seemed instrumental but I couldn't distinguish the instruments being played. They seemed like strings, but then I heard drums, and a second later I could have sworn I heard something from the brass section.

The pressure continued to build, but no longer felt like pressure as much as a kind of electric sensation in my toes, my legs, my shoulders and then the rest of my body. Recognition was immediate even in my dream state. It was the same sensation I had felt during our awakening that morning.

At the instant of recognition a particularly loud crack of thunder catapulted me out of the dream and into the present where the storm was no dream. I could still feel the same energy pressure from the dream, more intense in the real world, but now I sat on the edge of my bed, fully awake and alert. What I now recognized as memories filled my mind. Somehow I understood them each in their meaning, and yet I could not explain them if I tried.

I didn't realize until after the fact that I had picked up my violin from its stand and was playing unconsciously; playing along with the music from the storm, the same song that I had sung in my dream of more than a hundred years before.

It was like nothing I had ever experienced before: the feel of the energy, just short of electric, that flowed from inside me like before. This time though it flowed into my violin and the notes I drew from it. The music grew and swelled to a pitch, my hands flying as I played to the tune of the storm. I later realized that I wasn't playing a solo, but rather a part of a greater ensemble. I could both hear and feel the cello and viola among the strings of the storm and the timpani amongst the thunder's many drums. Then there was the brass, trumpets and trombones, in the lighting that crashed throughout.

At last I felt the song dwindle, fading into the distance with the storm as it too passed. I nearly dropped my instrument; my limp fingers barely kept the violin and bow from crashing to the ground. It felt like something was missing, almost as if something had been ripped out of me as I'd played and yet I felt more complete than any other time in my living memory.

A noise from the vicinity of my bedroom door suddenly caught my attention, and I nearly fell over as I turned around. My playing had woken up Tom and Kaya, both of whom stood, staring, in my open doorway.

It was Kaya that broke the silence. "Your talent then, I think we can safely say lies in your music." Nothing more was said about it.

I glanced then at my alarm clock, sitting on the little table near the head of my bed. It read 5:26am. My alarm was due to go off in four minutes. This finally made me move as I reached to turn off the alarm. It wouldn't be necessary since we were all already awake.

As I moved to put away my violin, I noticed that Tom and Kaya were still standing around my door. Something in their body language clued me in, so I gave them an opening: "Anyone for a cup of tea?" The relief was palpable as they nodded their assent. I had a feeling I hadn't been the only one with dreams that night. As we all moved toward the stairs and the kitchen, I wondered to myself what their dreams were like. I also had begun to realize just how our mother had intended us to learn exactly what she meant by being her children.

Chapter 4 — A Kind of Confession

Kaya walked into the kitchen first, switching on the light as she headed toward the hot water kettle on the counter; Tom got out our favorite mugs from a cupboard over the stove. I took a seat at the table and waited for them sit down.

We stared intently into our mugs of steaming tea and listened silently to the rainwater drip from every external surface. Somehow the sound seemed louder than it should be, and I caught myself beginning to distinguish the individual drops as I heard them.

"They were our past lives. Our souls' memories of them, weren't they?" Kaya broke the silence.

"I was a soldier once. And a master gardener." We all smiled a little at this information. It suited his gardener-cop persona perfectly. When he spoke again, he sounded bewildered, his eyes unfocused as if he were lost in thought. "They spoke to me. Not in words, but... that's the best description of it that I could give. They would give me bits of information, pass it through themselves to me kind of in images, but not quite that either." He paused, mouth moving soundlessly as he struggled for the words he wanted. "I... I saved people thanks to them. I..." He trailed off, I guessed for lack of words.

"You do that now, too, you know." I spoke quietly. "Or did you forget that you're a cop as well as a gardener?" I attempted to ease the awkward tension that had filled the room.

"I was a healer." This came from Kaya. "But not just like what happened yesterday afternoon. I mean with herbs, natural medicines and my cooking." Her eyes glowed as she shared this. "In the dreams... it was mostly animals - dogs, cats, horses, some cattle - and they all spoke to me, like the hawk did. But there were people too. Important people, or at least people who seemed

13

important to me." She paused then went on. "I think I saw my husband." Her voice filled those words with implication, full of an unspoken history.

My chest tightened at her words, and I reached out to touch her hand where it gripped the handle of her mug; trying to show the understanding I felt. Their eyes were on me, it was my turn to share. I'd always been the least open of the three of us, so no surprise registered at my not yet having said a word. Instead they just looked at me, expectant.

"I'm…." My dreams seemed so trivial compared to theirs. Finally, I plunged in and said it. "I'm a musician. I bring peace and happiness through my voice and instruments. I can't speak with animals, but I have a kind of influence over them through my music. In a part of the dream I played the flute for the horses and… they were listening, but not to the music itself rather to something held within the notes." I was talking fast now that I'd started. They betrayed nothing in their faces; they knew me too well. "Then I was in the storm. Well not this storm, but one from before, and I was watching myself sing with it, almost like I was in a concert. I could hear the orchestra in the storm, the notes and the different instruments and parts, even distinguish the key it was in." I'd been staring at the table, my voice getting more wound up as I talked faster and faster. My gaze lifted abruptly as I continued to speak, "The next thing I knew I was awake and the storm was real. I could feel it in me, not simply around me. It was like the music was at least a part of me, if not all of me. Then, when it was over… I thought I was going to faint, like Kaya did after the hawk." I felt a bit breathless as I looked at Tom and Kaya.

Unnerved, I picked up my mug and started gulping my tea. It was still hot, scalding my mouth and throat on the way down, but I couldn't feel it. Silence returned to the room, replacing the tension that had been there before.

"So will you be singing to the animals at the clinic tomorrow morning? Or would that be too conspicuous?" The last of the tension evaporated as we all burst out laughing.

While there were still questions we craved answers to, we knew we had some time to find them, or at least that we weren't the ones who could give them. It was now six o'clock and we wanted to start our day. It was a Sunday that none of us worked, but the early morning wasn't unusual; Kaya and I began to pull things out of the refrigerator and rummage in the cupboards for various breakfast items. Tom went to see what damage the storm had done to his garden, watering, for the same reason, being unnecessary.

Routine took over as we progressed through the meal. Our usual mindless banter returned, as we teased each other about various things that had happened the week before and what we expected to in the coming week. Tom did the dishes while Kaya and I went to change into exercise clothes. Sunday was Tom's weight lifting day so he stayed in the house; Kaya and I both stuck headphones in as we stepped out the front door. We never ran together for a myriad of reasons, the most important being the difference in trail preference. I headed for the bike path that wound its way towards the park, Kaya ran deeper into the neighborhood in the direction of the city.

I turned up the volume on my iPod as I settled into a rhythm. My dark-brown hair was pulled back into a ponytail that beat steadily against the back of my neck, in time with the crunching sound of my shoes on the trail. My hair was dark; some people mistook it for black instead of its actual deep brown and my eyes matched. My skin was a contradictory pale cream, the opposite of Kaya's rich brown skin.

Adrenaline surged as I picked up my pace in an attempt to keep pace with the rock pumping out of the headphones, the volume too loud as usual. I could see the trail curve ahead of me into the park. A soft layer of green appeared over everything, and, nearing it, I smiled as I recognized the storm's handiwork in the wet that dripped from everything. It looked, felt and smelled like spring. The cleansed air filled my lungs as I inhaled; the day seemed sharper, clearer. It felt good.

My run took me all the way around the park. It usually took me about forty-five minutes to make the trip. Today it took me less than forty. I stared at my watch when I checked my time. Despite our difference in height - me an average five-foot-seven and her five-foot-two - Kaya had always been the faster runner. It was another reason we didn't run together: we liked to go at our own pace, and it ground on her to have to slow down for me. As I looked at my watch I wondered just how much had changed since yesterday.

When I got back to the house I wasn't surprised to see Kaya already there, but she certainly seemed to be surprised to see me. She knew exactly which route I had taken, and, if her raised eyebrow as she looked at her own watch meant anything, she'd noticed the change as well.

I let her have the shower first, going into the basement to stretch instead. The Country music that Tom listened to seemed to double in volume as I opened the door to the basement. I'd been able to hear it the second I'd stepped into the house. He smiled as I came into his line of sight.

"Wow! That's a little loud isn't it?" I returned the smile as I stretched my quads.

"Hunh? Oh, no… it's the same as usual." He checked the volume on the stereo, a dumbbell in his hand; he'd been doing a triceps exercise when I'd come down. "Want me to turn it down?"

"No. No. Don't worry about it. It doesn't really bother me." I continued to stretch as he went back to his weights.

When I finished stretching, I turned towards the stairs to go take my turn in the shower. I paused on the first step. "Hey Tom?" He looked up. "Meditation tonight? Kind of skipped it this morning, I just realized."

"Oh yeah. I didn't notice either." He made a face. "How about after dinner? And it's your turn to make dinner remember? We don't want to give you an excuse to burn something." He smirked at me from his position on the floor; he was doing his own stretches now.

"Gee… thanks." I rolled my eyes. "I'll run that by Kaya when I get upstairs." I made a show of stomping up the stairs; his amused chuckle mixed with the music. I still wondered why I'd thought it was so loud. It seemed fine now.

I remained pensive as I made my way to the bathroom. Kaya was on her way out of it, wrapped in a towel as she headed for her room. "Hey Kaya!" She turned around, water dripping from the ends of her hair.

"Yeah?"

"Ummm… Tom and I were thinking about meditating after dinner, since we kind of forgot this morning." I paused a second for her answer. "Is that okay?" I asked when she didn't answer.

"Oh yeah, that's totally fine. Wow. I didn't even realize we hadn't meditated this morning. Guess I forgot. What with recent events 'n' all."

"I know what you mean! Right, so after dinner…" I turned then and went to take a shower. I could almost smell myself.

My mood remained pensive as I stood in the shower, felt the heat of the water as it poured over my head and neck. My mind raced as I thought back over the last twenty-four or so hours. The visit, the dreams, the little changes I'd noticed as well as the not so little. I struggled to fit it all together and make sense of what seemed like an unsolvable puzzle. The talents we'd each discovered somehow seemed to be the least of the issues. They made sense; or rather they fit in with what we already knew about ourselves. I had always been insanely musical, Kaya had always had a way with food and making people feel better, and Tom had always been the gardener-cop. That all fit. I just didn't know where the rest of it did.

When I finally stepped out of the shower and reached for a towel from the pile, nothing made any more sense than when I had stepped into it. When I entered the kitchen later to scrounge up some lunch, Tom was still upstairs in the shower, but Kaya sat with a book at the kitchen table. She looked up as I came into the room, her eyes serious. I knew that her thoughts of the last hour probably mirrored my own. She turned back to her book, and I went to find some food. Tom entered the room a few moments later with the same intention as I: food. We made sandwiches and sat at the table with Kaya. Jazz, Bluegrass and Folk music mingled as they played softly from the living room stereo.

Chapter 5 — Answers

The afternoon passed smoothly. Each of us kept ourselves busy with little tasks around the house and various other things that needed to be done by tomorrow. We kept the music on in the background, changing it around between genres but always kept it soft. A little blues, some jazz and classical as well as a little bit of bluegrass; I dug deep in my massive collection of CDs to keep up the variety.

Kaya kept reading her book that she apparently had to know the whole of for class tomorrow. Tom, no surprise, headed in the direction of the garden shed. That left me with my music.

Dinner was uneventful; I managed to scrape something together with some suggestions from Kaya and Tom. We took turns on kitchen duty since Tom and I felt it was unfair to make Kaya cook all the time; even if she did say she didn't mind. Just because she was in culinary school didn't mean it was the only thing she had to, and as a result she had to put up with our cooking a few times a week.

It seemed to take longer than usual to finish the dishes and put the kitchen back in order. At last we turned off the light and moved into the living room to form our circle on the floor.

Despite the anticipation that seemed to build between us, we had next to no trouble sinking into the meditation. The music still played softly, something classical now from the sound of it; it was soothing in the background. Though it wasn't usual to leave the music playing, our minds still emptied as we relaxed into the peaceful routine, despite its possible distraction.

I felt her before I heard her; heard her before I saw her.

"Good evening, children." I felt her smile warmly. "I already know what you have dreamt, what you have experienced since my last visit." She paused for a moment and tension increased slightly as we waited for her to continue.

"Of course I intend to give you some answers Tom. It is why I am here. To explain what you do not already know." I felt her sigh. "Not everything passes through in the memories, but that is the first answer I need to give. Pay close attention to your dreams, both now and in the future. They will be your guide, the only teacher you will have in the use of your gifts."

She looked much the same as she had the previous morning: the hair and eyes the same multi-color and her skin the same perfect brown. The only clear difference that I was able to detect in her was in the color of the dress she wore. This time it was in the Grecian style, a delicate shade of purple. I couldn't quite manage to pin point the more subtle differences.

"I will begin at the beginning." She paused, as if preparing herself. "The very beginning." The look in her eyes seemed like laughter. "There has never been a time when any of you were not human. It is through your souls that you are connected to me, the Earth, and related to each other. Your human lifetimes begin with the existence of humans. You will find that you have memories of times long before the most ancient civilizations began. Your gifts, fundamentally, have not changed; you have simply developed a greater grasp on how to use them to the greatest advantage with each lifetime. This is why your dreams will be so beneficial to you: they are the only way in which you can access whatever you have learned." She paused again, letting us absorb the information.

"When I first visited yesterday, these gifts were dormant. Yes, there have been little things that have slipped through. Tom's abilities with plants being one of the first times so much of a gift has shown itself before I have made myself known." A hint of honest confusion at this fact showed in her voice. "Then there is the very gift that drew you, Kaya and Lis, together when you met. You both have been able to communicate with animals, on some level, from a very early age. I will admit that this is again not the most usual circumstance, but I cannot seem to feel any anger at the situation. All of you have carefully concealed these talents, and they are the reason that you are even together." Her smile widened as she said this last. "Of course there is still more that you must know. I got sidetracked.

"The most important thing you must realize is the fact that you are not immortal. No matter how strong your gift, you are still capable of injury, or more importantly, still capable of being killed." Her smile ended abruptly. "You will find of course that, when it comes to illness, you have a stronger than average immune system. You have the deepest connection with all things natural. Over the millennia this has appeared to give your human bodies greater immunity to its…less pleasant attributes." It was clear she was selecting her words carefully.

After another of her pointed pauses, she continued with her answers.

"There is one final detail you should know about this connection. You might have already discovered that there is a kind of energy that is associated with your talents. I am referring, of course, to what you experience in your dreams. It is not something that would have shown itself before now." She seemed to wait for us each to give some sign in affirmation. Apparently she got it, though I don't recall giving an answer. "I thought as much. It is this energy that is the reason for my being so thrilled at your having already begun to work on meditation. This is not simply the way in which I will be able to communicate with you; it is also the way in which you will learn to concentrate the power of that energy." I felt an incredible sense of wonder as she continued to explain.

"This is the very essence of your connection to me and everything around you. You must use the control you have developed over your mind through meditation in order to develop the same control over your gifts. As you do so you will find that the power concentrates, becomes stronger, and forms a kind of "core" within you. If you do not have that control... the results will be much like those of the last day, only the odds of it betraying you become distinctly higher." Her face looked sad as she spoke these last words. It occurred to me then that this must have been the case at some point in the past. The thought didn't get much further; she continued. "This must be your greatest concern as you become acquainted with what I have just told you. You have always known that you were different. That is truer now than it ever was before. Protect yourselves and each other."

The vision of her in our minds suddenly vanished, but her voice whispered on in our minds. "I leave you now with my love my children. Never forget what I have told you." With these parting words, she seemed to leave us. Then, like an after thought, she spoke again. "Oh! And do not be surprised that your senses are more acute. You will grow used to it." Then we knew she was truly gone.

PART 2

Life Goes On

Chapter 6

The drawer clicked as it slid back into the file cabinet. Humming quietly I turned, manila folder in hand, to walk into the waiting room.

"Hey Lisbeth!" it was the secretary, Cassie.

"Hey Cas! How's the morning going in here?" My attention was on the folder in my hand more than the conversation, but she didn't seem to notice..

"Oh, you know, the usual. Nothing too interesting yet." She smiled.

I returned the smile, gave a little half-wave and walked into the waiting room. Next on my list was a routine visit; some vaccination updates and health check for an aging feline. I recognized the name on the file I checked, about to go through the door to the room beyond. It was a local family; I'd met them when they'd brought the cat in the year before. The cat's name was Emmie, and as I pushed the door open I saw that it was the missus who had brought her in this year, the kids must be in school.

I'd forgotten until that moment that I was still humming quietly to myself, the tune one I'd been working on over the weekend; I'd heard it in a memory dream. I was reminded sharply as I entered the room because everything with four legs or feathers in the waiting room had its eyes trained on me. I was faintly aware of a cat complaining, and a bird squawking, and stopped humming immediately. In the last two years I had gotten fairly good at controlling the need to sing, or in this case humming, while at work. It was clear it had an adverse effect on the animals in the clinic.

"Emmie." I called out the name of the patient, kicking myself silently for the slip up. The woman I'd recognized stood and came towards me, a large calico cat in her arms. It complained, loudly, and I just smiled. "Follow me through here." I directed. "How are you this year? The kids in school today?"

I forced myself to have a conversation with the woman as we walked into an exam room down the hall. The clinic was a fairly large one for a veterinary clinic. I flipped through the folder unnecessarily, my embarrassment almost back under control. I'd already checked what she was due for today.

"Right. Why don't we put Emmie on the exam table and I'll take a look." I put the folder down on the counter near the sink in the room, and reached to put on the mandatory gloves.

The check up proceeded after that, as any routine check should. I managed to stop myself from humming and the cat turned out to be fit as a fiddle. I was wrapping it up with the vaccination boosters when I heard raised voices somewhere towards the back of the clinic.

"I wonder what that could be?" I didn't fake the disinterest in my voice as I continued to give Emmie the shots she protested keenly.

I'd just finished the last one when someone knocked on the exam room door. This finally got my attention, and I went to get the door, pulling off my gloves as I went since I had finished the last shot.

"What's going on?" I asked as I opened the door. My surprise grew when I saw Dr. Dan Halle, my boss, standing in front of me with a slightly panicked look on his face. "What!? What's happened?" His anxiety was catching.

"We just got an emergency call from the track. They're insisting on having us send over Dr. Fournier." We walked quickly down the hall towards the large animal section of the building.

"Cas! Have someone finish up with the cat in exam room four for me, please." I yelled through the door to the office, barely remembering what I'd just been doing.

"No problem Lis! She all set with everything?" Cassie called back to me.

"Yup! She's all done." I called over my shoulder. I couldn't help but feel that something was really wrong; the sensation built as my anxiety increased.

Dr. Roman Fournier was the newest addition to the clinic staff, an Equine Specialist, who'd come from somewhere on the East Coast, or maybe it was studied there, I couldn't remember. As we reached the large animal section of the clinic in the back of the building, I stopped trying to remember. He was hanging up the phone as we walked into the room, hastily scribbling notes on a pad of paper as he turned towards us.

"Roman, this is Lisbeth Moore. Lisbeth, this is Dr. Roman Fournier. I know you've never worked with her before, but I think she'll be the best person to take with you this time. She's got a knack for calming them down." I blushed at the real reason behind the reputation I'd gotten since Mom's first visits almost two years ago.

"I'll take your word on it Dan. Right now I just want to get moving. Those stallions sound like they're in pretty rough shape." His eyes were trained on my boss as he spoke.

"Right. Lis?" This came from Dr. Halle.

"Yes."

"I'll let Roman explain the situation to you on the way. I know you haven't gone on many track calls since you've been here, but I'm sure you'll do fine." With this he nodded to the other man and turned to go back into the clinic. I just looked at Roman, waiting for directions.

"Right." He finally said, "Let's get going." He spun and walked swiftly to and out the door to the truck. I suddenly realized how tall he was as I hurried to catch up. Apparently everything we would need was already in the back of the truck, so I just opened the passenger side door and got in.

We sat in silence as he started the truck and pulled out of the parking lot onto the street. The anxiety I had felt in the clinic didn't go away as we drove. Instead it seemed to get worse as we continued in silence, his fingers drumming on the steering wheel. I hesitated to ask if I could turn on some music. In the silence I finally started to hum to myself again as I stared out the window, waiting for him to tell me what I'd been pulled into.

Finally he cleared his throat. "We're headed for the track. Specifically the Kennedy's stables. You ever been there?" He looked at me for the first time.

"Yeah. It's been more than a year since the last time though." I was suddenly unsure of myself. "They rent a part of the track stalls for the racing season every year. I think. Their home base is somewhere further south."

"Yeah that's right." He seemed a little relieved. I could tell now that he'd been a little doubtful of Dr. Halle's confidence in me; considering I'd been in the small animal clinic without exception since before he'd started there.

We were turning down the road onto the track grounds as we spoke.

"Yeah, so basically there's been a stallion fight in their barn. Apparently the handlers weren't quite doing their job and two younger stallions managed to get within kicking distance of one of their proven studs." He paused to check in at the gate before he continued. "Dan's the one who took the call, but I talked to them too before they hung up. The younger stallions are in the roughest shape."

"The stud knew where to aim, I guess, hunh?" I wanted to show that I understood the situation. It had stung more than I thought to realize he didn't quite trust me.

"Yeah, that'd be about right." I heard rather than saw the half-smile. "But those colts got some good ones in on him too apparently. They said he's got the least injuries, but they're not sure if they're not the worst ones." He paused. We'd reached our destination so we now sat in an idle truck. He was reaching for his seatbelt and the door handle when he added, "They still didn't have them separated when they called."

It hit me; that was why my boss had sent me along. Of all the techs at the clinic, I was the one with the most experience breaking up fights, however few and far between they were, in the waiting room. I forced myself out of the car as I processed this new information.

I was still quiet, operating in a kind of daze, as I gathered the basic gear we would need; we didn't need to ask directions, we could hear the stallion screams so we just followed them. I was humming to myself again.

There were two of the four stallions we had been told about still fighting in the open-air aisle between the barns. I could see the other two had finally been wrangled away from the fighting; each held by two grooms. I assumed out of fear they would only do more harm if put in their stalls.

The two stallions that still fought screamed viciously and bled profusely from multiple wounds. I immediately understood the source of the anxiety I'd felt since Dr. Halle had pulled me out of the exam room. I followed quietly behind Roman as we approached the scene. A few grooms still tried, futilely, to separate the remaining stallions, but they couldn't get close enough. Each time they thought they were, one of the horses struck out all over again.

"Dr. Fournier, you're here!" I could almost feel the relief behind the words. They came from an average looking man who stood off to the side, anxiously watching the horses. Judging from the quality of the suit he wore, I figured he must be the owner.

"Yes, Mr. Kennedy." His eyes were on the horses, not the man in front of him as he answered. I followed his lead.

"We've barely managed to separate two of the younger stallions. They're over there." He gestured nervously towards the two horses I had noted earlier. "We're still trying to separate those two." He was interrupted by a fresh scream. He winced. "I'm sure you can see that for yourselves." He paused, clearly unsure of what to do. I doubted he was around his horses very often. Noting the suit again, I was confident that that was a safe assumption.

"Right. Why don't I go take a look at the two you've gotten separated. I don't want them to lose any more blood than we can help." He started towards them as he spoke. I followed. "Lisbeth." I paused at the sound of my name.

"Yes?" I asked when he didn't continue.

"Uh." He looked unsure of how to say what he wanted. I waited. Then he came up close to me, as if he didn't want the owner to hear what he wanted to say. "Dan said you're good with animals in a fight. I can start working on the younger two by myself without a problem. The grooms will be able to help me. Why don't you see what you can do with those two?" I met his gaze and fidgeted.

"Not a problem. You should take this though." I smiled and handed him the things in my hands. "I'm going to need both hands." He nodded, seeming doubtful, and turned to follow the owner again. I returned to the fighting stallions, and took a deep breath.

I felt it immediately; my core of energy practically leapt out of my body towards the fighting horses. I had to act fast to rein it in, a little stunned by the reaction. Usually it was Kaya who had such strong reactions to animals. I focused on my breathing, counting a rhythm in my head to keep it consistent, then began to hum the same melody I'd had stuck in my head all day and move slowly in the direction of the horses.

I could see the shock written on the grooms' faces at the sudden reaction from the two animals. The screaming stopped abruptly when I was only a couple yards from them both, but the grooms still couldn't get close enough; they were still throwing a few kicks, unwilling to stop just yet. I increased my volume the slightest bit; my influence seemed slightly stronger when louder, and moved closer still.

The grooms managed to dodge in just as I heard thunder boom in the distance. I tensed, barely maintaining the quiet hum. Thankfully the grooms managed to get a grip on them and separate them before they realized I'd backed off. As they were being led away, I prayed the thunder had been my imagination. Either that or something only my oversensitive ears had picked up.

The sudden sensation that I was being watched closely made me look up. It was Roman; he stood motionless next to one of the younger stallions. He was staring at me, paused in the act of sedating the animal next to him. I didn't drop my gaze, but instead walked towards him. He seemed to realize that he was staring because he dropped his gaze, returning his attention to the syringe of sedative in his hand.

I moved to copy him when I got to our equipment. Although it had been a long time since I'd had to sedate an animal this large, I still remembered the dosages. Selecting a syringe, needle and bottle of sedative I moved to tranquilize the animals I'd just helped separate. I pretended not to notice the amount of attention the grooms were giving me with their looks as I proceeded to help Roman treat the four thoroughly sedated horses.

It took longer than we had expected. Each horse had received more than its share of violent contact from the other three, and there wasn't one among them that wasn't in need of stitches. The only good thing about the situation was that none of them had managed to break a leg or inflict any other lasting damage. We worked in relative silence, limiting our words to requests for a needle or what ever other tools we needed. The grooms helped as much as they were able, bringing clean water and dumping the buckets of bloody water when they got too dirty to use any more.

It had been almost two hours when I heard the thunder again and this time I knew I wasn't imagining it. I tried to hide my grimace and continue to work; storms were my major weakness when it came to my gift. Though my own connection to the earth chose to show itself mostly in my music, there was something about storms that seemed to make it incredibly difficult to maintain control over the core of energy inside me. I hoped fiercely that this one would hold off at least until we were in the truck again, but judging from how the wind was beginning to pick up, I didn't think my wish would be granted this time.

We'd reached the fourth horse when I heard a third peal of thunder, even closer this time, and started to get nervous. I didn't want to freeze up while I was working, it would be too embarrassing, not to mention difficult to explain. I focused on my breathing, hoping that I didn't look as nervous as I felt.

The fourth was the older stud, and he was in rough shape. Out of the fight, it was clear that the adrenaline involved and amount of blood loss had drained him. He stood calmly outside his stall, the sedation having taken full effect on him as well. Everyone still seemed anxious that he might react because there were at least four grooms hovering, even after he'd remained calm and sedated for the last two hours.

We continued to work in silence, trying to be quick since I was no longer the only one aware of the approaching storm. Until that point I had been pretty successful in hiding my nerves, but as the wind began to intensify and a few raindrops splashed across the dry dirt in the aisle, my control began to slip.

"Hey are you okay?" My head jerked up at the question, caught off guard after the hours of quiet.

"Yeah. I'm fine. Why?" I realized I'd answered a little too quickly when doubt flashed across Roman's face. I tried to relax a little bit. "Really, I'm fine. Maybe a little tired…" I shrugged instead of trying to say more.

"You just look a little tense is all." He turned back to sewing up the gash on the stallion's shoulder. I figured he'd given up on the subject, so I refocused on my breathing. The energy in my body fought against my control as the wind continued to pick up.

He continued to work methodically over the stallion's body, having started at the front he moved on from the shoulder wound to run his hands and a clean wet sponge over the near side of his barrel. We'd already covered the other side. Bloody water dripped onto the ground, but I didn't really notice. My attention was on my breathing and not the quickly approaching storm.

"Seriously, are you sure you're okay?" I almost jumped. Apparently I was wrong, he hadn't given up the subject. "You're breathing kind of funny, and you haven't been answering me. Can you hand me a fresh needle and more thread?"

"I'm fine really." I answered as I moved to get him what he'd asked for.

"Then why don't I believe you?" He was staring at me so intently; I could feel it on my face. Finally I met his gaze, and found myself staring into a pair of beautiful chocolate colored eyes. The worry that was there disconcerted me, but it did make me forget about the storm.

"I don't know." My voice sounded a little odd to my ears when I finally answered. "I guess you just don't trust me." I handed him the threaded needle, hoping to distract him. It didn't work.

"Your hands are shaking now." I looked at the hand holding out the needle and thread. Damn, they were. I sighed, fighting down the near panic that was starting to bubble up in my chest.

"I'm fine." I ground out between my now gritted teeth. "Would you just take it and finish taking care of the horse so we can get going?" He seemed a little surprised by the tone of my answer. He also seemed to realize he'd touched a nerve though, and did as I asked. I returned to my breathing, more difficult now that the rain was starting to fall harder.

The rest of the visit somehow went without further incident. We finished treating the four stallions, leaving the owner and trainer with positive outlooks for full recoveries. They had been lucky that none of them had lost as much blood as initially thought. None of the wounds had been deep enough for that. At length Roman ended his discussion with the trainer by informing him that they could expect his bill in the mail and that he would plan to come and check on their progress in a few days.

We were both safely in the truck just as the floodgates opened. The rain blew at a slant as it poured onto the ground and everything on it. I could barely make out the various grooms and other workers as they ran for cover from the torrential wet.

I barely registered that he had started the truck. Lost in the feeling of the storm that surrounded us now on all sides, and for me inside as well, I saw the lightning this time before I heard the thunder. They were almost on top of each other; the storm was moving faster than I'd thought.

Trumpets blared with the next flash of lighting and the timpani came rolling in directly after. The string instruments were in unison as they vibrated on the same note with an intensity equal to the winds they played within. I didn't recognize the melody this time, but felt it bubble up in my chest.

Suddenly I felt hands shaking me, a voice repeating my name in the distance and I was quickly jerked out of the storm into the truck. My ears rang slightly as I fought to reorient myself, eyes flying somewhat frantically around the truck in an effort to remind myself where I was. At some point in doing this my eyes locked on his, and held. It sank in fast then where I was: In the truck with Dr. Roman Fournier. I realized my mouth was hanging open and as embarrassment started to heat my face I snapped it closed, jerking my gaze away from his in the same moment.

The rain still poured down on the truck; I realized he'd pulled over. The truck idled on a shoulder of the highway almost back to the clinic.

Silence was thick in the truck. I probably could have sliced through it with a knife if I'd wanted to. It pressed down heavily on me as I waited anxiously for his reaction.

"What were you singing?" I groaned inwardly. Shit. I'd actually started singing? I didn't answer him right away, but I could tell he wasn't going to give up. His eyes were burning into my face as I stared out the window into the rain. I heard more thunder thankfully further in the distance this time. The storm really had moved fast; probably the reason it had caught me so off guard.

"Was I singing? I didn't realize." I tried to sound nonchalant, but he didn't seem fooled.

"I didn't recognize the melody. You..." I could tell he wasn't quite sure how to proceed. I wondered if he thought I was crazy. I laughed to myself at the thought. "You weren't singing in any language I could understand, but it was... beautiful." I finally looked up at him; shock filtered through my expression. It wasn't what I'd expected. "You seemed... I don't know, like you were in a trance. I couldn't get your attention the whole time I've been driving and..." He took a deep breath. "I got a little worried is all." His voice was kind of gruff as he said those last words. I smiled despite myself.

"I'm fine." I was still smiling. "I'm a little... sensitive you could say, to storms. They don't usually catch me quite that off guard. I'm usually pretty good at handling them." I could tell by his facial expression that he didn't quite buy my story. We'd been able to tell that the storm was coming the entire time we had been working. I decided not to dig myself any deeper. "I'm sorry I scared you. We should probably get going, they'll be wondering if we got washed away with the rain." I tried to laugh lightly when I spoke, but it stuck in my throat. The look in his eyes had me worried.

I was grateful when he didn't question me any more. His expression suggested he wanted to, but instead he started the truck and pulled back out onto the highway. We arrived back at the clinic without further incident. It wasn't until Roman turned off the truck that I noticed that my stomach was painfully empty - I hadn't had time for breakfast that morning and now we'd missed lunch - it was almost four o'clock.

We walked into the clinic the way we had gone out, not surprised to find it empty. This side of the clinic didn't see nearly as much use as the small animal section. We hadn't been in the building for more than a couple of minutes though when Dr. Halle came towards us. I guessed he had heard us drive up, though how I wasn't sure since the rain was just as heavy here as it had been at the track, and the roof here was metal.

"Roman! How did it go? Was it as bad as they thought?" I couldn't quite read his face but his voice was full of appropriate concern.

"Not even close. A lot of blood and plenty of stitches, but nothing broken and nothing that will cause lasting damage. They were more worried than was necessary."

The two men weren't paying me any attention, so when my stomach growled again, I decided to leave them to discuss the visit. Relieved that they didn't notice I'd left, I all but flew down the hall towards the office. I wanted my lunch.

"Hey! You're back!" Cassie almost shouted when I stepped through the office door. She was sitting in her usual place at the front desk, her chair swiveled around so she could talk to me.

I smiled and walked to where I usually stashed my lunch. "Yup. I survived. Did you guys manage here without me?" I teased.

Cassie just rolled her eyes. "Of course we did. How were things at the track? Dr. Halle said it sounded pretty bad."

"Well there was certainly more than enough blood. They were still fighting when we got there –"

"So that's why they wanted you to go." Cassie interrupted.

"I hardly think a knack for breaking up dogs in the waiting room is a recommendation for breaking up a stallion fight." I attempted a meaningful look; it didn't work. "Anyway, no it wasn't that bad. It just took us forever to go over all four and stitch them back together." I grabbed my lunch bag and a chair. My stomach growled again. "Nothing too serious, thank goodness."

"Oh. Well that's good news."

I waited for her to say more. When she didn't I turned to my lunch, intent on eating it before I had to get back to work in the clinic. I'd noticed that the pile of folders was still pretty high next to Cassie's computer. We probably still had a full afternoon schedule to wade through.

Cassie was still watching me from the corner of her eye as I continued to eat. I was on the verge of telling her to just spit it out when Meghan walked in, another tech. Tucked in the back of the room, out of sight of the front desk, she didn't see me right away. Grateful, I ate a little faster, knowing that she, like Cassie, would have questions. It wasn't exactly the most normal thing around here for a small animal tech to get sent out on a large animal emergency call.

"Yikes! Looks like someone got a little messy on that call." She'd seen me.

"Hey Meg." I replied, stuffing the rest of my sandwich into my mouth and chewing fast as I cleaned up the rest of my lunch.

"So I guess it was as messy as Dan said, hunh?" She'd come to stand over by me now, a file folder in her hand.

I swallowed. "That depends, what did he tell you?" I answered, tossing my now empty paper sack into the bin as I did so.

"He said Dr. Roman got called out to the track, Kennedy's stabling I think." She shifted her weight onto one leg, cocking her hip like she was settling in; I fought the urge to sigh; prepar myself for the questions. "He said they'd called about a stallion fight, between three of their youngsters and a breeding stud. Made it sound like they were really kicking the shit out of each other, and judging from the way you look at the moment, I'd guess those kicks were well placed and brutal." She bobbed her head in my direction, and I glanced down.

"Ah! What the hell!" I shot out of my chair. How had I not noticed what I looked like? I looked down at the chair: clean. Thank God.

"What, didn't you realize the state of your coveralls?" Meg asked, laughing. "You must've been wicked hungry, hunh? To forget about that." She nodded her head at my clothes again.

It took me a minute to answer her. I knew exactly why I hadn't remembered the condition of my clothes, and it had nothing to do with my hunger. "I guess. Wow I'm a mess!" I grimaced, as I looked more closely at myself. "Ugh. This is awful."

"I'll say! But hey, since you're back let's hear it." I looked up, not understanding the question. She didn't seem to notice, still talking. "How was it working with the new Doc?"

"Hunh? It was fine. Nothing special, why?" I tried to figure out where she was going with this, but got nowhere.

"Oh no reason. We were all just wondering. I mean he is a large animal vet and we all work in the small animal clinic, so...." She looked at me as if this explained everything. I still felt like I'd missed something. It wasn't a pleasant feeling.

Meg was struggling to answer my confused look, but Cassie beat her to it, taking over her friend's gape mouthed expression. "Lis are you really going to tell us that you really haven't noticed Dr. Gorgeous in the like six months that he's been here?" She looked just as absurdly offended as Meg, but for some reason I still didn't get it.

Then it clicked, and I felt like a world-class fool. " Whoa! Whoa, whoa, whoa! What – Wait… what?" The words stumbled out of my mouth as I fought for something to say that wouldn't sound totally idiotic. I wasn't very successful.

"You really didn't notice him, did you?" That came from Meg.

"No. I didn't." I could feel my face heat up.

They exchanged a look, neither of them saying a word. I just stood there, waiting for them to say something. Finally I took a huge breath and went for it; the situation couldn't get much worse, or so I hoped.

"Umm… Okay so I feel like I've missed something here. Was I supposed to notice this Dr. Fournier before? I mean, its not like we haven't had new vets here before, and we get good looking men in all the time with their pets and stuff. What's so special about this one?" As soon as the words were out of my mouth I snapped it shut. Two pairs of incredulous eyes stared back at me, and I was suddenly reminded of a pair of chocolate eyes locked on mine. I swallowed slowly. "Oh. Never mind, I know now." His eyes. "His eyes."

"Welcome back to humanity, Lis." Meg's tone was dry and I was reminded with that comment why we usually didn't get along. "I was beginning to think you really were a saint." I ignored that last comment, looking, instead, at Cassie.

She was laughing. "Oh Lis, you're too funny. What it must be like to operate with those blinders on!" She kept laughing, and I found myself smiling at her because of it.

"Yeah, I guess I usually do have tunnel vision." I admitted grudgingly. I was still feeling ridiculous and my face still felt a bit warm.

My comment had Meg snorting. "Only some of the time? Man sometimes I wonder if you'd see an archangel if he were in the room, let alone some hot guy with a sick pet." This just made Cassie laugh harder.

"Excuse me?" The voice came from the other side of front desk, and their laughter was abruptly cut off. "I've been waiting for a while, so I thought I would check to see what the hold up was?"

"I'm so sorry! I'll be right there." With that Meg vanished from the room, leaving me alone with Cassie. Neither of us said anything, I could tell she was fighting the urge to start laughing. Her lips were twisted with effort into an awkward smile.

"Right. I'm going to go change, I think." I said finally and headed out the door. Well at least someone had found some entertainment in that.

Chapter 7

I could hear Kaya on the phone, despite the distance, the moment I stepped through the door into the house. The heightened senses that the three of us now shared had proven the more difficult thing to get used to of all the changes in our lives in the last two years. Now it just made me smile; Kaya was jabbering away in Spanish in the kitchen, on the other side of the house. It sounded like she was filling someone in her family, her mother I guessed, in on recent events at the restaurant she worked at now. She had graduated from culinary school that spring.

My keys hung on their designated hook and my shoes ditched by the door, I walked slowly to join her in the kitchen. The rest of the day had gone almost too smoothly. No emergencies, and, thanks to Meg, no more inquisition rounds. She and Cassie had managed to field the questions from the other techs; something I thought they enjoyed far more than was really necessary. I shook my head at the memory as I walked into the kitchen. Kaya just smiled in my direction, never breaking from her steady stream of Spanish.

Since she was busy, I went to see what Tom was up to. I spotted him as soon as I stepped onto the brick patio; bent over the new vegetable patch in the back right corner of the yard, methodically thinning something or other. I had proven rather hopeless when it came to the gardens, despite Tom's best efforts to change that fact. Instead I did the one thing I could do well: admire.

In the past two years, the garden had all but exploded with life. The incident with the ivy that first day had been the most dramatic incident thus far, but while the rest of the plants were less forward about their reaction to Tom, their reactions in other ways were certainly no less obvious. Nearly every shade imaginable of the color green was visible in a single glance at our backyard. Then there were the roses that grew up the sides of the shed that granted vivid splashes of red and pink to the picture. It was the same with the marigolds, petunias, and various other flowering plants that he'd planted at strategic points throughout.

I took a deep breath, smiling as I exhaled. "Mmm… I can almost taste those roses today, Tom." He laughed, having finished with the vegetables he walked towards me, basket in hand.

"The rain always makes the air thicker, and the scent stronger." He gave me a one armed hug, grinning. "You should know that by now. That was one hell of a storm we got today, too. I don't think I'll be watering back here much the rest of the week."

"Haha! Yeah, I know what you mean. I got pulled out of the clinic to tag along on an emergency call." I sighed, recalling the day. "We got caught in it just as we were finishing up and had to drive back to the clinic in it." I tried to laugh at the memory. "It caught me a little off guard. I wasn't as on top of the weather report as usual…" I anticipated the question I could read on his face. Both he and Kaya knew how sensitive I could be to storms. There had been more repeats of my first night than I would have liked and I wasn't the only one who worried about it.

"What happened?" Leave it to Tom to ask me straight out.

"I managed fine until I got back in the truck…" I paused, unsure. "Apparently I went into a kind of trance. I remember the music, in the storm you know? Apparently I started to sing though." I winced at that detail.

"Awkward moment?"

"You could say that. I was with the new large animal vet, Roman Fournier."

"Ah." He looked confused. "Why were you sent out on a large animal emergency call? You've been in the small animal clinic for ages now."

Only Tom would ask the question I didn't know the answer to. "I have no idea. Cassie figured it was because of my reputation from breaking up the dog fights that happen sometimes in the waiting area." I pulled a face. Tom just laughed. "I know, right!"

"What do dog fights have to do with an emergency call?"

"It was a stallion fight – massive one – out at the track. Four stallions finagled their way loose and tore into each other. Made a bloody mess of themselves too!"

"Oh! That makes a little more sense, you were quite good with the horses when you used to go out before, but didn't they have it sorted by the time they called and stuff?"

"No. They didn't. There were still two of them fighting when we got there."

"Oh." He said slowly, comprehension dawning.

"Yeah." I copied his tone. "Talk about a little awkward. Apparently I haven't been quite as careful at work as I thought." Something clicked into place, just a little. "I think Dr. Halle has noticed something; probably my humming to myself? Something in the way Dr. Fournier asked me to help break them up…" I trailed off, suddenly feeling uncomfortable. I hadn't allowed myself to think about that as I'd finished up my day in the clinic, and talking about it now was forcing details of the day on my attention.

"Hmmm." He didn't say anything else for a while.

Moments later a sudden movement in the corner of my eye caught my attention, and I turned to see a badger limping towards us.

"Looks like Kaya's got a new patient." Tom said, shifting his basket around.

"Yup. I think I'm going to go and tell her about him. Why don't you finish up out here and come on in? Then we can get Kaya to tell us what all that Spanish is about, and figure out dinner." I smiled. I knew he wasn't going to let me get off quite that easy, he had more to say about what had happened this morning.

He smiled, too. "Sure. Sounds good. I'll be inside in a bit, just want to check a couple more things."

When I got back to the kitchen, Kaya was off the phone and pulling her kit out from on top of the refrigerator. It looked like I didn't have to tell her about the patient, she'd already heard him calling.

"Is he outside?" Yup, she already knew.

"Yeah, I just saw him limping towards the patio. Looked like he done something to his paw."

"Yeah, he's saying it got caught in a trap somewhere. Not in the neighborhood though." She added, anticipating my unspoken question. Kaya had had a steady stream of visitors of all shapes and sizes ever since her first visit from the hawk with the broken wing. She'd only had a handful of fainting spells since then, and all of them had been when either Tom or I were home; she had fallen into her role as a healer almost as naturally as breathing. At first it had made me jealous, that she had developed control of her gift so quickly whereas I still struggled with my own. I wasn't so much any more, but today I could feel it prickling.

"I thought that storm was going to cause problems." She stopped moving for a moment to look intently at my face. "I'm going to go take care of this guy, but then I want to hear about it. I caught a few pieces of what you were telling Tom."

"Thanks." I didn't have to say anything else. Although Kaya was younger than I by almost four years, a fact that should have meant my being in the mother role, she had always been the steadier, more mature of the two of us. I flipped on the hot water kettle and went to take down mugs for tea. Habit had me taking down three instead of just one; if I was having some they would want a cup too.

I stood, waiting for the water to boil, staring into space and soaking up the comfortable calm of the house, trying not to think about my day anymore. I heard Tom washing up in the sink by the backdoor; Kaya was still in the yard with the badger. I couldn't hear anything being said, she didn't talk to her patients out loud, but I could feel her working. I let out a relaxed sigh as I poured the boiling water over the tea bags in each mug and added various sugar cubes or honey as we each preferred. I heard Tom walk into the kitchen as I finished up. I handed him his mug as he set a small basket of vegetables on the counter next to the sink. He was on dinner duty tonight, I remembered as I glanced momentarily at the contents of the basket.

"Thanks." He took the steaming mug in his freshly scrubbed hands. I just smiled and reached slowly for my own. I would leave Kaya's to steep while she worked.

For a moment I just stood, inhaling the steam from my tea. "I'm going downstairs for a while, okay?" I looked up from my tea to his face.

"Ummm… okay… Call you when dinner's ready?" His face looked concerned, though we both knew what I was going to do.

"Yeah… Sure." I answered as I left the kitchen, walking slowly, still inhaling the steam from my tea as I headed towards the door to the basement.

As I walked I began to let a part of my day come into the front of my mind. The music from the storm had been deeply impressed on my memory; I began to hum the melody of it as I walked down the stairs into the basement. When I reached the bottom I turned to the right, going through another door. On my left was our gym set-up, but I didn't even glance in that direction. Instead I went through the door on my right, finally taking a sip from the mug in my hands as I did so.

When the three of us moved into this house three years ago my music had already been an important part of my life, having played piano and violin since my childhood; it had been my own personal niche in my family. The various posters and other odds and ends related to music now covered the walls of the room I entered, taking the place of paint or wallpaper. More of my ever-growing collection of CD's took up one wall, neatly arranged on shelves my dad had built me. Next to them, on the same wall, was my more recently begun collection of vinyl albums and a small box of cassette tapes, music I wanted but couldn't get in either of the other forms.

Walking into the room none of this grabbed my attention like it sometimes did; I was too focused on the melody playing in my head. I set the mug of tea on a coaster next to the piano that stood in the middle of the room. A baby grand, my college graduation present from my parents and the only possession

I cared for in the least, next to my violin. The coaster supporting my mug stood on top of a set of filing cabinets that stood along the wall closest to the piano. I didn't bother opening any of the drawers, what I needed was already out on the piano: blank staff paper and a pencil.

Still lost in the melody and beginning to recall some of the harmony of the music in the storm, I pulled out the piano bench and sat down in a smooth motion. As soon as I was sitting, my hands reached out reflexively to touch the keys, playing a few chords to refamiliarize myself with the feel of them. I hadn't played in a couple of days.

The next two hours were a blur after that. I played, the melody flowing from me to my fingers as they danced across the keys, and I wrote, the pencil flying in my hurry to get it down on paper. At some point I had flipped on my recording device where it sat on top of the body of the piano, recording the piece when I'd finally finished putting the pieces together.

It was a gentle knock on the door that finally pulled me out of the music. I twisted myself around on the seat to look behind me at the door, keeping my hands on the keys unconsciously. It was Tom; he stood in the door with a damp dishtowel in his hands.

"Sorry. Dinner's all set, we're just waitin' on you." He spoke calmly, but I could see on his face the effect my music was having on him. He was smiling a soft, understated smile. I returned it.

"I'll be right up." Standing to follow him upstairs as I picked up my now cold mug of tea.

"That's the music from the storm this afternoon." It wasn't a question. We were at the top of the stairs now.

"Yes."

As we moved towards the kitchen I could smell the food, my mouth watering in response. Over the last two years Tom and I had done some catching up with Kaya in the cooking department. Thanks to the more acute senses, particularly that of taste, neither he nor I were able to tolerate our sometimes-burnt attempts. The more accurate sense of smell had also come in handy and between the two we had both become far more adept in the kitchen. It was something that we knew made Kaya much happier about letting us take turns at dinner duty.

As I walked into the kitchen now I could see that the vegetables he had brought in earlier had been turned into a brightly colored salad; he had also roasted some of them and they were now plated with the steaks he had done on the grill. The scent of the spices of the marinade filled the air. I could pick out the smell of roasted sweet peppers mixed in with the tangier smell of the BBQ sauce.

"Mmm." I made appreciative noises, becoming aware of just how hungry I was; my late lunch had worn off hours ago.

Tom laughed as we each took our usual seats at the table, and I felt the atmosphere of the room relax as we settled into the mealtime routine. Someone had put on some quiet music that now filled the room around our usual chatter about the day. I avoided talking about the more important part of my own. I didn't feel the need to bring it up again. So instead we teased Tom about various details from the station, and Kaya filled us in on the day's gossip from the restaurant.

As I ate I relaxed, the music that had been pouring through me only moments before finally ebbing away. It did that, came on so strong that I couldn't hold it in and then, as soon as I had gotten it down on paper, it just left, as if it's purpose was done; it had been recorded and remembered. I sighed as I thought about it for a moment. It made my gift the most difficult, of all ours, to control and it was that fact that had been bothering me from the beginning.

I grabbed a new file from the pile and checked the name as I walked out to the waiting room. I didn't stop to talk to Cassie, and thankfully she was too busy with someone at her desk to speak to me either.

The day had been busy, but uneventful; consisting mostly of routine check-ups and a few minor injuries. As I walked to one of the four exam rooms I chatted inanely with the owner of the boarder collie whose name was on the file I held. They were new to the area, and it was their first visit to the clinic.

"Alright, Jet, let's get you up here." I muttered to the dog as I moved to lift him onto the table. He squirmed a little as I lifted him, caught by surprise. "There you go. That's not so bad now is it?" I muttered softly to him as I set him on the table.

The owner didn't hover, but sat in the chair provided in the corner as I began to run my hands over the dog, doing a mental check. Eyes were clear. Legs: nothing at odd angles. Back and hips: nothing sticking out too much or overly sensitive.

"How old did you say he was?" I asked, pulling out my stethoscope.

"He's just turned one. My husband and I got him just before we moved here." The woman answered. I just nodded as I listened.

I continued my exam, checking breathing after I'd finished with the heartbeat, and then checking gut sounds.

"Everything seems to be in order here." I pulled the earpieces out as I spoke, clipping them around my neck. "It looked like he was due for some vaccination boosters when I looked at his file." She nodded. "I'm going to go get those. I'll just be a minute."

As I ducked out of the door, I all but ran into Meghan.

"Oh! Hey Lisbeth." She looked a little too happy to see me.

"Hi, Meghan. Haven't seen you much today. How are you?" I asked as I walked. Apparently we were both going in the same direction.

"I'm pretty good. Its been busy this morning, guess everyone wants to get their pets up to date before school's in full swing, hunh?"

"I guess." I kept walking, not really listening, just letting her keep talking.

"Yeah." She gave a little laugh and kept talking. I tuned her out as I selected the bottles I needed and then the syringes and needles I would need as well.

"Have you seen Dr. Fournier today?"

My head flew up, not quite registering the question.

"What?" I asked, my heart suddenly jack hammering in my chest for some reason or another.

"I just asked if you had seen Dr. Fournier yet today. I would have figured he'd want you along for a check-up on those stallions. I mean, why would he take someone else when you'd been there already?" She shrugged as if the question were obvious.

I took a deep breath, trying to settle my heart while avoiding the reason behind my reaction. I didn't want to go there just now. Finally I answered her, "No. I haven't seen him."

"Oh." I sighed in frustration at the disappointment I heard in her voice.

"Meg, why on earth would he want me along? Small animal tech remember!" I tried not to sound too sharp as I answered. "Besides, why do you care anyway? What's it to you if I go on the check-up visits or not?"

"Oh… no real reason. I was just curious I guess. And it did seem like the logical thing to happen." I couldn't quite read the look on her face, but there was something about it I didn't like.

Sighing again I turned, hands full, and headed back to the exam room I'd just left. I didn't want to deal with this right now. In fact, the whole reason that I hadn't seen or talked to Meg all day was for that exact reason. I'd known she'd still be too curious. The whole clinic had taken an interest in my romantic life at some point or another over the years that I had been here. I had been single the entire time and some of the other techs just couldn't quite wrap their minds around that fact. That or the fact that I liked it that way.

I stood outside the door for a moment to collect my thoughts before I went back into the room. I didn't need to be sticking needles in the wrong places, nor did I need yet another animal having a weird reaction to me. Yesterday had been enough exposure for at least the rest of the week.

An hour later I walked into the office to get my lunch; Cassie was busy again at the front desk when I entered. The rest of the office was blissfully empty as well, so that I was on my way out of the office when Cassie finally realized I was even there.

"Hey Lis! Hang on a second." I froze, and sighed, no avoiding her now. "Right, she'll be due for a check-up again next year then." I could hear her smile.

"Okay, I'll look for the reminder in the mail as usual then." I heard the owner respond. "And the bill of course."

Cassie gave a little laugh. "Alright. We'll see you next year then. Hopefully no sooner." It was the owner's turn to laugh, the sound fading as she left.

I still didn't turn around. I was feeling frozen to the spot, waiting for Cassie to say something.

"Right." I jumped a little; she stood right next to me now, her own lunch in her hand. "Its time for my lunch break too, and I haven't talked to you all day!"

I stifled a groan. Cassie and I were old friends, having started working at the clinic at almost the same time, but I knew that she was going to be just as curious as Meghan and I wasn't in the right frame of mind to deal with either of them today.

"I know." I finally said when we started walking to the break room I'd been planning to avoid. "How has your day been? Every time I've been in the office you've been busy." It was obvious I wasn't going to be avoiding them today, but maybe I could distract them enough so that they wouldn't get a chance to start on me. It never worked, but I was feeling more inspired than usual to try.

"Oh, not bad. The usual mess of things to sort through. You know the filing, the schedule, etc. And of course managing to keep the peace in the waiting room." I smiled; knowing my cue, then tuned her out as I walked over to the furthest corner of the break room. I might not be able to avoid them, but I still wanted to try. I shouldn't have bothered.

"Hey Meg! How're you?" Cassie sat down across from me as she gave a little wave in the direction of the others.

"I'm good. Haven't talked to you much today! Looked like you were busy." I dug into my lunch as they went through the same conversation I'd just had with Cassie a moment before.

"Hey Lis, what's up?" It was Jess; she'd slid in next to me while I'd been eating.

"Hey Jess." I tried not to mumble after I swallowed my mouthful of food. "Not much. What about you?" I'd hoped she would take the bait; she didn't.

"Nothing special. Hey, so what happened yesterday? I heard you got pulled to go on an emergency call at the track yesterday." I just nodded. "So what happened?" I could tell she was trying to keep the extent of her curiosity out of her voice; I had to hide a cringe.

"There was a stallion fight in the Kennedy's stables." She kept looking at me, waiting for me to continue. Finally I sighed and obliged. "Four of their stallions managed to get loose, three young ones and one of their older studs; apparently they were in a fighting mood because they were still at it when we got there. Well two of them were, they'd managed to get the other two of them separated by then at least."

"Oh geeze." Jess breathed. "That sounds nasty."

"That's for sure. All four of them were a mess, covered in blood. It took us hours just to get them cleaned and stitched back together."

"Nothing broken then?"

"Nope."

"Well that's lucky." I could tell that Jess was genuinely concerned so I relaxed into the conversation a bit.

"I know. They were wicked angry; I have no idea what started the fight, didn't ask. The younger ones had some of the deepest wounds though; the older stallion knew what he was doing. His cuts were shallower, though they sure bled enough." I rolled my eyes. "I think I gave Meg a fright when I got back yesterday. My clothes were covered in blood." I laughed a little to myself. "I kind of forgot how nasty I was. I missed lunch..."

"Oh. Hungry, hunh?" We shot each other wry smiles.

"You could say that." I turned back to my sandwich for a moment, chewing slowly.

"So..." I looked up at the new voice. It was Sera, another of the techs on lunch break. "You said they were still fighting when you got there?"

"Yeah." I swallowed. "I think they must've called as soon as the fight started. I think they were figuring it would be worse than it was." I paused, waiting for the question I knew would come next.

"So that's why you got pulled to go, hunh? Needed the expert fight lady to break it up?" I could hear the laughter behind the words.

"I guess." Maybe I would get out of this after all; if all they were going to tease me about was going in the first place, maybe I wouldn't have to deal with the Roman issue after all. I tried not to get my hopes up.

"Okay, so we've all been dying to know." Just my luck, it was Jess. "How was it working with the new Doc?" She exchanged a meaningful glance with the three other women who sat or stood around me in the corner.

"Nothing special." I answered. "Was it supposed to be?" They groaned collectively.

"No." Jess answered a little to quickly. "We were just curious. I mean, he's been here almost six months and none of us have worked with him yet. Somehow he's only been working in the large animal clinic, and hasn't done any small animal shifts yet."

"Oh." I felt their eyes on me as I sat eating, trying to ignore them.

"Lisbeth I know you're not blind." This came from Cassie.

"Well, sometimes I wonder." Meg contradicted. "Only our Lis could go on a call with the Dr. Roman and come back saying it was nothing special. I mean, I know I'm not the only one who's noticed those eyes!" They moaned again, but this time with a different kind of frustration. I sighed in my head; why did this always happen to me?

"Seriously guys. What's the big deal? Yeah, I noticed the eyes. They're kind of hard to miss." Frustration had me mumbling.

"I knew she wasn't blind." Cassie muttered.

"Oh for God's sake!" I crumpled the remains of my lunch and stood up to leave. "Guys, I don't care whether or not the new vet has gorgeous eyes or a six-pack, or whatever else. He could be five feet tall and be balding with a wart for all I care!" I took a deep breath. "I don't know why I got picked to go on that call. It makes even less sense to me than it does to you. And Meg, I don't know if I'm going on the follow up call or not and quite frankly I don't care if it's me who goes or not, okay?"

They stared at me. I'd taken a lot of teasing from them in the past. In their minds I was being stupidly stubborn about staying single and they'd been trying to change that fact for years. Why was this different? Why was this bothering me? I'd been walking as if on eggshells all day without any real reason. Why? My frustration finally overwhelmed me and I just turned and pushed my way out of the room, tossing out the remains of my lunch as I went. I could feel their eyes on my stiff back, but I ignored them. I was too busy holding back the tears. Why was I crying? Ugh.

I was just outside the office door when I heard the voice calling my name from the other end of the hallway.

"Lisbeth?" I didn't need to turn around to see the owner of that voice, I already knew who it was. "Lisbeth Moore?" It was closer now; I wanted to melt into the floor.

"That's my name." I turned around to see he was directly behind me.

"Oh. Hi." Now that he had my attention he looked like he wasn't sure about what he wanted to ask me; shoulders hunched awkwardly and hands shoved in his coat pockets.

"What?" I said, my embarrassment making me bite off the word rather than just say it. "Did you want something?" I attempted to soften my tone.

"Ummm…" I could just see him shifting his weight around. "Yeah. About yesterday." He paused; I froze. "I was going to go out to the track again tomorrow and check on those stallions. I was wondering…" He trailed off and I relaxed a little as I realized he was just as uncomfortable as I.

"Wondering what?" I prompted.

"Well, I was wondering if you'd come with me again tomorrow. You know since you've already seen them once, I thought it would be a better idea than finding someone else to go." I felt my heart rate start to pick up speed as he spoke; I took a deep breath.

"Sure. Why don't I just clear it with Dr. Halle before I leave tonight." Why couldn't I say no?

"I already did." My eyes flew up to meet his. How had I forgotten how tall he was? "He liked the idea actually. Sounded like he's been wanting to get you out on some of the track calls." He shrugged, seemingly unaware of my reaction; I still stared at him mutely.

"Oh." I finally managed. "Okay. Guess I'll just see you tomorrow morning then." He nodded.

"I'm going to leave first thing, so I'll just meet you out back in the morning if that's alright?" It was my turn to nod.

We both stood there for a moment. My heart rate was slowly evening out again, but now I joined him in the fidgeting. It felt like one of us had something more to say, and I had a feeling it was him. Lord knew I didn't have anything more to say to him; I was trying to avoid him.

"Ah… was there something else you wanted to ask me?" I finally asked. This time it was his turn to jerk his eyes down to mine.

"Oh. No. Sorry. Didn't realize…" He trailed off. "Right, sorry, I'll see you tomorrow morning then?"

"Yeah, I'll meet you out back." I answered, confused. He was already walking back down the hall, his steps measured as if he were trying not to walk too fast or too slow.

I stood where I was for another moment, absorbing what just happened. It looked like I was going to be spending some more time with Dr. Fournier after all. For some reason I wasn't quite sure how I felt about that fact. I sighed, and why did he have to be so tall? At least six-foot-three was my guess; made me feel like a shrimp when he stood that close. With an inward groan I gave myself a mental shake and spun on my heal. There was still work to do, the afternoon was supposed to be as busy as the morning had been, and I had even more of a reason to avoid the others now than before. They could find out on their own that I was spending tomorrow morning on my own with their favorite veterinarian.

It was eight o'clock in the morning and we were already pulling out of the clinic parking lot onto the road. Roman had been ready and waiting when I'd arrived at my usual time: 7:50. The clinic opened at eight.

It wasn't long before we were on the highway, weaving our way through the thinning traffic.

"Do you mind if I turn some music on?" I finally broke the silence that had begun before we'd even gotten into the truck to leave.

"No, go ahead." He gestured at the dash with his elbow, both hands on the steering wheel.

I sighed in relief. It was a rarity for me not to have a tune playing in my head, but today was proving an exception and I was dying for some music, so I reached eagerly for the power button and tuning dial. The instant my finger hit the power button music poured out of the speakers, not the radio, but a CD. I realized that this must be his truck, the one he drove on calls, and his CD. My curiosity piqued in spite of myself; the music that came out of the speakers was tasteful, a mixture of classical, folk, and what sounded to me like jazz. I paused in turning the radio on instead, to listen to the song.

"Do you like it?" I jumped a bit in my seat when he spoke. "Sorry, didn't realize you were listening that closely." I could hear his smile before I looked up and saw it. He was watching me intently.

"Watch the road." I continued to listen and he just chuckled, turning his eyes back to the road.

"I was just wondering if you liked the song." He said again a moment later, eyes back on the road. "It's a friend of mine's band. Not everyone who hears it enjoys it." He explained, contorting his face a bit as he said those last words. "He likes to…take artistic liberties when it comes to genre." Now he glanced sideways at me.

"I like it." I said slowly, still listening. It was on a different track, but it had the same feel as the previous. "Nice lyrics." I chuckled when someone started to sing. I saw him wince out of the corner of my eye, but he didn't try to turn it off.

"I'm glad you like it." Was all he said and we sunk back into silence; just listening.

Finally my curiosity got the better of me. "Do you –" I bit my lip, wondering if I should ask, or what it was I even wanted to know. He looked over at me, a question on his face. "Do you play anything? I mean, anything musical?" I stammered over the last of my words, suddenly self-conscious. I took a deep breath and clarified, "I was just wondering. You said this was your friend's band so I thought maybe you played too?" I stared out the window as I spoke.

"I'm in the band." I stared at him. "What?" He was laughing.

He was in the band. I couldn't believe it. He played music! This wasn't happening, couldn't be happening.

"Which instrument?" I finally stammered out.

"Guitar most of the time, acoustic and electric, but I play some piano and keyboard too for him sometimes." He was still laughing; I forced myself to stop staring, my face starting to burn from embarrassment. "Depends on the song, I guess."

"Oh." Was all I could manage. I went back to listening, another track was playing; the songs were short.

"So." He coughed, I guessed to hide that he was still laughing at my response. "What do you play? I already know you sing, but what about any instruments?"

I looked at him, trying to make myself answer the question. As I did, I noticed that his hair was kind of long, dark brown, though not as dark as my own, and a little wavy. "Piano and violin mostly, but yeah I sing and I've played the flute a bit. Haven't tried guitar yet; I want to." I stumbled over the words, rushing to answer the question before I let myself look at him much more closely; it was too... dangerous.

"Wow. Impressive."

"I'm not in a band though." I added, still uncomfortable; he'd remembered the singing. As we turned onto the driveway into the track grounds though, I started to relax, knowing an escape was at hand. "How long have you been playing?"

"Oh, years. Piano as long as I can remember; guitar I picked up as a teenager and never stopped." He grinned. "How about you? How long have you been playing?"

"Piano as long as I can remember - five, I think - was when I started that. Then, Violin since I was about six, so I guess I've been playing that since forever, too." I realized I'd answered without thinking and paused.

"What about flute? You mentioned that." He prodded.

"I picked that up to play in band, my school didn't have an orchestra. Then voice has just kind of been for fun, never really thought about getting any training." I shrugged; figuring I'd finish what I'd started. "Never intended to do anything much with any of it. I guess..."

He didn't respond; instead dealing with the gatekeeper and driving the truck over to the closest parking spot to the Kennedy stables. The owner was waiting for us before we'd even parked; it struck me as odd. I snuck a look at

Roman as I pulled various items from the bed of the truck, he didn't look like he'd noticed anything unusual; I decided not to say anything.

We started with the younger stallions since they had been hurt the worst, moving our way through them as methodically as we had when we'd stitched them back together. There were no surprises in them, no major infections or swelling, so all we had to do was refresh their bandages and give them some antibiotics. It seemed clear that the track grooms knew what they were doing; everything was neat, clean and organized - the horses especially.

"Right, let's take a look at your stud then, shall we?" Roman said as we finished up with the third youngster.

"Right this way." Mr. Kennedy gestured to the aisle at large with his hand. It struck me again as funny; like I was the only one not in on the joke.

I followed behind; moving slower on purpose, and used the kit and buckets I carried to make it appear more normal. The older stallion's stall was further down and on the other side of the barn, but we arrived there quickly.

A cursory glance at the stall, and the horse in the stall, showed nothing amiss. This part of the barn was just as neat, clean and organized as the rest had been. Figuring that this was going to be as basic as treating the other three had been, I moved to set down the equipment and take out what we would need. As I did so, I caught the look on Roman's face from the corner of my eye, and I froze. Something wasn't right.

"Who's been in charge of taking care of this horse since I was here last?" His voice was stiff; I got the impression he was trying to hide his frustration.

"I'm not sure." Mr. Kennedy's self-assured façade vanished as he spoke.

"Find out." Roman reached for his stethoscope as he entered the stall. "I'd like to have a word with them." I looked up sharply. Something was wrong; what had I missed?

I moved quickly to slide through the stall door just behind him. The smell hit me first, but then I saw it too, and for once I was really sorry that I had sharper senses than the average person. It was the smell of infection. Roman was already running his hands over the swelling that had developed in various places; apparently the smell didn't bother him like it did me. Then I realized what it was that had made Roman so upset: the stallion stood with his head low to the ground, eyes closed, breathing shallow; he had a fever, a serious one.

"Do you want me to go get some Bute from the truck?" I knew that the first priority would be to get the fever down.

"No." He said, then elaborated. "They'll have some closer here in the

46

stable, we'll just wait for them to get back." He turned back to the horse, his face full of focused concern.

I turned and left the stall. In that case the next thing would be to get ready to drain those swellings; I could already tell that they were the source of the smell. Outside the stall it wasn't nearly as pungent, and I realized that the absurd cleanliness of the barn seemed to mask it. It was concentrated within the stall itself. I forced myself to pay attention to the work at hand, not wanting to think about what that could potentially mean; I started to hum to myself, attempting to distract myself further.

"Here he is, Dr. Roman." Mr. Kennedy was back, groom in tow.

"Good." Roman came out of the stall, finished with checking the horse's vitals. "Mr. Kennedy, I am sure you have some Bute in a feed room nearby. Would you mind getting some? I thought you would have some closer than our truck."

I didn't look at his face, but I had the feeling that this request didn't quite sit well with the Mr. Kennedy. He mumbled something in response and left. I barely registered the oddness of the situation; since when did the owner do whatever a veterinarian told them to do? I focused instead on the conversation between Roman and the groom. Roman wasn't bothering to disguise his frustration now, I could hear it clearly in his voice as he spoke. He'd only waited long enough for Mr. Kennedy to be out of earshot.

"Why wasn't someone called before now? The infection has gotten a much stronger hold than if it had just happened overnight. There's the track clinic here on the grounds; it didn't have to be me who treated him." He bit off the words, motioning for the groom to look at the stallion behind him as he spoke. I stood quietly and watched them both as I waited to see how this would go.

"I don't know, sir. He looked healthy when I checked on him last night." The groom spoke quietly. "I been keepin' the bandages clean like we always do. Checkin' his temp every time we did, and there hasn't been anything wrong with him. It wasn't until this morning that anything seemed off."

"We?"

"Me and the other grooms that work here, sir." He was stuttering with what I assumed to be nerves. "But it's just been me takin' care of his bandages and such." He rushed to clarify.

"Right. Well…" Roman trailed off; the groom's hands clenched in white-knuckled fists. I looked at Roman, wondering what he was thinking. His face seemed carefully blank.

While I waited for him to continue, I started to pick up the things we would need to create drains for the swelling, and the antibiotics for the infection. All the while still listening hard for what would happen next. It didn't take him much longer.

"Okay." He took a deep breath and shifted his weight a little. "Regardless of what you're telling me, that stallion still has a raging fever, infection, and his wounds have swollen with infectious puss, so, I don't know about you, but something isn't quite matching up here between your story and the facts." He just let the words hang in the air between them.

"I didn't check on him last night." The groom whispered a moment later. "I didn't change the bandages like I was supposed to. I overslept…" He trailed off, and we all guessed what he'd been doing last night and sleep wasn't it. Given the bloodshot state of his eyes, I guessed at least some alcohol had been involved.

"Alright. Well now we're getting somewhere." Roman looked at me now. "Let's get some sedative in him. We'll need to drain the swellings and clean those wounds again."

"Already set to go." I gave a little smile in an effort to lighten his mood. His intensity was making me nervous too. I gestured towards the stall door behind him. "Shall we?"

His response was to turn around and open the door; I followed close on his heals, hands full. The groom didn't move, just stood silently in the aisle. I glanced at him briefly as I walked past; tears streamed silently down his thin cheeks. I frowned slightly, but kept walking. We needed to get to work before the infection had a chance to get too developed. If he felt bad maybe he should have thought about that before neglecting his job.

"Here's the sedative." I held out a syringe of clear liquid.

"Thanks." His voice was tense. I ignored it and organized the supplies I had in my hands so that we could work efficiently; settling back into the tune I'd been humming before. Neither of us spoke as we started to put in drains, cleansing the infected wounds. We were already in the process of dosing him with antibiotics when I heard footsteps in the aisle.

"Mike!" My head jerked up, and I stopped humming, at the sharpness of the words. "What're you still doing here? Get back to work." It was Mr. Kennedy.

"Yes, sir." Came the mumbled reply from the groom whose name must be Mike.

"Here's the Bute you asked for, Dr. Roman." He stood in the doorway now, hand extended, polite smile and tone back in place. I narrowed my eyes slightly at the change, but kept my mouth shut.

"Thank you, Mr. Kennedy." Roman answered, reaching out to take the white tube, his voice sounding completely unaffected. He pulled off bloody plastic gloves, and started to spin the dial on the syringe to adjust the dose. I kept my own gloves on as I piled up rubbish to be tossed out, and dealt with the needles and other remnants of our work. When I finished I straightened up to see another groom standing in the door, garbage bag in hand.

"Thanks." I smiled a little and dumped my pile into the bag, stripping off my own gloves to add to the mix. The groom just nodded his head, tied off the bag and left. I shrugged; neat, clean and organized fanatics – whatever, it had its uses.

Roman was talking to Mike when I stepped out of the stall, carrying the remains of what I'd brought into it.

"So he'll need to get two grams of this twice a day for the next few days. I'll call and check on how he's doing then and we'll adjust it if we need to." Roman was explaining. "Got it?" Mike nodded fervently. "Right, now I need to talk to you Mr. Kennedy." I watched Mike's face flash with anxiety at Roman's words before quickly pocketing the Bute and vanishing.

"Yes, Dr. Roman?" Mr. Kennedy looked up at him expectantly. Neither seemed aware that Mike had left; Roman simply looked at the man before him, his face unreadable.

"Mr. Kennedy, I think that we need to get something straight." Mr. Kennedy's eyebrows rose into his hairline, apparently he hadn't been expecting that any more than I had.

"And what might that be?" Was his only reply.

"None of these horses were seriously injured by the fight, so there was no reason not to just have the vet on call at the clinic here at the Park to treat them." Roman paused here for a moment. "Why, then, did you call me in when I'm working at a clinic a far further distance from the track, when there was nothing wrong that couldn't have been handled by any of the well qualified veterinarians working at the clinic here?"

I caught myself as I started to move closer to the pair. Mr. Kennedy wasn't answering; his face expressing what seemed like simple indignation.

"Well?" Roman pushed. "There had to be some reason."

"I think that you know why I called you and not someone else closer." Was all he said.

"No. I don't think that I do know, Mr. Kennedy. Why don't you elaborate on that for me? Enlighten me as to why someone else couldn't take care of your animals."

"My horses get the best Doc. If you're going to tell me that that isn't you, you're wasting your breath." I struggled to hide my shock at the ice that coated the man's voice. Whatever I had expected, from either of them, it wasn't that.

"I'm going to call the clinic when I get back. The stallion's records will be transferred to them and one of their vets will take over his care. There isn't anything that I would do that they aren't equally capable of doing." He paused for a second, taking a calming breath. "Do you understand me? I have other clients to take care of in my new position, and I can't keep wasting time coming all the way up here when your horses get in fights."

"What's that supposed to mean?" Mr. Kennedy took a half step towards Roman; he didn't even blink at the movement.

"You know what I mean. I'm not the only one who can break up those fights and I'm not the only one who can clean up after them." Roman turned to me suddenly. "Lisbeth, let's go. We're all set here. You can expect a bill, Mr. Kennedy." He didn't give me a chance to answer, instead turning as he spoke in the direction of the truck. I moved to follow him; stunned into silence by what had just happened, none of which made any sense.

I had to move quickly to catch up to him. He had forgotten, in his frustration, the difference in our height and stride length. Rushing to put what was left of the supplies I had taken with us into their proper places in the bed of the truck, I had just managed to close the door by the time he had the truck in reverse. The next five minutes seemed more like an hour, his frustration, no longer held completely in check, giving the silence an uncomfortable edge.

After the first five minutes though, I decided that there were too many things unexplained for me to sit in silence for the whole ride back. I flicked the CD back on and turned up the volume. The rhythm of the music that pulsed through the speakers helped me relax and by the time it changed to a second track I could feel him relax too. He was the one who finally reached for the volume, turning it down to a more convenient decibel for conversation.

"I'm sorry about that." He kept his eyes on the road.

"Its alright. Shit happens." I shrugged and forced a laugh.

"No, I'm really sorry. I shouldn't let him get to me like that. Its just…" He trailed off, and I saw his hands tighten on the steering wheel.

"Do you want to talk about it?" I felt my heart start to race a little when he turned to stare at me.

"Do you really want to hear it?" He whispered.

"I think I do." I answered truthfully. "I don't know why, but I do."

He didn't say anything for a minute. Deciding where to begin, I guessed. My curiosity became almost unbearable as I waited for him to speak. What could possibly make him so angry? I'd felt it, seen it in every one of his actions during the visit, and heard it in every word he'd flung at Mr. Kennedy before we'd left. I was beginning to wonder if I had pushed my luck too far, when he finally spoke.

"What have you heard about me? Around the clinic I mean?"

"Nothing really." The truth of that statement hit me hard as I said it. "I haven't been listening, really. I guess I've always been a bit deaf when it comes to office gossip." I winced at the memory of Cassie and Meg's words two days before.

"Hmmm." His eyebrows knit together in response. "So you don't know that I used to work here at the track? As one of the chief vets on the staff, covering a majority of the emergency calls." I shook my head, wanting to hear more before I said anything. "Yeah, until about six months ago. Things went a little wrong with some people involved with a case around then and… I decided I'd had enough. Now I'm where you see me: working for Dr. Halle."

I didn't respond to what he'd said for a moment. Letting the music fill the cab as I mulled it over. Watching his hands on the steering wheel again, I voiced the first of the questions that filled my head.

"Why did Mr. Kennedy call you then when the fight broke out? Why didn't he just have one of the other vets at the track take care of it?" He didn't answer right away.

"You know how I said that anyone of the other vets was just as capable of breaking up fights as I was?" I nodded. "Well, that's not exactly true. I was the unofficial bouncer, if you will, of the track. I was the one who took care of the fights when no one else could break them up." He laughed a little. "It basically boiled down to my being the biggest of our group." It was my turn to laugh, remembering how I'd felt when he'd stood right next to me the other day.

"But that doesn't explain why he called you. I would have thought that they could have managed to break it up eventually. I mean they got two of them split by the time we got there." I felt like I knew the answer but asked the question anyway.

"He didn't trust them to do it. Stupid really, the horses only got hurt more seriously because it takes me longer to get here than it would have for any of the others." The edge crept back into his voice. Both of us kept our eyes on the road in front of us. I heard him take a deep breath. "I'm not really sure why though. Maybe what he said is the truth - "

"And he thinks you're the best?" I filled in.

"Yeah."

"Mmm." Was all I could think to say.

"Don't you want to know why I left?" He said, making me jump. I'd been attempting unsuccessfully to fit the puzzle pieces together.

"What? Oh, should I?" I replied caught off guard.

"I don't know. I just thought you'd be more curious."

I didn't answer him right away. He had no idea just how curious I was about him; too curious and I didn't have the faintest idea why that was. There were valid reasons behind the things Cassie and Meg had said about me, and I knew that.

"Do you want to tell me? Since you brought it up."

"I got in a fight with one of the other partners in the practice." My jaw dropped. "I was getting burned out; too many long shifts and owners just throwing their money around. I guess I snapped." He laughed a little, trying to ease the tension replacing the music, but I saw his knuckles whiten on the steering wheel.

"That doesn't explain why you left though." I still felt confused. "What – "

"I fought with the one person in a higher position than me." He interrupted, face suddenly rather grim. "He didn't want to fire me... so I quit."

"Still... why? What was the fight about?" This wasn't making sense.

"I'd gotten into a... bit of a disagreement with one of the owners whose horse I was lined up to do surgery on. It was a gorgeous colt – fast – but it had broken its leg, and badly." He glanced in my direction as he spoke. "I knew when I looked at the colt that it would've been the humane thing to put it down."

"The owner didn't feel the same, did he?"

"Didn't understand would be an understatement. He refused to understand." He shook his head. "I have no idea what he was thinking, but it definitely wasn't about the horse."

"The horse was that fast, hunh?" Amazement at the situation he described filled my voice.

"Apparently he was. Either way, something in me just snapped at his attitude towards that horse." He took a steadying breath. "I knocked him out."

"You did what!?" I asked, mouth agape with shock yet again.

"I punched him." He shrugged tense shoulders. "That colt was standing in its stall, all but dead with how much tranquilizer I had to give him. I just couldn't stand it anymore."

I took a minute to absorb what he was telling me. It was difficult to imagine him getting that angry, but then I thought about his reaction to the stallion's infection and it didn't seem quite so impossible. Mr. Kennedy's behavior on the other hand seemed much more justified, now that I knew Roman's history at the park. As I thought it all over, I realized that none of what he'd said really bothered me. I didn't really care about what had pushed him to leave the track for a clinic in the suburbs of Chicago that rarely saw any large animal patients. No, it was something else entirely that was bothering me; and it had more to do with me than with him.

"Why did you want me to go with you when they called the other day? Why not someone else? I mean, if you're so capable of breaking up fights then why did you need anyone with you at all?" I watched his face carefully.

He didn't answer. The CD changed tracks again as I waited for him to answer. I watched as different emotions seemed to flit across his face; fighting to keep my heart rate reasonable as I waited for him to answer. I wasn't sure why it mattered so much what his answer would be, but it did.

"I had two reasons." He didn't elaborate right away. Then he explained in a rush, eyes on the road as the words poured out of his mouth. "The main reason was because I wanted to talk to you. You didn't seem to notice me at the clinic so I thought that it would be a chance to get you in a different... situation so that I could talk to you for once. I've been watching you for months; curious." He glanced at me as he paused briefly. "But my other reason was that I didn't want to come back by myself, and especially not to have to fit back into my old place breaking up the fights." He sighed. "I knew you had a reputation for breaking up fights with the big dogs and such in the waiting room. I thought maybe you'd be able to help with the stallions, show them that I'm not the only one who can be of... assistance. Really though I just used that to justify why I really wanted you to go with me." He winced slightly, and I noticed a little fresh color in his face. Blushing? He looked in my direction again and I could see the nerves clearly on his face; his forehead wrinkled with concern, mouth turned down slightly in a frown.

I didn't respond right away. We were pulling off the highway, almost back to the clinic. I used that time to think of a reply. But what did you say when the first guy to catch your eye in years confesses that he's "curious" about you and goes to such lengths just to talk to you. I had no idea and wasn't much closer to figuring it out when we pulled into the parking lot of the clinic.

Roman parked the truck and turned it off, but didn't move to get out. He sat, turned in his seat to watch me, his eyes intent my face.

"I'm really not sure what to say to that." I finally decided to go with the truth.

"You can say whatever you want. No pressure." Yeah right, was all I could think; I'd never felt more pressured in my life.

"Can I meet the rest of the band?" It took him a minute to understand what I was asking.

"You mean you're not mad at me?"

"Of course not! Why would I be?" I grinned at his confusion.

"I don't know, I just..." He blinked, shaking his head a bit. "I guess that's what I get for expecting the worst." He chuckled softly. "But yeah, of course you can meet the band! When do you want to?"

"How about this weekend? You could pick me up here." I picked a date out of my head at random. I hadn't thought quite that far ahead of my answer. "I could bring my violin, maybe?" I suggested.

"Sure, that would be great." We both moved now to get out of the truck, relaxing as what was happening sank in.

Our hands bumped as we both moved to open our doors and my heart lept in my chest. I smiled shyly and looked up at him as I pulled my hand back. He just chuckled, seeming much more like himself now that we were back at the clinic. I swallowed nervously as he did; my nerves flooding back as I walked through the door. It had occurred to me belatedly that I was now going to have to face a legion of questioners the instant I stepped into the office. I would prefer a firing squad.

Chapter 8

The man and woman seated before me were deep in conversation, sitting directly across from each other with their eyes focused intently on one another. The man was speaking, but I couldn't hear a word of what he said. I could only guess from the focused expression on the woman's face and the fact that her lips weren't moving.

The room in which they sat was small but with a high ceiling, and furnished in the style of a previous century; heavy drapes and furniture with complimentary upholstery and in a formal design. The woman, who looked vaguely familiar, had golden-blond hair tied back in a style from the same century as the room, and eyes a deep blue in color. The man wasn't the least bit familiar looking; average height with hair a ruddy-blond color. He looked sturdy and strong in a way that was complimentary to a similar strength in the woman.

I still could not hear what was being said as I made these observations of the scene; I could feel tension sizzling in the air, but was unsure whether it came from me, or from them. As I waited a sudden breeze blew through the window I now realized was open, and, in blowing the drapes, drew my gaze to the corner opposite the couple. In it stood a beautifully designed harp of what seemed to be a dark cherry wood, and it shone in the sudden sunlight from the window.

As soon as I'd looked away, my gaze flipped back to the woman's face to see something wet on her cheeks reflect the same light as the harp. The man lifted his hand and cupped her cheek, wiping away the tears with his thumb in an intimate gesture. As I watched she leaned into the caress, tears continuing to stream silently as she did. Although I still could not hear what was being said, I knew that he continued to speak through all of this because, moments later, a blissful smile spread across her face.

Before I could even begin to wonder what could possibly have been said, the man was leaning over and kissing the woman in a way that made my heart ache; the woman reached her hands up to cup his face in return as I felt my heart wrench again, painfully. Then it was like someone had switched the volume on and I could finally hear what was being said when they broke the kiss.

"You're not running away from me?" The woman spoke thickly through her tears.

"No I am not." Was all the answer he gave.

"Is this a dream?" She laughed lightly as if in disbelief. "Are you really still here, sitting in front of me?"

Then the volume switched back off, and the scene went black. I was left wallowing in confusion until comprehension struck.

This was another dream. I had been watching myself.

My eyes flew open as my body jerked upright, heart pounding, as I took in the room around me; my own, I realized. I closed my eyes and breathed evenly in an effort to settle myself. The dreams still had this effect on me sometimes. There didn't seem to be any exact reasoning behind how or when they came; they simply came and went, imprinting themselves on, or rather into, my mind as they did. It was impossible to forget them; the room and the two people who had been sitting in it were burnt into my mind, still visible to me as I sat with my eyes closed.

I puzzled over what I had seen in the dream, keeping my breathing rhythmic as my heart settled back to its natural beat. After about ten minutes, I still hadn't come up with any ideas for what she could have said to him to provoke such a reaction. I opened my eyes, sighing deeply as I got out of bed. I knew I wasn't going to be able to sleep any more now, so there was no point in trying. Instead I pulled on a pair of sweats and tied my hair back in a messy bun as I walked down the stairs to the kitchen. I wanted a mug of tea while I tried to figure this out.

The smell of frying bacon and eggs filled my nose as I descended the stairs and walked into the kitchen. It smelled like I wasn't the only one who'd had dreams tonight; I just made tea when something kept me up at night, but Kaya started cooking things. There had been more than one instance over the last few years where Tom and I had awoken to a multi-course breakfast because Kaya had been up at night.

I glance at the clock as I walked into the room; it read 3:36am. I sighed in frustration: only about five hours of sleep. I had been hoping for more, having gotten a bit behind in the last few weeks from some later nights than usual, and a few earlier mornings for various reasons. Kaya heard the sigh and looked up from the bacon frying in front of her.

"Couldn't sleep?"

"Dreams. You?"

"Same. Want some tea? I was going to make some."

"Sure."

"Want some food?"

"Yeah. The smell is making me starving."

I smiled to myself as I picked up the hot water kettle and filled it in the sink. That was the extent of our conversation; lapsing, instead, into a comfortable silence while we each moved around the kitchen. We didn't need to say anything as I poured water over tea bags and Kaya loaded two plates with bacon, eggs, and toast. She left some for Tom for when he woke up later. At least one of us would get a good night's sleep.

"So." Kaya began, breaking the silence at last as we both sat down at the table. "Let's hear it." It wasn't a question. She picked up her fork and started eating, waiting for me to start talking. It looked like I was going first.

"I really don't know how to explain it." I began. "It was so...odd." I took a bite of the eggs on my plate. They were perfect, as usual.

"Well, who was in it?" Kaya appeared determined that I be the first one to talk this time.

"There were two people." I started after swallowing another mouthful. "A woman, blond with blue eyes, and a man, average height with brown hair. I couldn't see his eyes because his back was to me the entire time." I paused, thinking, unsure of how to continue. "While I was watching only the man spoke; I never saw the woman's lips move. I couldn't hear anything though. Not until the very end; the last, oh, four or five sentences of the conversation. It was weird."

"The blond was you?"

"Yeah."

"So it was a memory? Not just a dream then."

"Yes. Yes, that I know for sure too. There's no way a regular dream would keep me up like this, or bother me this much for that matter." I sighed and ate some more; bacon this time, perfectly crisp.

"Hmmm." She didn't elaborate, just kept eating, but knowing her she was thinking hard. "What did they say? The part that you heard I mean."

"I couldn't quote it, but the woman was saying something about being amazed that the guy hadn't run away from her. Like she'd admitted to something that should horrify him, you know? And the man was saying something about how he would never do that." Kaya gave me a look as I spoke. She knew that if it was one of the memory dreams I would definitely be able to quote it word for word, you didn't forget those dreams, not a single detail. I was glad she didn't say anything about it.

"I think you know what that dream was about." Was all she said, and I ducked my head as the answer to it flashed suddenly in my mind.

"She'd been telling him…" I broke off; embarrassed I hadn't seen it right away. It seemed so obvious now. "She'd been telling him about Mom. I'd been telling him about Mom, I mean." She just nodded slowly at me, not saying a word.

After that we sat for a while, eating in silence, while we thought over the implications of what I had just said. My own mind ran through the image of the dream over and over and over. I searched for clues to why this dream had come now. There was something nagging at the back of my mind, like there was something ridiculously obvious I should be seeing. I went over the details of the room, nothing stood out. I thought about the man and woman who had feature in it, but I'm not in a relationship, so that didn't raise any alarms. Finally I gave up, deciding that it was Kaya's turn to talk about why she was up so late, or maybe I should be thinking early.

"What about your dream? What's got you up at three am, making breakfast?" I tore off a piece of my last strip of bacon.

"It was a very old memory, from centuries ago." She sipped at her tea. "It was confusing as well, I don't really know where it was."

"Not in North America this time then?" So far our dreams, all three of ours, had been limited to taking place on the continent we were still living on; and we generally recognized the locations.

"Yeah, or at least that's what I think. It seemed like it was in a rainforest."

"South America then?" I asked, getting an idea.

"Maybe…" Her eyes were distant, unfocused' I guessed she was remembering the dream.

"Kaya?" Her eyes refocused at the sound of my voice. "Do you think that this has to do with your current heritage? I mean, I know we supposedly don't have any kind of connections with our human heritages, but still…I'm almost always Caucasian in my dreams. There have been few if any exceptions."

"And I've always been the same way." I jumped at the male voice; apparently Tom was awake too. "I've pretty much always been Caucasian."

"Exactly," I tried not to let my surprise show. "So do you think that maybe there's a connection there?"

"I guess." She whispered. "I've never really paid attention to my skin color in my dreams. Never occurred to me to do that." She looked up at me, eyes a little bewildered.

"I can't really say that for sure, you know, but don't you think that that makes sense?" She didn't respond so I decided to let it rest. There was more than enough time to think about it later. Instead I turned to Tom, who was sitting down at the table with his own plate of bacon and eggs. "So what're you doing up?"

"You know me Lis, I smelled the food." He grinned. "Besides, it's not really that early anymore, the alarm was going to go off in less than an hour anyway."

"Oh." I looked over at the clock in surprise. It read 4:48am; our alarms would be going off at 5:30.

"Yeah, so Lisbeth I happened to catch the end of what you were saying about your dream." I looked up in surprise from my tea. I hadn't even noticed him until a moment ago. "Relax." He raised a finger to his ear. "I was still upstairs at that point. Your senses aren't messed up." His face split in a grin so I stuck my tongue out at him. Sometimes it was too easy to forget how annoying he could be.

"Okay, so what would you like to say?" I tried to look more annoyed than I was; it was hard for me to stay mad at him for long.

"Right. Did you forget about a certain someone you met for the first time in this past week?" He looked at me, one eyebrow raised as if the answer were blatantly obvious.

"Uh?" I didn't get it.

"Seriously?" The eyebrow lifted higher into his hairline. Okay, what was I missing here?

"Oh!" How had I not realized it? "Roman Fournier." I whispered his name, as it sank in.

"Who?" Kaya asked.

"The doctor I went on that emergency call with on Tuesday." I explained, realizing that Kaya didn't know quite as much about what had happened during that trip as Tom did.

"Had to patch up some stallions at the track right?" I nodded. "What does he have to do with this?" Her confusion showed on her face.

I sighed, opening my mouth to explain from the beginning. Tom beat me to it.

"They got caught in that huge thunder storm that came through, and, um, Lis didn't quite manage to stay quiet..." He finished vaguely, the look on Kaya's face making it clear she understood what he was getting at.

"Oh." Was all she said.

Tom's words hung in the air between the three of us.

"Yeah, well there's a bit more to this than that, actually." I whispered; my brain racing furiously over the events of yesterday in the truck.

They both looked at me when I spoke, faces curious. I gulped, throat tightening with nerves as I realized I was going to have to explain it all. It almost felt worse than dealing with Cassie, Meg and the others at the office given Kaya and Tom knew me even better, and they wouldn't fall for any evasions if I tried them.

"Roman asked me to go with him, when he did a follow up call on those stallions yesterday." I stopped, struggling not to rush while also not sure how to continue from there. No one said a thing. "We got going on the topic of music, which by the way he actually remembered my singing, and I'm going to go see his band, well play with his band really, on Saturday, which is tomorrow." I stopped again, letting my abbreviated version of yesterday's events sink in.

"You have a date?" They said simultaneously, dumbfounded looks on their faces.

I sighed; should have expected that reaction.

"Yes, I have a date… of sorts." I mumbled.

"How on earth did this happen?" It was Tom. "You haven't gone on a date since that disastrous prom experience, and that was senior year of high school!"

"I know." I didn't appreciate the reminder of that night; teenage boys could be real jerks.

"Am I dreaming? Did you really just tell me that you are going on a date tomorrow?" Kaya's voice was equally doubtful, and she didn't even have the extensive experience with my love life, or rather lack there of, that Tom did.

"No." I was getting a little frustrated now. "You are not dreaming. I am going on a date tomorrow. With a man who has seen me react to a storm, and remembers what he saw!" My voice rose as I spoke. They were missing the most important point of all of this.

"Oh. Right." They said together. Silence.

"Your dream was about telling him. Whether or not you could…or should." Kaya whispered bluntly into the quiet.

"Yes." I answered. Silence again.

As we sat in silence my mind raced. Thinking over what this would mean for me, for all of us.

"How on earth did music happen to be the topic to come up for conversation?" Trust Kaya to avoid the real issue at hand.

"There was a CD from his band in the player and when I went to turn on the radio it came on instead." I explained grudgingly. "It was really good, and it just kind of went from there I guess."

Kaya and Tom exchanged a meaningful look.

"What?" I asked, getting a bit nervous.

"I'm not sure, actually." Kaya answered.

"Okay." I said slowly.

"Why don't you elaborate on your conversation a little? You know, fill in some of the details for us." Tom asked.

I sighed. "Why? So you can make fun of me?" I gave him a dirty look. "Make fun of my blinders?" I mimed wearing a pair, finding that I couldn't help laughing a little at myself as I did, remembering my earlier conversation with Meg and Cassie at work.

"Maybe." Tom was grinning at me again, so I stuck my tongue out at him like I had before. He just laughed; it was my typical response to his teasing so he didn't really react to it anymore beyond laughter.

"Come on, I want to know more. And maybe it can really help us figure this out." Kaya tried to reason. I couldn't see her logic, but figured it couldn't hurt. If I couldn't trust the two people I was closest to, then who could I trust to talk to about this? I couldn't think of anyone.

"Okay." They both grinned; I winced in response, wondering if I'd made the right decision. I opened my mouth; too late now.

"He said that he's been watching me. At work." I found it wasn't as painful as I'd expected and continued. "He just started at the clinic something like six months ago, and I hadn't really noticed him before. He's been working specifically in the large animal part of the clinic."

"Whoa, how's he managing that? You guys don't exactly get a lot of calls for large animal stuff." Tom looked confused already.

"I'm not sure honestly." I shrugged. "Like I was trying to say, I hadn't really noticed him until this week."

"But it seems he noticed you?" Kaya filled in.

"I guess. Anyway, what pretty much happened was that on our way back from the follow up we started talking about some other stuff, like why he'd left working at the track – "

"Wait a minute. He worked at the track clinic before?" Tom interrupted. "That doesn't make sense. Why would he leave?"

"I didn't understand that at first either. He said it was because of a couple things: burning out on the work, and it didn't help that he got into a serious fight with one of his partners." I saw understanding dawn on Tom's face. "Yeah, kind of a mess really, but basically it made him decide to leave, and now he's working at Dr. Halle's clinic."

"Where he has now noticed you." Kaya finished for me.

"Yup. But about the music conversation –"

"Yeah, let's hear more about that!" Kaya interrupted me this time, making me laugh a little bit.

"It was a very, I think I would call it, natural, conversation. It just happened. Like it was meant to." I looked at both of them to see if they understood. "He said he's played piano since he was tiny and then picked up guitar when he was a teen." I smiled at the cheesy image this presented in my mind; the stereotypical order of events. "I kind of got the impression that he's mostly self-taught. Though he didn't actually say that." Then again neither had I, but somehow I had the feeling my conclusions were right.

"Hunh." Tom and Kaya said at almost the same time.

"What?"

"I don't know." Tom answered.

"Me neither. It just seems so weird. I mean, you never seem to notice anyone, haven't in years. Now all of a sudden you're going on a date with a guy and he seems perfect for you!" Kaya's voice sounded as confused as I felt.

I couldn't find an answer. Roman, perfect for me? No way, there was no such man in existence. I was too weird, too quirky... wasn't I? Then I thought about how I'd felt, talking to him in the truck, and I wasn't so sure anymore.

"I think Kaya's right." Tom continued. "I don't know what's going on here, but one thing is for sure: this guy must have been made to order. He plays piano and guitar, is in a band, and he works with animals for his career." He stared pointedly, making me blush and drop my eyes to the plate in front of me.

"He didn't even seem bothered by my reaction to the storm." My hand flew to my mouth the second the words snuck out. I gasped. They were right. Uh oh.

After my unintentional admission, I stood quickly to clear the dishes. We seemed to have reached a mutual conclusion that there was no point in talking the subject to death when there was so much to think about first. As I stood, loading the dishwasher, I heard the first beep of the alarm upstairs. It was time to really begin the day; we each turned to walk into the sitting room, ready to begin with meditation as usual.

Chapter 9

I handed Cassie my previous patient's file as I reached to grab the next from her desk. I moved slowly, my short night making me disoriented with sleep deprivation. Thankfully the day had been a slow one so far, allowing me to take the time to be accurate rather than speed along numbly, hoping I was doing things right. Cassie didn't seem to notice; although, to be honest, it wasn't the first time she had seen me sleep deprived for one reason or another.

I left the office without saying a word to my friend, just bobbing my head in acknowledgement. The day had been uneventful as well as slow, in more ways than one; I hadn't seen Roman once since I had arrived at the office this morning. I hadn't even glimpsed him out of the corner of my eye, and it was making me wonder if I had imagined yesterday.

I nodded at Meg as I passed her, walking in the opposite direction, not making any more effort for her than for Cassie; I pushed open the door to the waiting room and read out the name on the file, making an effort not to look too under-whelmed.

The rest of the afternoon continued in as uneventful a fashion as it had begun. I continued in a zombie-like state, focusing on doing my work correctly rather than quickly; going through the files piled on Cassie's desk and the various drop-ins that showed up throughout the day. Nothing out of the ordinary came up though, and when it was finally time for me to sign out and head home, I was more than ready for a nap before I tried to do anything else.

Just as I was picking up my keys to walk out the back door to where I had parked my car, I felt someone tap on my shoulder. I sighed, and turned around slowly, feeling all the more keenly how tired I was now that I was being prevented from getting home for a nap as quickly as I wanted to. It was Roman.

"Hi." I closed my eyes for a second to stop myself from showing my exasperation. "What's up?" I asked, when he didn't say anything.

"I just wanted to tell you that I'll pick you up here at about ten tomorrow; we're having a jam session at my friend's place sometime around eleven. Will that be okay for you?"

"Yeah that'll be great." I forced a smile. "I'm planning to bring my violin, that still okay?"

"Yeah that'll be great." He frowned slightly. "You okay? You don't look so good."

"I'm fine." Did he ever miss something? "Just a little tired, couldn't sleep last night." I opted for the truth since he'd actually noticed how shitty I was looking today.

"Oh."

"Yeah, I'm headed home now, going to take a nice long nap." I gave a half smile as I thought longingly of my bed.

"Hmmm…okay, well I'll let you go then so you can get some rest." He shrugged and turned to leave. "I'll see you tomorrow."

"Yeah, see you tomorrow." I mumbled, and followed him out, sleep hanging heavier on my eyes the longer I tried to keep them open.

I got to my car, and starting it, drove slowly and carefully home. I wasn't in the mood to end up in a ditch, or wrapped around a pole somewhere for that matter. The moment I walked through the door I stripped off my shoes, dropped my purse by the door and fell onto the sofa that was conveniently near by when I walked into the sitting room. I was out when my head hit the pillow, and didn't wake up again until Kaya came through the door two hours later, only to eat dinner and crash back into bed a few hours later.

I felt dramatically better when I woke up with my alarm at 5:30am with my usual energy; I was relieved when we made it through breakfast and meditation without a single word being said about my imminent "date". I was trying not to think about it too much, not sure how I felt about the whole thing anymore. It wasn't as if I knew what I was doing exactly. I was happy, too, that I ran alone; another way to avoid odd questions, as well as use up a little bit of my confused energy in the effort of running.

It wasn't until I stood in the shower, hot water running over my head, neck, and back, that I finally let myself think about who I was meeting in an hour at the clinic, and where we were going after that. I needed to pack my violin; it still sat in its stand in my music room where I had played it last. I had decided during my run that I would pick out a few pieces of music to take with me, just in case I would want it. It had also occurred to me that I had never played any of my storm music; for some reason I felt it might not be a bad idea to take some of that, too. After all, maybe they would be able to help me play it with all the instruments I heard it with; I wasn't sure why I wanted to do this, but it didn't seem like a bad idea, so I didn't question it.

I turned off the shower, and grabbed a towel as I stepped out to stand in front of the mirror over the sink. My thoughts shifted. As I looked at myself in the steamed up mirror, studying the reflection with a mixture of emotion. My skin looked even paler today, standing out more than usual against my deep brown hair. My eyes had dark circles under them, the product of the previous night's sleeplessness. I'd always liked my face, not that it was anything spectacular, but my eyes matched my hair, my lips were full and curved, and my nose was straight. I smiled and laughed a bit as I studied myself. I didn't see anything spectacular enough to make Roman watch me like he'd claimed; I was far from being a stunner, though I was equally far from ugly by any standard.

I laughed outright and started to towel dry the rest of my body; I wasn't usually the kind of girl to get hung up on her looks. I finished and wrapped the towel around myself to walk across the hall to my room and get dressed. Fifteen minutes later I had finished with my make-up and was packing my violin. I was running a little bit later than I'd planned, but when I went to pick a few sheets of music out of my piles, I paused.

I was holding a piece of music from a storm that had come during the night, about a year ago. As I looked over the music I could hear it play vividly in my head, and it stopped me in my tracks. Something in the corner of my mind told me that I should put the music aside, leave it at home, but somehow I couldn't quite manage to do that. Instead I held onto it as I picked out a couple other pieces of music that I had bought, rather than written, for my violin and another random piece of storm music for the piano; I didn't look at it this time, not wanting to waste even more time getting lost in it as I had with the other. That done, I carried everything up to my car, and, taking a moment to do a mental check of what I had with me, drove to the clinic to meet Roman.

When I pulled into the clinic parking lot, he was already there in his truck. He got out as I parked and it hit me for the first time that he was really incredibly attractive, not beautiful, but attractive. I realized that he wasn't wearing his usual coveralls for work and gulped; we weren't at work now.

I took a moment to breathe before getting out of my car and opening the trunk to get out my violin case and the bag I'd put the music in. I felt a little giddy with anticipation, and it was a struggle not to start giggling hysterically for no reason whatsoever. I took another deep breath, attempting to stifle the urge. I shut the trunk and looked over at him. He had walked over to the passenger side of the truck, and had moved the seat so that I could put my violin behind it.

Walking over to him, I noticed that my legs were steadier than my nerves had led me to expect, and I reached him without making a fool of myself. I put my violin where he indicated before looking at him, I didn't trust myself. The moment that I did, I froze, eyes locked on his. The look in them made my insides melt involuntarily, and I wondered how I had managed to overlook this for so long. The word blind flashed through my mind and I glanced down sharply, trying to hide the wince I knew flashed over my face.

"Hey you okay?" I could hear the concern and the frown in his voice.

"Yeah, I'm good. You?" I avoided his gaze.

"I'm good, too." Was all he said, but I could tell from the sound of his voice that he wasn't satisfied. "Why don't we go, they're expecting us."

"Okay, cool." I was relieved that he didn't press the issue. I wasn't feeling completely myself at the moment and needed a minute to get a grip on how I felt.

As far as I was able to tell, Roman wasn't nearly as unhinged as I was at the idea of being near me outside the workday; it was an observation that forced my errant mind back into my body, embarrassed. When I did, I noticed that he had turned on the radio, and a Blues station from the city was coming from speakers. I was happy to notice as well that we hadn't gotten that far, not quite on the highway yet, because it meant that I hadn't been sitting silently for too terribly long.

"This is nice." I observed about a piano piece that was being played just then.

"Yeah, it's a nice piece." I could hear the relief in his voice; maybe he wasn't as comfortable as I'd initially thought. I looked over at his face when he didn't say anything else. He had his eyes on the road, and both hands on the wheel in front of him. Definitely not as comfortable as I'd thought; I immediately felt myself relax.

"So where exactly are we going? You didn't say where you usually meet up. Are we going to your friend's place?" I asked conversationally.

"Ah, yeah, we're going to his place. He lives in the city, but he's got a good piano so we generally meet at his." He still didn't take his eyes off the road, effectively avoiding me by checking to change lanes in the mirror opposite me, but I could tell he was relieved to have me in charge of the conversation; his hands relaxed on the wheel and his shoulders eased back into his seat.

We drove for a while just listening to the music: more bluesy piano stuff. I closed my eyes for a little while, just enjoying the music since we didn't seem to have anything else to talk about. The initial tension was gone though, and it didn't feel awkward to sit without speaking. Instead it felt comfortable.

As I listened I studied the sky for any signs of cloud mass. I had checked the weather quickly before I'd gone for my run earlier, but I was still slightly anxious. I was happy to see the clear skies forecasted reflected in the baby blue stretching out above us.

While I had slept solidly through both my nap and the entire night, I had also had little snippets of my dream playing in my mind throughout. There had been slight variations to the scenario, though; little things that I knew were a result of my own overactive mind, but they still stuck in my memory. Little things changed, like the color of the woman's hair, the height of the man, and then in the last variation I had been able to hear some more of what had been said. Altogether connecting the couple in my dream to Roman and myself. It hadn't really bothered me when I'd woken up this morning, but now that I was sitting in the truck next to him, it all came flooding back.

We were getting into the city before I, tired of my own thoughts, began to feel like we should have some sort of conversation, no matter how mundane. My mind was on music so that was where I began. "I brought some music with me."

"What, sheet music?" He sounded surprised at the sound of my voice over the radio.

"Yeah. I grabbed a couple of things for violin and piano, just to have with me. They're stuff I know… so…" I paused and shrugged, unsure of how to explain that I'd written two of them.

"What are they? Anything I know?" He asked, warming to the conversation.

"I'm not sure. The stuff for violin is an old Irish folk song." I smiled; it was my dad's favorite. "I don't remember the name of it at the moment, but then the stuff for piano is mostly classical."

"Oh. I guess I'll wait until I hear you play them then." He was smiling now too, though still not looking at me. We were in the city now, so I figured he wanted to pay attention to where we were going. "We've got another like twenty minutes or so." He abruptly answered my unspoken question.

"Oh! Okay. How'd you know I was wondering that?"

"Lucky guess." He looked at me now, laughing a little himself as he did.

I just smiled, forgetting what I had just been talking about. It came back to me when he turned back to the road.

"Yeah, and then the other couple of things I brought with me are multi-part." I was suddenly confident enough to tell him I'd written some of what I'd brought. "They're some stuff I've been messing with; stuff I wrote myself."

"Really?" His tone was carefully curious, making me wince a little. "You didn't mention before that you'd studied that formally." I couldn't figure out what he meant by saying that; it took me a moment to reply.

"I haven't." I paused a moment, carefully figuring out what to say next. "I got a lot of theory from my piano and violin teachers over the years. I guess I just kind of kept it up, started playing around with arrangements and such. Now I've written several pieces, but of course I have no idea if they're any good with the actual instruments…" I paused again, knowing that this was a huge lie as I said it. "I've only ever played them out on the piano."

"Oh! We should see if we can play whatever you've brought with you with the group!" He sounded really enthusiastic as he said it. "It would be nice to play with something that wasn't just my friend's work. It gets a little boring playing that all the time." He twisted his mouth a little as sarcasm dripped from his voice. I smiled involuntarily; this was going to be fun.

We were pulling into a parking garage now. I had lost track of where we were going while I'd been talking. I looked around in surprise. We were in the more upscale part of town and I could feel the nerves returning as I took in the cars that were parked around us. It was full of BMW models and Audi's and various other makes and models that I didn't recognize in the least, although I thought I did see a very new looking Honda Civic somewhere. Then I heard him laugh and my head whipped around to glare at him, embarrassed. His head was tipped back in a full belly laugh and I felt my face heat up as I watched. Clearly my reaction had been plain to see on my face.

"Not quite what you expected, hunh?" He said, when he'd gotten his laughter under control.

"No. Not exactly." I answered, trying to sound as miffed, as I'd felt. It was difficult with him laughing like that though, it was contagious and I was finding it difficult to maintain a straight face. "Can we go in?" I asked minutes later, when he didn't even move to get out of the truck.

"Oh! Yeah, of course. They'll be wondering where we are." He was still laughing, although more muted now, as we both got out of the truck. I got my bag of music and violin out from behind my seat before he could come help me; then I followed him to a door in one of the walls of the parking garage that took us into the apartment complex I had noticed next to it on our way in.

I was thankful to find the inside of the building less overwhelming than the cars in the garage had been. The floors were covered with a plush tan colored carpet, and the walls were painted in a similar shade and had a simple dark wood trim along their base; it was all very clean and neat, but not ostentatious. It made me feel a little less apprehensive about who I was going to meet, to walk into a scene that felt so much more normal than the garage. Although I wasn't sure why I should be nervous in the first place. It wasn't like I was his girlfriend that he was bringing for the first time to meet his friends; or at least I didn't think I was. My heart rate picked up a little at the thought, remembering what he'd said about watching me for the last few months. Maybe they did think he was bringing his girlfriend.

We walked down the hall a short ways, me following behind him, until he stopped at a door on the right side of the hall and knocked. I could hear people yelling to come on in; they seemed to know who it was, and I got the impression Roman's prediction would be right.

I tried to relax when Roman just smiled and opened the door, but somehow I couldn't quite manage to. My nerves were back, just for a different reason this time. As hard as I tried, I couldn't help wondering what they would think of me. I had no reason to; I'd never met them before and there was a chance that I would never meet them again, but for some reason, it was vitally important to me to make a good first impression. I swallowed hard and followed Roman into the apartment; a smile fixed firmly on my face.

"Roman!" Was the collective yell we heard as soon as we walked through the door. "You finally made it man! What the hell took you so long?" Asked the man walking over to where we stood by the door. I noticed that there was a small group of men all seated on the various sofas and love seats arranged in the sitting area just to the side of the door; I counted about five guys already here.

"Sorry, Jason, traffic was ridiculous so it took longer than usual." Roman explained. I caught the name Roman used, and finally looked at the man it belonged to. He wasn't as tall as Roman, though he looked like he was more muscular, and had black hair with warm brown eyes. I thought I could hear a whisper of a foreign accent in his voice too.

"You must be Lisbeth, then?" I froze for a second before realizing he was talking to me.

"Yeah, that's me." I answered a little late, finally unfreezing and returning his warm smile; I was able to avoid the handshake though since my hands were rather full.

"It's nice to meet you. Roman said you two work together?" He continued to smile, and I began to relax; I liked him already.

"Yeah, I'm a vet tech at the clinic he's working at now." My voice gained strength as I elaborated.

"Good, good." Was his only response, as he clapped his hands together in a gesture that told me he was eager to start the session. "Why don't we introduce you to the rest of the gang then. Oh, and Roman said you play; I see you've brought an instrument so let me know what you want to do." He spoke as he walked to where the rest were seated, none of them having moved since we'd entered the room. Roman moved to stand nearer to me, seeming to sense my increasing nerves at to the group of unfamiliar faces.

It was Roman who introduced, what I now saw I'd estimated accurately to be, a group of five men. I focused hard to connect the names with the faces and store it all away into my memory. There was Billy: a blond man from the city who played the flute. Then there was Damian: a tall, thin man with a hank of black hair that played electric and upright bass. Chris was younger than the others, with short blond hair that had been spiked with gel, and played saxophone. Mike, a slightly pudgy, flaming redhead, I was told was the drummer, which left Mark, a tall athletically built man, who apparently played trumpet. I spent a moment wondering why no one played guitar, but promptly remembered that Roman had said he played.

"Right. Let's get crackin'!" Jason said, once Roman had finished with introductions, and turned to walk across the apartment into a room on the opposite side. He had disappeared into it long before any of the others had moved from their seats. All of them, seemingly unaffected by their friend's enthusiasm, took the time for another drink from their beers before standing to make their way after him. I followed Roman, listening to their casual conversation.

"Hey Chris! Its good to see you. How was the visit home?" Roman asked the saxophone player.

"It was good. It was good." I noted a London accent. "My mum and dad are doing well, and it was nice to see all the rest of the family."

"Good to hear." I got the impression from his intonation that there was a history here I wasn't aware of, but I didn't have time to think about it.

"Hey Damian!" Roman engulfed the thinner man in a bear hug. I was struck by the difference in their looks; one tall and sturdy with warm looks and the other tall but thin and shockingly pale against the black hair.

"Hey Roman." He responded, a small smile on his lips.

I watched as Roman repeated the process, greeting the other three members of the group, before he turned to me and placed a hand on my shoulder. He caught my eye as we walked towards the room Jason had disappeared into, and I sensed read some of my confusion there.

"Some of us had trips to make, so we haven't met up in a while." He said by way of explanation. "Jason's all excited to get going because he's had something in the works since we met last, and he wants to get going on it." He laughed quietly. "I guess you could say you were lucky when you asked to meet them all this weekend."

"Oh. Yeah, I guess that was lucky." I was glad my voice didn't squeak; my nerves had settled faster than expected.

As I walked through the door I was immediately struck by the size of the room. It was about half again as big as the room we had just left, and full of everything a musician could possibly want. A Baby Grand piano sat in the corner just across from the door, and along the wall across from it stood various speakers and amps for the numerous guitars that stood in stands arranged in front of them. Then there were, of course, a handful of music stands and chairs; all but two already claimed by the rest of the guys. One of these stood directly in front of the door Roman closed behind us; the other stood amidst the group, arranged around the chair I'd observed first.

Roman caught my gaze for a moment before motioning for me to take the chair by the door, setting my violin on the floor just below the piano as he went to fill the other empty seat. Neither of us spoke - it was impossible to hear anyway over the sound of tuning instruments that now filled the room. I wondered as I took my seat, how Jason's neighbors put up with the noise, but it occurred to me, that the room was most likely sound proof.

As I settled myself into the chair I heard a change in the noise, Jason was playing the beginnings of something on the piano. I didn't recognize the sound of the melody, so I listened closely, trying to make it out; one by one the others followed his lead, without a word, simply falling into the flow of the music as if they'd never stopped playing. Soon I was caught up in the ebb and flow of its melody, and I closed my eyes as I relaxed and let it flow through me.

The next two hours flew by; the men shifting seamlessly from melody to melody, taking breaks as necessary to empty spit valves and such but never stopping at the same time, maintaining continuous sound. The music ranged from simple folk arrangements to bluesy and jazzy pieces, and a few I recognized as Jason's genre mixtures. My ears rang with the silence when they finally stopped.

I didn't speak; didn't want to be the first to break the silence. It took a moment for anyone else to say anything, and I could tell by the looks on their faces that they were still in the music, even when they finally did.

"Not bad for having a month off." Billy finally joked. Laughter effectively broke the silence and left a sense of relaxed energy to fill the room.

"Let's give that new thing I've got a try." Jason pitched his voice over the laughter.

"Sure, Jason, let's see what's got you all excited." Roman teased. "I hope it's good!" I couldn't help joining in the laughter this time.

"Lisbeth, would you mind playing a violin part for me?" Jason caught me off guard. "You don't have to if you don't want to." He added immediately, my surprise evidently visible on my face. "I just thought I would ask."

"No, I'd like to play." I smiled. It would make me feel more comfortable to play with them. "Do you have a copy of the music for me?"

"Yeah, right here." He pulled a piece of sheet music from the stack that sat on the piano. "There you go." I looked it over as he handed the rest of the stack to the others.

I liked the look of the piece, not too difficult, but I had a feeling it wouldn't sound as simple as it looked. I stripped off the light jacket I'd been wearing, draping it over the back of my chair, and went to get out and tune my violin. When I turned back to my chair a few minutes later, a music stand had appeared in front of my chair. It made me smile as I adjusted its height and arranged the music across it. The piece wasn't long, so I wouldn't have to do much page turning.

The rest of the gang was already playing through some of their parts, so I took a moment to look over my own. It sounded like I had expected it to. A moment later Jason asked everyone to stop playing, so they could run through it; giving us the tempo, and a couple of bars before starting.

For a first time run-through, I was amazed at how smoothly it went; especially for myself since I had neither played the song or with them before. It had flowed smoothly, and quickly, the melody an upbeat combination of an Irish folk song, some classical lines, and a little bit of rock. While it might have made a purist cringe, I found it exhilarating; my experience with the storm music had made me appreciate ingenuity more than the ruling guidelines of genre and composition.

"I like it." I said when we'd finished. "It's good."

"Thanks." I looked up at him. He grinned widely; I'd only told him what he already knew. I grinned back, laughing lightly at the ego. The others joined me, ribbing on Jason about kissing up to the ladies while giving him their own compliments.

"Hey Lisbeth?" It was Roman, trying to get my attention over the noise of the other's voices.

"Yeah?" He motioned for me to go over by him. "What is it?" I asked, once I stood next to him; his body was difficult to ignore as he wound his arm around me and spread his palm over my waist. I forced myself to ignore the small shiver that trembled through my body.

"Would you want to play something for us? You said you brought music with you…" He trailed off at the end of the request with a shrug that made me smile.

"Sure, no problem. You guys can have a break then." I could see by the look on his face, I'd interpreted the request correctly.

"Hey Jason!" Roman shouted to get his attention, and I saw the corners of his eyes crinkle in silent amusement at our casual stance; for once I didn't care. "Lisbeth is going to play some songs for us. She brought some music with her."

"Oh." His brows lifted. "Okay. We can take a little break, I guess." I could see he'd wanted to keep working on his own piece.

"I won't be long, I promise, Jason." I said by way of placating him.

"Okay." He sighed and gave in.

I went over to my chair to pull out my bag from underneath and get out the music I had brought. I figured it would be easiest to start with the violin pieces, since I already had the instrument out of its case and tuned. I didn't wait for the others to quiet down to start; instead, I just started straight into the music, letting it fill the gaps in the noise until it was the only thing to be heard.

The piece I selected was classical, and it ebbed and flowed within itself so that I felt myself begin to move with the motion of the tune, feeling every note. I felt the remnants of my nerves fall away as I fell smoothly into sync with the movements of the instrument I held. It was over too soon, and left me feeling on edge, unfulfilled, so I continued, moving directly into the piece I had subconsciously placed behind the one I had just finished. This piece was different, an old Irish traditional piece I'd had around for ages; the one that was my dad's favorite. I felt a blissful smile spread across my face as I played the piece, memories of other times I had played it for my family flashed across my mind.

When I finally finished that piece, I was startled out of my reverie by a loud burst of applause that made me jump in surprise. It took me a moment to focus my gaze on the group of men in front of me; they were looking as dumbstruck as I was feeling. I had a moment of déjà vu, and then remembered a similar scene in one of my dreams: I had forgotten the effect that my gift had on those listening to my music; I was glad I had just been playing violin, and not singing.

"That was amazing." Damian whispered.

"How did you learn to play like that?" Chris added. I blushed a little slightly; slef-conscious.

"I don't know." I was as truthful as I could be. "I just love to play I guess, and practice helps."

"Whatever it is you do, that was...unbelievable." Jason's voice sounded thick.

"Lisbeth?" It was Roman speaking now. "Would you play the piano pieces you brought?" His voice sounded even thicker than the rest had, and when I met his gaze, I found my eyes locked there by the intensity I saw. I felt my throat go dry, and it took me a moment to speak.

"Yeah, I guess I could do that." I broke away for a second to look guiltily at Jason. "That is of course if you don't mind, I know you wanted to go over that piece some more."

"Of course I don't mind. Go right ahead!" He almost sounded insulted that I'd asked; I had to suppress a laugh, knowing perfectly aware of why he didn't care anymore.

I put away my violin, not wanting to leave it out while I played the piano. No matter what Jason said, I knew he still wanted to go through his piece again, and we had already been playing for about three hours straight. My instrument taken care of, I picked up the rest of the music I had packed, and walked over to the Baby Grand. Jason moved over to the chair I had vacated so that I could sit on the piano bench.

I took a deep breath as I sat; spreading out the music in front of me, not paying close attention to which piece came first, simply settling into the instrument. I played a couple cords to test the keys and sound; took another breath and began to play.

I didn't realize until I began which piece of music had shifted its way to the top. It was the same song that had caught me up so thoroughly just looking at the sheet music that morning, and it caught me up just as strongly now. A thought flashed briefly in my mind that I'd intended to play this piece with the band, not as a piano solo, but I didn't spend much time on it. As the first chord rang in my ears I heard a faint rumble of thunder in the distance, and again at the second, third and fourth. I didn't react as I continued to play, feeling the piece play itself in my mind as my hands drew it out of the piano in front of me.

About two lines into the piece, I saw the first flash of lighting, and heard the sound of brass instruments in it. I was conscious of what was going on now, but I was still unable to stop, the piece took control of me, pulled energy from my core and brought the storm's song, written on the paper in front of me, to life outside the apartment.

Conscious now, I began to feel panic nip at the edges of my mind, vying with confusion and fear for control; it took a few moments before my years of meditation kicked in, allowing me to breathe deeply and calm myself, regaining control of my mind. The effect was instantaneous; I was able to control the actions of my hands again and immediately began to slow the tempo. Yet I knew instinctively that I shouldn't end the song, so, playing the piece embedded in my mind, I looked up from the paper and searched for Roman amongst the people in the room.

The men were at the one window in the room, observing the storm that, to them, had appeared out of nowhere. The sky had been perfectly clear when I had started playing. It wasn't hard to find the man I sought; he stood directly in front of the piano, his eyes as intense as before, but filled with a different emotion. What had been an intense awe was now an equally intense concern, edged with a fear that as barely overridden by something I wasn't prepared to recognize.

Neither of us said a word. I knew he was reading my face as I was his; I hoped that he would see beyond the new calm that had taken over my mind. He continued to stand where he was, and I played on, skipping repeats until I reached the end. I tried to ignore the storm that was raging just outside the room we were in, but it was impossible. I could still feel every beat, every note, as if for the first time.

It wasn't until I played the final chords that I began to realize what exactly had happened; looking down at my hands as I lifted them from the keys, I suppressed the knowledge. It would have to wait until I was home and could talk to Kaya and Tom; I wasn't ready to bring Roman into the mix, even if it probably wouldn't be much longer before I did.

We stared at each other again after I'd finished; the moment he realized I was done, he moved around the piano to my side. I couldn't read the look on his face.

"Are you okay?" I could both feel and hear the emotion in his whisper.

"Yeah." I whispered before looking up at his eyes.

My heart squeezed a little when I looked over at him, seated beside me on the bench, as I remembered what I had seen in his eyes mere minutes before. We didn't say anything else; there wasn't time as the rest of the group filtered back over to us; the storm having dissipated, the skies clearing. It made me a little more comfortable to know that the storm took longer to dissipate than it had to build up; it meant that some part of it had been natural.

"I think it's your turn now." I smiled as naturally as I could at Jason.

"You sure you don't want to play more?" He asked, the effect of my music still visible on his face.

"Yeah, I'm sure. I think you've had enough of a break." I looked over at Roman, and he returned my smile. One storm was enough for today.

"Alright, if you're sure." He didn't look as disappointed anymore. "C'mon guys, let's give this another go."

There was a collective sigh as the rest of the gang returned to their seats. It occurred to me as they did, that they seemed oblivious to any connection between my playing and the storm. I stored away that observation for later.

I got up and took out my violin again, shifting through the music on my stand to find Jason's piece. Roman had moved back to his chair and was picking up his guitar; the rest of the group following suit.

It was as if we hadn't taken the break, playing the piece even more smoothly than the first time, and once we had finished the second run through Jason jumped straight into working on specific details and sections of it so that we spent another one to two hours just on that piece. When we were finally finished it was after four o'clock in the afternoon, and I was in need of a break. As we began to put things away, I looked around the room, glad to see that I didn't appear to be the only person that felt that way. We had been playing for almost five hours straight between us, and my fingers were screaming at me for a break, red from pressing down the strings.

"Right, who's for a drink?" Mark said to the room at large. There was a collective chuckle in response.

"I'm up for that." Mike and Billy looked at each other and grinning.

"Same here!" Damian chimed in. I looked over at Jason and couldn't keep from smiling when he grudgingly agreed.

"Alright. Drinks are in the fridge."

I looked at Roman, curious at his silence, and found that he was looking at me, with a thoughtful expression on his face. I swallowed, forcing myself to keep smiling as I held his gaze. Finally, after a while, I pulled my eyes away from his and went to pack my violin back into its case; focusing on maintaining the calm left from playing with the band. As a result, I was in the middle of putting my music back into the bag I'd brought it in before I realized that Roman stood in front of me, watching.

I felt him more than I saw him when I did notice, pausing in my movements - waiting - not wanting to be the first to break the silence. After a moment or two, impatience got the better of me, and I looked up at him. His eyes were a dark brown with concentration, and he wasn't smiling; I could tell he was thinking hard about something, but I wasn't sure I wanted to know what exactly that was. Not watching what I was doing, my eyes on his, I finished filling my bag, and stood, slinging it over my shoulder in the process.

"If you want to ask me something, I'd rather you'd just ask. Don't just stand there staring at me, coming up with your own answers." My voice sounded flat to my ears for the way my pulse jumped.

He didn't answer right away, just continued to stand there, looking at me. Then, before I could even register the motion, he was directly in front of me, and I was staring up at him, neck bent back.

"This may be one of the craziest things I have ever done." His voice was low. The next thing I knew, he was kissing me; softly, a gentle pressing of his lips against mine, but a kiss none-the-less.

I was stunned, overcome by this response to the events of this afternoon. He didn't try to deepen the kiss, simply pulling away after that one simple meeting of lips. As he did, I found myself staring at him again, something I was slightly embarrassed to realize I'd done a lot of throughout the day; we stood like that for a moment, neither of us spoke.

When he bent in to me again I was prepared for the kiss, and as I felt his lips meet mine, I leaned into it. Suddenly aware, as I did, of my heart racing, breath shortening, and a heat curling through my body where it pressed lightly against his. This time it was me who pulled away first, slightly overwhelmed at the response my minimal experience hardly prepared me to handle.

I couldn't quite meet his eyes as I pulled away. Aware of the hand that had wound its way into my hair while the other was pressed firmly against the small of my back. I could also feel his eyes search my face, gauging my reaction. I guessed he was wondering the reason for the hot flush that had flooded my face.

"Definitely one of the craziest things I've ever done." His voice sounded thick, and just a little strained, but he smiled as my eyes flew to his, laughing a little as well. "God, you're beautiful." He stated it simply, but I still felt myself flush again at the words.

"Maybe you really are crazy." I mumbled. His eyebrows shot up a bit at whatever he caught of it.

"I'm not that crazy, Lisbeth." When I didn't respond to that, he sighed. I dropped my eyes from his, staring at his chest instead; heat flooded my face yet as embarrassment surfaced again. I heard another sigh. "Are you going to tell me who you are?"

I stiffened at his words; not ready to give the answer he was asking for. So I stalled for time as I decided what to do. Thankfully he didn't push.

"You know who I am." I finally settled on, still avoiding his gaze.

"You know what I mean." He pulled his hand out of my hair now, an action that left me surprisingly sad. "Are you going to tell me who you really are?"

I sighed and for the first time faced the fact that I would eventually have to tell him. There was no point feeding him a lie in the mean time.

"I will." I stated simply. He just looked at me and waited for me to continue. This time it was me who put some distance between us, taking a deep breath and a step back from him at the same time. "I can't tell you right now... but I will, I promise." I looked back up at his face as I spoke, hoping he would read the sincerity of the words in my own.

"Okay, then. I trust you." He didn't wait for me to reply, instead he turned slowly and walked out the door to join the rest of the guys. When I followed him a few minutes later, carrying my violin and bag of music with me, I found him chatting casually with his friends, drink in hand.

He didn't avoid my gaze when I sought his, wanting to check if everything really was ok. He simply walked over to draw me into the group, effortlessly working me into the conversation and effectively distracting me from further thought on the topic.

It ended up being almost six o'clock before we finally left Jason's apartment, returning to the overwhelming garage of cars to get into the truck and head home. The drive back to the clinic parking lot was an uneventful one; we listened comfortably to the radio, chatting about whatever we felt like while thoroughly avoiding the one thing we both knew we needed to talk about.

The tension that had filled our drive that morning, however, was completely evaporated, and thanks to its absence the drive passed by much more quickly than it had before. We didn't say anything about future plans as he dropped me off by my car in the clinic parking lot. We both knew that we would be seeing each other again on Monday in the clinic, so there was no need to make plans now. On the drive back to the house though, my mind began to replay the events of the day in slow motion noting every detail and raising more questions than I knew what to do with. When I pulled into the driveway and parked I wasn't surprised to see that neither Tom nor Kaya were there; they would've had their own plans for their Saturdays.

I took my things out of the car and walked through the door, into the house, a plan slowly forming in my mind. I needed answers to the questions crowding my head; and there was only one person who could really help me, more than either Tom or Kaya, and that was Mom.

Chapter 10

Fifteen minutes later I was seated, cross-legged, in the middle of the living room floor; our usual place for meditation. It felt odd, meditating alone; it was a first for me. Regardless, my breath evened out swiftly, my heartbeat settling with it into a steady rhythm, and my mind emptying so that I sat in a calm, controlled silence.

I had no real idea of how to go about doing what I was attempting to do. I was only able to guess, based on her previous visits, that meditation was the key as she had only appeared to us during a few of our meditation sessions; never during our dreams or any other time. So now I sat, legs crossed, deepening my meditation and waiting, completely unsure of whether or not I was doing the right thing. Only aware of the fact that I desperately needed to talk to her. To, at the very least, ask the questions if not get the answers.

I have no idea what point I had reached when I had finally done the right thing, but I was suddenly confronted with a familiar image on the backs of my eyelids, and an even more familiar voice in my head. She sounded the same as she always did, her voice a little low for a woman, and warm without sounding husky. The sound of it made me smile in my mind, while my face remained smoothly focused in the meditation. As on the previous occasions when she had visited, though few since the initial introduction almost two years ago, her face and form were vaguely reminiscent of various people I knew; different people each time. Her dress was a vaguely Grecian style, and a deep blue this time; while the color of her clothing changed constantly, the style of it never did, and it draped perfectly around her body as she stood there, in my mind, looking back at me with her multi-colored eyes. Returning her gaze, I felt her knowledge of my dilemma, though she had yet to say anything; so I laid before her, in my mind, the questions that were crowding it, and simply waited for her reply. I wasn't sure what to think when I saw a look of absolute surprise fill her face.

"So." She began. "It appears you have made a discovery." She paused, her face thoughtful, and I felt myself grow impatient for her to continue her answer. She smiled when she sensed my anxiety. "This is truly the first time that you have had this particular talent through your gift. I am not sure how to answer your questions." She explained. "I don't know for sure whether it will happen again, or not. There is a chance that you can control it, and there is also the possibility that you will never have full control." She lapsed back into silence; I mulled over what she said in combination with what I already knew.

After a moment she spoke again, and as I listened I knew that she had been listening to my thoughts, combining them now with her own conjectures and knowledge.

"Let's review what we do know: that you hear the music in storms, record it on paper as well as on a tape, and generally don't touch them again for one reason or another." She didn't crosscheck her information with me, but I nodded mentally in agreement anyways; grasping at that false sense of control it gave me to give rather than have my opinions assumed, even if assumed correctly. "Now we have learned that if you do play the music again, whether or not you recreate the entire instrumental arrangement, the storm will be recreated, again regardless of whether or not the present weather is predisposed to a storm. We also know that your reaction to the music was much like Kaya's to the hawk when she healed for the first time; the energy was taken from you against your will, you did not have a choice in the matter." She paused and looked at me studiously, or rather at my memories.

"Yet you regained your control, didn't you? You were able to shorten the length of the storm, skipping the repeat signs and even slowing the original tempo for a moment." She spoke slowly, her face thoughtful; I wasn't quite sure yet what she was getting at. "You made a conscious decision not to end the storm, but to let it run its course, playing the rest of the music rather than stopping in the middle. Yet you would have been able to, to stop I mean."

It began to sink in then what she meant. "Yes, my daughter." She smiled at me now; she'd known the second I had reached the answer. "You can recreate the storms, but you might also be able to control them: their beginning and end, the middle, and perhaps even the effect they have, their final result."

My mind went haywire, new questions pouring forth in both fear and amazement as I struggled to wrap my mind around the concept of being able to control the storms whose music so often controlled me.

"I do not have the answers to your questions, my child, and unfortunately you will not have the help of your dreams either." Her eyes were concerned as she spoke. "This is the first time that this talent has surfaced, in all your lifetimes. As a result the only way to find those answers is through your own searching. I only wish that I knew what it was that triggered its appearance now, instead of before." Her voice trailed off a bit as she spoke, and then the look of concern deepened and she burst out suddenly, "Who is this Roman Fournier?"

I was stunned at the question, completely unexpected, but that quickly changed as I felt laughter well up in my chest. She sounded so perplexed. Then I felt my face begin to heat at the tone of her voice as she asked the question; she sounded every bit the part of a mother. I wondered what she had seen in my memories of the day to make her sound so protective through her confusion.

"My dear it would seem that you are situated in the middle of two turning points in this lifetime." Now I understood. "I do not know why this talent has made itself known now of all times, what the catalyst for this might have been; and I don't know what its potential might be. I only know that time will make it clear." Maybe I didn't understand. "Oh my child." She paused, her face filled with an emotion I couldn't quite pinpoint; then she reached out with her hand, as if she would have touched my face were it possible. "Trust yourself. Trust your family. Trust him. All will come clear, if you simply allow yourself to believe in yourself." She vanished then; left me with an empty mind, to sit in the middle of the living room floor.

I sat motionless for a moment or two after she had left me; soaking up the peace before I let my mind return to the information she had filled it with. When I did open my eyes I was struck by a singular thought: I was on my own. She had not had answers for me, no little bit of knowledge that had escaped my dreams to tell me. No, instead, she had told me that I was alone in the search for the answer to my questions, and that she didn't know how long it could take to find them. In the midst of the confusion she had left me in, however, it occurred to me that she had left me with one key: Roman.

I heard the car doors slam from where I sat on the sofa with my book, and knew that at least one of my housemates had returned. I didn't bother to move, waiting until I heard the door open to look up from the page. When I did, I saw that both Kaya and Tom had returned, their arms weighed down with brown paper bags; it appeared they'd been out grocery shopping.

"Hey, you're back. How was the date?" Tom asked as he made his way to the kitchen.

"It was good." I answered vaguely, getting up to see if there was more to bring in. "How was your day?"

"It was good. Uneventful." Kaya answered for him. She watched me carefully as she spoke, following Tom into the kitchen with her armful of bags.

"That's good." I walked past her to go out to the car and get the last couple of bags that I could see were still sitting in the back of the car. As I did, I forced myself to organize my thoughts, preparing to face the questions I knew they would be bombarding me with the moment I walked into the kitchen.

"Right." Tom started, the moment I walked through the kitchen door. "Spill. What happened?" I smiled at his excitement as I set the bags in my hands on the counter and proceeded to empty them.

"Where to begin?" I asked teasingly, avoiding the topic while trying to mask my growing nerves. "I mean, it's been a busy day; where do you want me to start?"

"Let's start with when you left the house." Tom said sarcastically, arms crossed over his chest as he looked at me archly. I smiled; aware, as he was, that I was being evasive.

"Right." I quickly put away the frozen or refrigerated items that had been in the bags I'd grabbed and grabbed a chair at the table. The rest could wait a bit. "When I left the house." I took a deep breath and glanced at Kaya; she had been unnaturally quiet this whole time, and it made me a little apprehensive. I tried to shrug it off as I continued to talk to Tom. "I went to meet up with Roman at the clinic. Then he drove me to his friend's place in the city."

"Ok." Tom prompted when I paused.

"Ok, what? We met up with his friends there, the ones in the band, and I pretty much just listened to them rehearse. I brought my violin, so I played with them a bit, but otherwise it wasn't anything very spectacular." I cringed at my blatant lie. I wasn't sure when I had made the decision to avoid the topic of the storm, but apparently I had. Neither of them said anything just stared at me, their faces incredulous. "What?" I said guiltily.

"We saw the news Lis." Kaya said then. "The storm was breaking news. You know it's not exactly every day that a massive thunder storm shows up out of now where on an otherwise sunny day, and then vanishes without a trace." Her voice was like acid, and I knew that she'd been more than a little stung by my lies.

"Oh." Was all that I could manage to say; head ducked and cheeks flushed.

"Yeah, that's right." That was Tom. He wasn't sounding so excited now. "Care to tell us what actually happened on your date today?"

My face got even hotter as he spoke, my guilt increasing. I should have known that it would make the news. There was no way that the storm would have escaped the notice of the entire city of Chicago; the reactions of Roman's friends alone should have told me that much.

"I'm sorry." I said, looking up at last. "I shouldn't have lied like that. I guess I just...got a little nervous about it when it finally came to telling you." I ducked my head again. I'd always known I would tell them; all I'd done was to create another issue by skating around it instead of just coming out with the truth the first time around. "I did meet Roman at the clinic, and he did drive me to his friends in town. We messed around for a few hours; me listening, them playing; nothing very out of the ordinary with any musical rehearsal. Then Roman asked me if I would play for them, violin and some piano; he knew I had brought some music with me, and of course I'd brought my violin thinking I might play with them on some songs or something." I paused for a breath. "One of the pieces I brought was one of the storm songs, the ones I write down after hearing, you know? I played it on the piano after I'd played some stuff on violin and..." I trailed off, unsure of how to explain what had happened after that. They looked at me; waited for me to continue.

"What happened after that Lis?" Kaya prompted after a moment; her voice had lost its acid and was again filled with its usual levels of concern.

"It was, I'm not sure how to describe it, odd, I guess. When I had just looked at the sheet music before leaving, the music had gripped me, playing in my mind, like I was in the storm again, but when I actually played it..." I looked at them both in wonder. "It was like it had linked into me. I had no control, I simply played the first chords and then I was locked into it, my core energy flooding into each note I played. I panicked, when I lost control; I wasn't sure what I should do. I eventually remembered that I needed to use the meditation techniques; you know breathing and that kind of thing? I was so relieved that I was able to regain control the moment I began to concentrate on it."

"Wait, you regained control that quickly? Then why did the storm run its course? Why didn't you stop it?" Kaya's voice rose with the question.

"I don't know why I didn't, but yes I did regain control that quickly. It was odd, you would think that it would take longer to control something so new - "

"Actually I wouldn't. You remember how quickly I was able to control my own talent, with healing?" Kaya interrupted sharply.

"Oh. Right." I remembered what Mom had said earlier, about my new talent acting like Kaya's initial experience with healing.

"So, it actually would make more sense, given our own history, for control to happen so immediately." She elaborated.

"Yes, it would." I whispered, lapsing into silence for a moment, lost in thought.

"Keep going Lis. What happened after that?" Tom said after we'd sat quietly for a minute or so. "After you regained control."

"I slowed, the music I mean, and almost stopped." I caught Kaya's eye as I spoke, and rushed to answer the question I already knew she would ask. "I don't know why I didn't, Kaya, but I do know that something in me prevented it. I don't think its possible for me to, to cut off a storm. It let me alter the tempo, and even cut out repeats and things like that, so I can certainly alter the music, but I can't change when it ends. I have to play from beginning to end. Or at least that's what I think it has to be at this point." I shrugged, trying to make the point that none of this was definite.

"How much do you think you could alter the music, and thus the storm, do you think?" Tom's face was eerily serious.

"I don't know, yet." I raised my hands in a gesture of uncertainty. "It'll be a question of trial and error now, I think."

"You've already talked to Mom, haven't you?" Kaya spoke up, her tone wry.

"It was the first thing I did when I got back." I looked her dead in the eye. "I didn't see the point in waiting."

We sat in silence for a moment then. Each of us lost in our own thoughts. I knew that they each had more questions to ask me. I got the impression as well that Kaya was slightly miffed at the fact that I hadn't waited for them to try and get in touch with Mom. Although I didn't really understand why; it was probably just one of her things where there really was no reason for how she felt. After a few long moments of silence, I began to wonder what it was they weren't asking, or more importantly, what it was they were thinking.

"What's the matter guys? What aren't you asking?"

They didn't answer right away, looking at each other as if unsure which of them should speak first.

"I don't know if we have the same question to ask or not." Kaya began. "But I know what question I want answered." She paused, biting her lip before blurting out her question. "Did any of the others with you connect what was happening? Did anyone realize?"

I let out a breath of relief as I realized what she was worried about. Being able to create storms wasn't exactly the most normal trait for a person to have. "Only Roman." She didn't look convinced. "Kaya, I don't know if you've realized what kind of effect my playing or singing has on my audience, but they weren't exactly in a state of mind to notice much beyond the storm and the fact I was playing. That connection would have been too much."

"But Roman?" Tom asked.

"He was just focused on me the entire time. We were focused on each other, actually."

"Oh." They reacted simultaneously. I stifled a laugh at the look on their faces.

"Yes, so don't worry about it Kaya. No one had a clue." I smiled as I remembered the rather dazed expressions on the men's faces as they'd re-gathered to play again.

"Ok, well then, answer my question then." Tom said.

"Okay, shoot." I said, wondering what he would ask.

"Why now? Why has this talent shown up now, not in a previous lifetime or never? Did Mom have any ideas as to what triggered it?"

"Neither mom nor I have any ideas as to why now, Tom." I sighed. It was the question I'd been pondering while reading. "I wish I did. It would make it a bit easier, to at least know why."

Tom just nodded in response. "Mom didn't have any ideas either, hunh. Did she have anything helpful to say about all this?"

"No, not exactly." I stuck out my tongue. "She pretty much just confirmed what I had figured out on my own, not really adding anything important." I frowned, remembering her parting words. "Actually... She seemed to feel that this was something major. That there had to be something really important happening for a new talent to show up like this."

Tom and Kaya simply nodded in response. None of us seemed to have any answers. As we sat in silence, I glanced over at the microwave clock to check the time. It was about 7:12pm; close enough to dinnertime, so I stood to start rummaging around the recently stocked kitchen. It was my turn to cook. As I started the stove to boil water for pasta, Tom stood up from the table and walked into the living room to put on some music. Kaya continued to sit, staring as if in a trance at the surface of the table, lost in her thoughts. As curious as I was to know what they were both thinking, I let them be, focusing instead on the pasta with vegetables and meat sauce that I was making.

I heard a Moody Blues song start to ease its way out of the speakers as Tom walked back into the kitchen. I smiled, dumping handfuls of diced peppers into a saucepan, as my mind flicked back to the music Roman and I had listened to that day in the truck. It seemed that blues music was the order of the day. As I cooked, images from the day at Jason's apartment flashed back through my mind, not in any particular order it seemed, just little clips on shuffle. It wasn't until my mind hung up on one particular moment, that I paused, halfway to the saucepan with a jar of tomatoes.

It was the moment, during the storm, when I'd found Roman staring at me with an odd look in his eyes. I hadn't been able to recognize the emotion I'd seen then, but now I realized what I had seen, and as I did, something that Mom had said suddenly clicked. Roman was the key to why this was showing now; he knew more about me than I had ever guessed, because it had been recognition I'd seen mixed in with the awe in his eyes this afternoon. I upended the jar of sauce into the pan as the idea hit me, not even registering the spots that splattered onto my shirt from the pan; I was too stunned.

I felt Kaya's eyes on me as I turned around slowly to face her, trying to grasp the idea that had just occurred to me. Kaya stood up and walked quickly over to me the moment she saw my face; judging from the look on her own I had a feeling I was a bit pale.

"What is it Lisbeth? What happened?" Kaya asked as she moved.

"I -" I broke off, not sure how to say what I'd just realized. "Roman – " I tried again.

"What about him, Lisbeth?" She was looking me dead in the eye now, hands reaching up to rest gently on my shoulders. I didn't answer, just stared down into her warm brown eyes. "Lisbeth. What is the matter? What about Roman?" She pressed, saying each word slowly, enunciating each perfectly.

"Lisbeth?" Tom was standing with us now, and I looked up at him before answering.

"He recognized me." They didn't get it. "Roman recognized that I was the source of the storm, that I'm…" I trailed off, but neither of them spoke, waiting for me to finish the sentence. "That I'm a Child of the Earth."

I saw them both freeze, and knew my words had been crystal clear. We stood like that for a couple of minutes, until I remembered the sauce in the pan behind me, and spun suddenly just in time to save it from burning to the pan; judging from the smell I hadn't acted a moment too soon. Even as I turned off the stove, no one spoke. I didn't wait for them; finding that focusing on the food helped to keep me from letting the idea of Roman's already knowing what, or rather who, I was overwhelm me. So I simply proceeded to finish preparing the meal, and plating it for the other two, before walking, with plates in hand, to the table. They followed me, still speechless.

Sitting down at the table, I picked up my own fork to start eating, wanting to do something other than sit in silence, but not wanting to be the first to break it. Yet, I still couldn't quite bring myself to take a bite, feeling like the issue at hand needed to be resolved before I could. Looking up from my plate at the other two, I saw that they seemed to feel the same; both of them had forks hovering over their plates of pasta, neither taking a bite. Tom was the first to sigh and sit back from the food, looking expectantly at Kaya and myself.

"Alright, we clearly can't avoid this issue, now can we?" He spoke bluntly into the silence. Kaya and I looked at each other for a moment and then let out a sighing breath as we also sat back into our chairs.

"No, we can't." Kaya agreed.

I simply nodded; I'd already said enough.

"What're you thinking, Tom? What exactly is the issue?" I asked, after waiting a moment for them to say more.

"I think that would be pretty obvious, Lis." Kaya said. "How did Roman know you? How is it that he, of all the people that we have known since our awakening, recognizes who you are? Who we are? Doesn't that strike you as a little odd? Oh, and maybe just a little worrying?"

I grimaced at her sarcastic tone. It seemed that I was developing a talent for making Kaya pissed off tonight; it wasn't exactly normal for her to have acid so thick in her voice so often in one night, let alone in the space of maybe a half-hour.

"I was going to tell him anyway, Kaya. You know that." I whispered to her from my seat across the small table. "The dream."

"Just because you dreamed it, doesn't mean that you were going to do it now." Tom's sharp tone made it clear he was more put out than he let on. Of course Kaya and I were both staring at him now; all three of us knew just how false his comment was. Our dreams were our lessons in our individual talents; however, the lesson times were not necessarily consistent. Our dreams were more often predictors of an event approaching, in which we would need that specific information.

"Ah, Tom, I'm going to pretend you didn't just say that." I shot him a questioning look. He pursed his lips a bit in response and didn't look at me. It let it be.

"Ah yes, I'd forgotten about your dream." Kaya brought the conversation back on course. "I remember now." She looked quite a bit happier at that information. "When are you going to do it? Tell him, I mean." She looked up at me expectantly.

"I don't know yet. I guess it depends, on Monday at work, I mean. We didn't make any future plans, considering we already knew we'd be seeing each other at work anyway." I ducked my head, wincing a little as I did at the weakness of my explanation.

"But you are planning to tell him, right?" She looked worried again.

"Yes! Yes! Of course I'm going to tell him." I rushed to reassure her. "I don't think he's going to let me not explain myself. Not after today." I sighed, leaning forward over my plate of food. "I'm so scared, Kaya. I don't want to have to tell him. I'm so scared of his reaction." I looked up at them both, knowing my panic would show on my face. The concern and pity that mixed in their faces confirmed the thought. "And yet I have no choice. The first man that doesn't run away from me just for being me, and now I have to tell him this."

The tears started then; leaking out of my eyes until I just couldn't hold them back any more and I broke down into sobs. I was thankful that neither of them moved, simply sitting there and letting my tears run their course. It was embarrassing enough for me to break down at all, let alone having to deal with them getting all worked up over it as well. When the tears finally stopped though, and I looked back up at their faces, I could tell that leaving me alone hadn't exactly been their first choice of actions.

"Sorry, I'm sorry." I muttered, sitting up and picking up my fork again. "We should eat this before it gets cold." I tried to forget the fact that I'd just been crying, and dug into the pasta. I felt a little better when they followed my example; saying nothing as we ate, and maintaining the silence as we cleaned up and went through the motions of putting the kitchen back in order for the night. In fact, it wasn't until we were going our separate ways for bed that any of us said a single word.

"Lis?" I heard Kaya ask softly from behind me. "Are you going to be okay?" She asked when I'd turned to face her. I sighed; she was only asking because she cared.

"I'll be fine, Kaya. Really." I looked at Tom as I answered as well, knowing he would have wanted to ask the same question. Neither of them seemed to believe me, but they kindly let it go.

"Okay. If you say so." Kaya glanced at Tom. "Good night guys."

"Good night." Tom and I answered in unison, making all three of us smile as we headed the rest of the way upstairs to bed. I was more than a little happy as I settled in beneath the covers that the day was over. What I now had to look forward to the next day and the many days to follow after that didn't exactly have me psyched up for the future, but at the moment, all I was worried about was ending the present.

Sunday had passed quickly and simply, my sleep dreamless and restful, and, before I was ready for it, it was Monday, the end of that day arriving long before I'd even registered it's beginning. I had spent the workday hours avoiding in every way I could think of, the question that was nagging at the corner of my brain and in the pit of my stomach. I had continued in much the same mindset as I'd worked my way through the schedule of check-ups and the few emergency visits that peppered the day. Walking towards my car now, still in the zone of the workday, I didn't react when I looked over to see Roman leaning against the hood of my car, waiting for me.

He'd already changed out of the coveralls he wore for work, dressed now in what appeared to be well-worn jeans and an old t-shirt. He looked comfortable; leaning against my car the way he was, perhaps a little too comfortable, and a bit expectant. I swallowed sharply, he made my old Honda Accord look like a mini version by standing next to it, but it wasn't that that made me slow down; it was the look of absolute determination that he gave me as his eyes met mine. It was immediately clear to me that he wasn't just expecting answers; he wasn't going to accept anything less. Remembering what I'd realized the night before, it made me stall for time it before I had to start talking.

"Hello Roman." I said when I was close enough for him to hear.

"Hello Lisbeth." Neither of us said anything more until I was standing directly in front of him; as I did, I realized that his truck was parked right next to my car. For a moment I wondered how I'd managed to miss that when I'd parked this morning; it was a momentary thought though because as I met his gaze my senses went on red alert, nerves humming with awareness. The sensation jerked me solidly into the present moment.

"How was the rest of your weekend?" I hoped my voice was steadier than I was feeling at that moment. "Do anything else fun?"

"Nothing out of the ordinary. How was yours? You get up to anything interesting?"

"No, not really. Finished a book, helped out my housemates with some stuff, nothing spectacular."

"Mmm, that's cool." He shifted himself so he wasn't leaning on my car anymore. "So where are you headed now? Do you have any big plans for tonight?"

"No." I raised an eyebrow at him, wondering what he was getting at. Who went anywhere on a Monday? "No plans. I'm headed home right now, as usual. I thought you spent so much time watching me over the last few months, did you miss the fact that my social life is pretty much nonexistent?" I tried to sound sarcastic, but I wasn't sure it worked. He just looked like he was trying not to laugh. Well, I tried. "Ok, Roman, what do you want?"

"What? Why do you think I want something? Can't we just have a conversation?" His face looked a little too innocent as he said that, hands raised like I'd been attacking him. I frowned, not convinced. "We were having a conversation weren't we?"

"I'm not sure that's what I would call it." My voice was low. "More like an evasion session. Out with it." He sighed dramatically and dropped his hands.

"I think you know what it is I want, Lisbeth. Do I really have to say it?" He was serious now, not even the hint of a smile on his face. His eyes seemed darker with the gravity of the moment.

I didn't answer him immediately, standing there instead and thinking over the right way to answer that. Somehow I knew that there was more than one answer to the question he was asking. One I wasn't quite prepared to give while the other I didn't have the choice not to. I smiled and laughed a little as I thought, reaching a hand up to his face before I gave him my answer.

"Somehow that question doesn't seem to be as easy to answer as it should be. Oh, I know what it is you want." I said when I saw him start to look away at my words. "There just isn't one simple answer to give you though. That simple answer would be, me, you want me. The real, complete answer though, is that you want answers and you want me, but you're not sure you're going to like what those two together will mean." I wasn't sure where the tear came from that rolled down my cheek as I spoke, but I didn't try to wipe it away. My dream might have warned me that I would have to do this, but it hadn't done much more than that; I felt the terror I'd been suppressing the last couple of days, grip me completely and make every word I said a struggle.

Roman brushed the tear away for me, his fingers lingering on my face. I could see the confusion in his eyes as he did, and felt my heart wrench at the sight of it. Wasn't life full of little ironies; the first man I finally think things could work out with, and he's the one I run the greatest risk of losing. I fought back a hysterical giggle as it occurred to me how Hollywood-esc this moment seemed; like something out of a cheesy romantic movie. As soon as that thought popped into my head, I forced it back out. I wasn't going to be able to make this work if I couldn't talk for laughing; and it was now vitally important that I make it work.

"So, where are you headed to now?" I pulled my hand back from his cheek; he followed my example, shoving his hands awkwardly into his pockets.

"I'm headed home too, I guess."

"Oh, okay." I said softly, thinking. I smiled as it hit me. "Hey, would you want to come over? Right now I mean, you could follow me home in your truck." I paused and ducked my head a bit, hoping that it wouldn't sound too out of the blue; I mean I had just been crying. His eyebrows shot up; clearly he hadn't been expecting that. "Of course only if you want to. I just thought…" I trailed off, face flaming.

"Ummm, ok. I guess that works."

"Okay, so…" I paused; we were both still just standing there. "Should we go?"

"Oh, yeah." He turned immediately towards his car, then stopped and turned back. "I'll follow you." He confirmed, and walked over to the driver's side of his truck. I copied him, walking the few steps that it took to be even with my own driver's side door. I took a long breath as I sank into my seat and buckled up. My nerves were returning in full force now that I wasn't in front of him. I was full of new doubts and concerns about telling him; as much afraid of what I would be loosing if he did think I was a crazy person, as I was of the consequences if he turned out to be someone I shouldn't have trusted with potentially dangerous information. I understood now why Kaya's chief concern had been how much anyone had noticed on Saturday; it made me wonder how it hadn't bothered me before.

I eventually turned the key to start the car, and backed out of my parking spot. A glance in my rearview mirror as I started to pull out of the parking lot told me Roman was right behind me. I felt my breath catch in my throat a bit at the glimpse of him in the mirror. I was glad it wasn't that long of a drive to the house, and turned my eyes back to the road, focusing on my driving for the next fifteen minutes, Roman right behind me.

Turning off my car after I'd parked in the driveway, I kept myself on autopilot, not letting myself wonder whether I was doing the right thing or not. It had just seemed like it would be easier explaining what I had to explain to him, if I was in the one place I really felt comfortable with the topic; the one place I had always been able to speak freely about it: home.

Roman caught up to me as I walked around the house, purposely going directly to the garden rather than walking through the house. I was glad to see that neither Tom nor Kaya's cars were in the garage; it meant I could do this alone.

I tried to relax as I walked, counting out a steady rhythm as I fought against hyperventilating with nerves, focused on the green scent that filled the air as we stepped into Tom's masterpiece of a garden. The moment that I set foot on the patio, I knew that I had done the right thing, and as I turned to face Roman, I felt confidence replace the nerves. He had lagged behind me, eyes wide as they took in the garden around him, and was still standing in the middle of the lawn, several feet away from me. I smiled at the look of awe on his face; despite having lived with this in my own backyard for the last couple of years, I wasn't immune to its beauty, so I had no difficulty understanding his feelings.

"It's beautiful, isn't it? It's Tom's masterpiece." He didn't answer, just turned to stare at me instead of the garden. I laughed softly; Tom's garden tended to have this effect on people. For a moment we just stood like that, looking at each other without saying a word. I waited, hoping that he would ask and save me the trouble of breaking the ice; after almost five minutes, I gave up.

"I don't know where to begin." I'd concluded that honesty would be the best approach. "How much do you already know? I know you already know something, just not how much or what."

"I know very little, but the little that I do know I think is pretty key to this whole deal." His voice sounded surprisingly steady.

"If you already know what I am, then why not just tell me? Or ask me about it?" I asked bluntly; I was pretty confident about what it was he knew. "And, more importantly, how do you even know in the first place?"

"I didn't ask because I was worried that I was wrong. I'm not asking now because, now, I want to hear it from you first. I want to hear it from your own lips, no one else's."

"But how?" I asked. "How did you even know we existed? No one…"

"I'll explain that after you tell me." He avoided my question.

"Ok." I sighed, my mouth suddenly dry, and took a moment to steady myself before speaking. "I am Lisbeth Moore, a Daughter of the Earth, an old soul born at the very beginning of human time on earth, whose connection with the earth itself has given me a gift that expresses itself through my music and an extreme connection with the weather on this planet." My voice was flat, and direct in tone; the spoken words felt incredibly hollow for all the information they delivered. "Now tell me how you knew."

"My mother was one of you." It was enough to send me into shock.

"Your mother? But… how?" I stammered out. "She told you? What she was I mean."

"Yes, she told me. She told me after my father passed away. She died about ten years ago." He explained, his expression pained as he spoke. "I don't know why." He added a moment later. "I guess she just wanted me to know." He shrugged, not offering any further explanations.

"Oh." Was all I could manage to say; I was still frozen. He smiled sheepishly at my silence and ducked his head. Finally, I took a deep breath and cleared my throat to speak. "Well that explains your lack of surprise at what I just said. Roman, what did your mom all tell you? About us, I mean; did she tell you her talent, or anything like that?"

"She just told me she was a "Child of the Earth", and that her connection had been primarily with plants. She always did have beautiful gardens. Though nothing like this of course." He amended, looking back around our jungle of a back yard. "Though I suppose there aren't many gardens in the world like this one." He smiled, looking back at me. I nodded; that was definitely true. "She also told me that, although she had always been alone, there were others like her in the world. I guess not all of you are lucky enough to end up in a group like you and your housemates have."

"I guess not. Roman, where was your mom from? Was she American?"

"Born and raised French. She met my dad there and then they both immigrated here to Illinois immediately after their marriage. My cousin lives in the family home now, in Lille. Why does it matter?"

"It doesn't really, I guess. I was just curious because all three of us are American, and we've never met or heard of any like us in other countries." I shrugged. "What about your dad though? Did he know about your mom?" His face clouded over a bit as I spoke; I almost regretted asking.

"I'm not sure if my dad knew or not, but then again we weren't exactly close." As much as I wanted to, I didn't push him to elaborate; His face had clouded over completely now, and it was quite clear to me that I'd stepped on a nerve with the questions I'd asked.

"Oh, I'm sorry." I tried to find a way to divert the conversation. I hadn't really expected telling Roman about my secret to go quite this smoothly. I felt like I'd forgotten something, left out some important detail, but nothing came to me. Then two things occurred to me at once: one, that it was my turn to cook again, and two, that the only other two people who might think of other questions or details were going to be home in about an hour.

"Lisbeth? You okay?" Roman's voice made me jump a little. "Sorry."

"Oh! I was just thinking, sorry!" I explained. "Ummm… why don't we go in the house? I need to start working on dinner since it's my night to cook; maybe you could stay? Tom and Kaya will be back in about an hour or so from work, so it won't be that long." I waited for an answer.

"Ah, sure. Why not?" He sounded a bit surprised. "Can I do anything to help?"

"We'll see. You might be able to make yourself useful." I teased as I turned to walk into the house through the back door.

"So did your mother teach her son to cook? Or are you like most single men these days: barely capable of pouring milk over their cereal let alone frying an egg or boiling pasta." As I'd intended, he laughed again.

The next twenty minutes were spent in easy banter as we teased and complimented each other on our cooking skills. I found out that his mother had in fact taught him how to cook, because he helped me turn the simple rice dish I had intended to make for dinner, into something quite a bit better, though I was sure only Kaya would be able to completely appreciate it. As we worked the conversation shifted; going from casually teasing and light, into much more personal territory. It started innocently enough with simple questions about each other. Nothing out of the ordinary for two people getting to know one another.

"So what's your favorite color?" I asked, laughing lightly as I checked the rice.

"Hmmm… burgundy. What's yours?"

"Really? Deep Purple."

"Hunh. So what's your favorite genre of music? And you can't just say everything, name a genre."

"Probably classical, although I do actually listen to everything." I smiled. "What about you?"

"Blues."

"No surprise there." I cut him off with a snort.

"What's that supposed to mean?" He demanded; pointing the knife he was using in my direction. I didn't take him seriously though, considering he was smiling as he did it.

"Oh, you know, it's only the one genre I've heard from your radio; it was on when I turned it on, but I'm pretty sure it's on your presets too." My voice was thick with sarcasm.

"Very funny. Here's another question then. What's your favorite instrument to hear played? Miss. Musical."

"Miss. Musical indeed." I took the chance to point my own knife in his direction. He didn't take me any more seriously than I had him. "What is this, a trick question? I'm not going to say guitar just to make you happy."

"Oh, I'm so sad." He mimed wiping away a tear, making me giggle a bit. "You won't hurt my feelings, shoot. What is it?"

"Piano." I fought to keep a straight face.

"Oh, well, you see now you've gone and flattered me anyway. You see, you kind of forgot that I play that too."

"Yeah, I know." He just stuck his tongue out at me, looking so childish I just laughed all over again.

After that we continued to work in silence; taking the rice off the stove while we finished preparing the vegetables and started sautéing them. We moved comfortably in the kitchen. Working smoothly with one another in a way that almost made me uncomfortable when I became aware of it. We seemed to anticipate each other's movements, never in each other's way. Then of course there was the way that he seemed to know exactly what to add to the dish and when, despite having never made it before. He also seemed to know just the right things to add, that weren't part of my original recipe.

With the two of us working together this way, it seemed to take less time than usual to go through the steps of the recipe; I knew the vegetables and rice hadn't actually taken less time, I just hadn't noticed the time as it passed. So it felt like no time at all before we were scooping the rice into the frying pan with the veggies to pan fry on a low heat for a few minutes, the final step in preparing the dish. I took a deep breath as I mixed the rice in with the rest of the ingredients, inhaling the rich aroma of the spices we'd added to it. I felt my mouth water as I teased my senses with the smells I inhaled.

I felt his eyes on my face before I looked up and saw him watching me. His face was more serious than before, but not in the way I'd been afraid to see. I set the spatula down on the counter beside the stove, and turned so that I was facing him completely. He was standing just a couple of feet away from me, in front of the sink but with his body angled towards me. I ran my eyes over his body, studying its language, trying to perceive what had caused the change in attitude. Then, when my eyes reached his, it clicked. They were dark, the outer edges of the irises almost as black as their pupils; the emotion I read in them causing my breath catch in my throat, my hand grasping vaguely for the edge of the counter.

Neither of us spoke as he moved slowly towards me, and cupped my face gently between his hands. My breath trembled in and out from between my lips as I waited, prepared this time for the kiss. It was nothing like our first; that had been a test, a foot in the water before the plunge. This was it. His hands wove their way into my hair as his lips fused to mine. My own hands were touching him before I even realized what I was doing, running over his shoulders and up into his hair. I felt myself melt as an even more intense heat than before built inside me. Then, before I was even conscious of my reaction, he broke the kiss.

I followed his mouth as he did, not wanting it to end, but he put a finger to my lips. I pouted a little at being thwarted, but focused instead on getting my embarrassingly heavy breathing back under control. When I finally looked up at him again a moment later, I could tell he'd been watching me again. The determination in his eyes, alongside the desire unsettled me.

"God you're amazing." That didn't answer my silent question.

"Why?" I wasn't sure how to express what I wanted to ask.

"It doesn't matter if you start a cyclone that tears down the entire city, or if you get so lost in a storm that you become part of it."

"You saw more than I thought, didn't you?"

"I guess." He shrugged. I saw his gaze dip to my mouth and smiled; I hadn't been the only one who'd enjoyed the kiss.

"Hmmm." I wasn't sure what else to say.

"Lisbeth?"

"What?"

"I don't think now's quite the time." When he looked at my mouth again, I laughed.

"I guess not, hunh?" I pouted a little as I looked up at him. "You're really not afraid of me." It wasn't a question. Then something else occurred to me. "Why me, Roman?"

"What do you mean?"

"I've been single, pretty much my entire life; the only dates I've been on have been disasters, and more often than not, guys just steer clear of me completely rather than even have a conversation with me." I paused for a moment to let that sink in. "So I'm asking, why me? When you clearly could date whomever you wanted." He snorted. "Why me?"

"I think I need to set some things straight here. First, don't even start on why I'm attracted to you. That would be clear to anyone who took a good look at you." I looked down as he spoke, but his hand caught my chin and pulled my eyes back to his; my face was burning. "Secondly, where are you getting the idea that I'm so much more experienced than you are? What makes you think I haven't been in the exact same position you are?" I didn't move, not sure what to say to something so unexpected. "Lis, I might not have been single my whole life, but I can tell you that I'm not that far off from it."

"Oh." Was all I could manage to say to that. "But... why?" It was his turn to laugh.

"Most women don't like the fact that I'm actually dedicated to my job." He smirked at the thought. "Loving animals is all well and good, just not actually taking care of them."

"They wanted you to be dedicated to them. Right?" I reached up to rest my palm against his cheek.

"I guess that's it." He shrugged and looked at me with worried eyes. "I guess I just didn't care about them enough to do that. I love my job too much, but, maybe -"

"I think I'm the one woman you could have found that would never ask that of you. Roman?"

"Okay." He brought one of his own hands up to rest on top of mine. "You really have to be the most unselfish person I've ever met."

"You have to be the craziest man I've ever met." I chuckled.

"Well I guess that makes us the perfect pair then." He said, shifting slightly closer to me. "Neither of us thinks they deserve the other." What reasons did he possibly have to be thinking I'd reject him? He wasn't the one recreating major storm systems simply by playing music on the piano.

"How can I? Deserve you, I mean." I asked after a moment; my voice thick with emotion.

"I just... I don't know... I guess, I just..." He couldn't come up with an answer, and after a few minutes he just gave up.

"Yeah, ah, Roman? You're not the one recreating storms on the piano. I'm just hoping you won't run away screaming the next time I get caught off guard by a storm because so far, you've proven a little too perfect, and how is it possible that I could deserve perfection."

"Oh really?" He raised a speculative eyebrow.

"Yes, really."

"Then I would like to know how it is that I deserve the one woman who has an even stronger connection to the animals we take care of than I do? How can I deserve her when she's one of the most beautiful, compassionate, intuitive, and intelligent women I've ever met?" It was my turn to raise a brow. I was hardly all that. "You are most definitely all that Lis. You forget that I watched you for months before this last week. Some things just can't stay hidden." He smiled at the disbelief that I was sure was written plainly on my face.

"I think you really are crazy." Was all I said before I gave in to temptation and pulled his mouth down to mine, standing on my tip-toes in the process to bring myself that little bit closer, and wishing desperately I wore heals to work.

I had just managed to meet his lips in a soft initial kiss, when I finally felt his hands grasp my waist and lift me so that I sat on the counter behind me. Neither of us hesitated to deepen the kiss and I felt the heat kindle inside me again. Just as I felt myself melt completely into the kiss, I heard two car doors slam in the driveway. I jerked back sharply and groaned. It meant Kaya and Tom were home, right on schedule. I tried not to wish they'd been late, just this once. Instead I settled for looking longingly at his mouth, curved now into a smile, and moved to slide off the counter to stand again on the floor.

"They're back." I explained, just seconds before I heard Kaya's voice yelling from the door.

"Lis! You here? Whose truck is that in the driveway?" I didn't have to answer because a moment later she answered herself by walking into the kitchen. "Oh!"

"Kaya, this is Roman. Roman, this is Katarina; better known as, Kaya." I hastily introduced them, trying desperately not to think how I must look right now. She didn't say anything though I was sure she hadn't missed a single detail of the scenario, so I simply introduced Roman again when Tom came into the room a moment later.

"Tom, this is Roman. Roman, this is Tom." The two men shook hands, and I noticed Tom giving Roman a once over. I stifled a laugh; he was such a big brother sometimes it was absurd.

"Right, well I've invited Roman to stay for dinner. I hope that's okay." Neither of them said anything to make me think otherwise so I continued. "We've got things about set, so dinner can be ready whenever."

"Okay." Was Tom's shrugged response.

"Sounds good." Was Kaya's. "I'm going to just go clean up. I'll be back down in a bit." She smiled at Roman as she turned to leave the kitchen. If Tom was the classic older brother, then she was my mother; the age difference non-withstanding. Then I remembered that the stove was still on and turned quickly to turn it off, sighing with relief when I saw the rice hadn't burned yet, though judging from the smell it hadn't been far from it.

The meal went as smoothly as I could have hoped for. It seemed like Tom and Roman hit it off right from the start, since they kept talking through the entire meal. I managed to catch a few phrases about sports, then later about something in the news recently; so I assumed they were doing some male bonding. Kaya and I did manage to break into the conversation a few times though, asking questions about what was going on down at the station or at the clinic. Roman retold the story of why he'd left the track clinic, and then went into a few other entertaining anecdotes from working at the track. Listening to them, I started to understand why he'd burned out so quickly; He was barely in his thirties, and he would've only graduated from vet school a handful of years ago. It sounded like he threw himself into work more than just a little hardcore.

Without a pause in the conversation, dinner was over before I realized, moving smoothly into the washing up. I smiled at Roman's surprised expression when he saw just how clean we left our kitchen. We all liked things clean, but Kaya tended to be a bit obsessive with the kitchen; it was her special place, in a manner of speaking. When we'd finished with that though, Tom didn't even hesitate before turning on the hot water heater.

"Tea, anyone?" He asked, as if our visitor's presence was normal.

"Sure, I'll have some." I answered.

"That'd be wonderful." Kaya smiled.

"Um, sure, if you're all having some." Roman chimed in.

Tom just nodded at each of our replies, and then turned to retrieve four mugs from the shelves. I could see him struggle for a moment as to which mug to give Roman. We each had our usual mugs, which he pulled out without hesitation, but he wasn't sure which to give our guest. He made a pretty quick decision though, so I was pretty sure no one else noticed; it made me realize how few guests we'd had since moving in here. It was almost sad.

"What kind of tea would you like, Roman?" Tom broke into my thoughts. I could see he'd already put a tea bag in each of the other three mugs; he didn't need to ask us, he already knew what we'd want.

"What've you got?" He asked, walking over to look at the options; he pointed out one he liked and Tom pulled a bag out of the box.

"Okay, why don't we go sit in the living room? No point in sitting in here." Tom suggested, motioning towards the mugs sitting on the counter.

"Okay." I was surprised at the suggestion. We almost always sat in the kitchen when we had tea.

"And Roman, there's honey and sugar in that cupboard if you'd like some. And milk's in the fridge." Tom gestured widely in the direction of the cupboard.

Tom and Kaya turned then to walk into the next room, leaving Roman and myself to stand in the kitchen. Roman was still looking a bit bewildered as to where Tom had meant.

"This one." I pointed directly at the cupboard he was looking for.

"Thanks." He sounded relieved as he reached up to take out the honey and pour some into his mug. I inhaled the steam from my own mug as I waited.

When he'd finished stirring in the honey, we both turned to follow the other two into the living room. When I looked up to see where to sit, I saw that both of them had taken the two individual seats, leaving the sofa open for Roman and I. Kaya caught my eye and smiled; I stuck my tongue out at her in response. They weren't exactly being subtle. I sighed, and walked over to the empty sofa, not wanting to pause for too long. Roman followed my lead, settling in next to me on the sofa while he blew on his steaming mug; I held my own in both hands, and inhaled the steam, smiling peacefully. We sat for a few minutes in the silence; for once there wasn't any music playing.

"May I ask a question?" Roman broke the silence.

"That would depend on the question, I think." Kaya replied carefully.

"What's your specialty? I mean, I already know that Lisbeth's is music and weather, and I can easily assume that Tom's is plants, considering the garden. But I don't have any clues as to what your specialty is." He spoke just as carefully.

"How do you know that the garden is Tom's handiwork? It could be mine." Kaya avoided the question.

"Lisbeth said that it was Tom's masterpiece, so I assumed..." He trailed off, sounding confused.

"Oh." She looked at me abruptly. "So you told him today?"

"Yes. I did." I stood, suddenly feeling uncomfortable. "I'm going to put on some music. Any requests?" I set my mug on the coffee table in front of the sofa, and walked over to where the sound system was set up on the side of the room. No one had voiced any suggestions, so I took my time, looking over the assortment of CD's carefully organized next to the CD player.

"Well, in that case I suppose I can understand your curiosity." Kaya was continuing. "Lisbeth's specialty is really just music, she just has an added connection with the weather, particularly large storms."

"Thanks for clarifying for me, Kaya." I threw over my shoulder when she paused for a moment.

"You're welcome." She tossed back. I laughed and went back to choosing music. "Tom's specialty is rather obvious when you know the garden is his baby, if you will; plants just can't seem to get enough of him." I could hear the smile in her voice. I pulled an old disc from it's spot on the rack, and stuck it in the player. It was an old Nanci Griffith album, one of my favorites; perfect for a quiet evening among friends.

"Kaya, you have yet to give him the answer to his question." I teased as I went to sit back down; feeling better now that music played quietly in the background.

"I'm getting there." She frowned at me; she liked dragging things out.

"I'm just thinking he'd like an answer, you know, to his actual question."
She gave me a look and I couldn't help but laugh.

"I'm getting there." She turned back to Roman, making a big deal out of
ignoring me. "My specialty is in healing. I can mend various wounds, broken
limbs, and minor illnesses."

"Wow." Was Roman's monosyllabic answer. I rolled my eyes; here was a
primary example of why we didn't tell people about ourselves.

"Yeah, I guess wow fits." Kaya's mouth was curved in a half smile; amused
with his response. "I've only really worked with animals so far. We get a
variety of patients coming for visits, despite being in such a developed area. I
treated a badger just last week." The look on Roman's face was priceless, his
mouth hanging open and eyes bugged out. Kaya was clearly struggling not
to laugh, her lips pressed tightly together now that she wasn't talking. "And
of course I have a knack with herbal treatments; very few of our customers at
the restaurant I work at, leave ill."

"Have you tried healing humans yet? Or just animals?" Roman asked
when he got his voice back. Kaya didn't answer, her face looking a bit stressed
as she looked in my direction.

"She knows that she can." I began for her.

"I've had dreams about healing humans, but…" She trailed off for a
moment, not looking anyone in the eye as she continued to explain. "The
dreams are all set centuries ago, when we would have been accepted as the
norm; back in the time when we were almost newborn. Now, I'm forced to
ignore human hurts and focus on the animals, and even then I have to limit
myself to only healing the ones that come to me. I can't let anyone see; my
gift is too special, you know?" She looked up at Roman, her face wet with
silent tears.

Tom and I looked at each other, feeling panicky. Among the three of us,
it was simply understood that we must keep our gifts a secret, letting no one
know they existed. For Tom and myself, this was a much simpler task than
it was for Kaya, but because we all accepted these things as normal, it never
occurred to either of us that it might be causing her pain. We were both
appalled to see her finally voice how she felt.

"As someone who sees extreme animal pain on a daily basis, I can
empathize with how you feel. It isn't easy to walk by while another living
being is suffering." Roman spoke slowly. "I wish there was a way for me to
help, but as it seems you already know, this day and age is definitely not
designed in a way that would allow you to be accepted."

"Yes, it is something that I have been forced to accept over the last couple
of years. My only comforts are the animals I help, and the people I help
indirectly at work."

"Sneaking drugs into people's food, are we Kaya?" Tom teased in an effort to make her laugh.

"Yeah, loads." Kaya replied, equally sarcastic.

After that, we sat without speaking for a time, Nanci Griffith's music slowing issuing from the speakers to fill the silence. My tea had cooled enough to drink, so I sipped at it carefully while I drifted amongst my thoughts. I remembered cooking with Roman after he'd taken my news about being a bit more than human without even blinking, and of course I remembered our kisses. I smiled and hummed softly in the back of my throat at the memory, a pleasant one. As I did, I happened to glance down at the watch on my wrist. It was almost nine o'clock.

"Damn! How did it get so late?" I exclaimed.

"What? What time is it?" Roman asked.

"Almost nine. Do you need to go?" I looked at him, stupidly hoping he'd say no.

"Yeah, I suppose I should get going." He replied slowly, taking a last swallow from his mug to finish the tea.

"I guess I'll walk with you out to your truck." I half mumbled, feeling suddenly shy. "If you don't mind."

"Okay. Let me just get my shoes from the back door." We both stood up from the sofa at almost the same moment.

"Good night, Kaya, Tom." Roman said before turning towards the kitchen. "It was nice to meet you both, and thanks for dinner."

"No problem, it was nice meeting you, too." Tom gave half a wave, not bothering to get up from his seat.

"Yes, you're welcome any time, Roman. It was nice to meet you." Kaya agreed from her seat before she stood and went to give him a brief hug. Roman, looking a bit surprised, returned the embrace, then went into the kitchen to return his mug and retrieve his shoes from the back door.

"Alright, I'll be back in a minute." I said, before following him. As I left the room I heard Tom and Kaya whispering between them as they got up to take their own mugs into the kitchen. I met Roman in the hallway leading to the front door, and we walked in silence out to his truck. When we reached it, I saw that by some miracle he wasn't parked in; they'd opted to park me in rather than the unknown truck.

"That was great." Roman said when we reached his driver's side door. "Thank you for inviting me to stay."

"Like Kaya said, you're welcome any time." I smiled and shrugged; happy they'd all gotten along. "So, I'll see you tomorrow then?"

"Yeah, you will." He turned to open the truck door. He was about to get in, when he paused and turned around. The next thing I knew, he was kissing me again; just as passionately as when we'd been interrupted earlier. When he broke it several minutes later, we were both breathing hard and smiling.

"Have dinner with me?" Roman puffed out, eyes on mine despite the dark.

"I just did."

"I mean like a date; dinner and a movie. This Friday night, I can pick you up at around seven and we'll pick a movie during lunch break tomorrow. I'll find a place for dinner, my surprise." His breath evened out now and he sound more and more excited as he spoke.

"I -" I didn't know what to say. Somehow this felt so different from meeting the band, or having him stay for dinner. Then I kicked myself. What was I worrying about? This wasn't high school. "That sounds great."

"Good. I'll see you tomorrow at the clinic then." A huge grin split across his face as he turned to get into the truck and leave. I couldn't help but to return it as I stood there and watched him start the truck and back out of the driveway. Then, feeling like an idiotic teenager, I stood there and watched his taillights as he drove away. Finally, starting to feel the chill of the night air, I hugged myself and went back into the house. The length of the day was finally hitting me.

Chapter 11

I heard the truck pull into the driveway as I stood in front of the bathroom mirror, examining the final touches I had just put on my make-up. We had picked one of the movies playing at a cinema nearby, some romantic comedy that sounded interesting, and were going for dinner at the restaurant Roman had picked beforehand. He hadn't even told me how formal the restaurant would be, so I'd had to guess at what to wear, with a little help from Kaya, since I hadn't been on a date in about a decade.

I wasn't quite satisfied with my eye shadow when I heard the knock at the door, but since neither Kaya nor Tom were home, I had to let it be and go answer the door. Already wearing the heels I would wear for the date, I had to take my time negotiating the stairs, but when I opened the door I immediately felt massively underdressed; Roman stood on the stoop dressed in a black suit with a deep red tie that stood out against the crisp white shirt. The jacket was unbuttoned, and he stood, slightly angled to the door with a hand in pocket and the other holding a bouquet of roses and baby's breath. I felt like I'd just stepped into a dream; it felt like a moment out of a movie, every cliché imaginable fitting the man standing in front of me. Then he looked up at me, and I knew there was nothing cliché about him.

"Come on in, I'm almost ready." I said when I finally managed to get my voice to work, and walked back into the house.

"Okay, no hurry." He moved to follow me into the house; I saw a small smile flick across his face and guessed he'd noticed my reaction. It made me glad I had my back to him so he wouldn't see me blush.

I walked quickly over to where I'd set my jacket with my purse earlier, to pick them up. It was still comfortably warm, but the nights were getting cooler as we got closer to September. Now that I wasn't looking at him I calmed down a little; still aware that he stood only a small distance away, but I always was. This week at the clinic I had seen more of him than before; he found me at my lunch break if he was there, and he'd been waiting for me at the end of every day; of course then there were the numerous momentary sightings where I would feel someone watching me and look up to find him looking at a set of x-rays or whatever he happened to be reading, or talking to. When I had collected my jacket, and checked my purse, I ran a smoothing hand over my basic outfit - long black slacks and deep purple top - before I turned to tell Roman I was ready to go.

"Are you sure that I shouldn't put something else on? I feel like I'm underdressed…" I groaned when I looked at him again.

"You look wonderful, no need to change." He laughed and held out his hand for me to walk with him.

"I'm not so sure you're right." I mumbled and took his hand. "Where are we going anyway?"

"You'll see," was all he said; I wasn't comforted.

As we walked out the door to the car we didn't talk, simply enjoying each other's presence as we went through the motions of getting in, starting the truck and backing out of the driveway, and sorting out what music we would listen to. It struck me, as I went to change the radio station that it had taken almost no time at all for us to feel comfortable with each other. It had been just over a week, but it felt like centuries; it made me think about how Mom had ended our conversation last Saturday.

The drive to the restaurant was still quiet; both of us just listening to the music that pumped softly out of the speakers; I'd settled on an oldies station that was presently playing an Elvis song. I wasn't paying very close attention to it though; staring instead out the window, attempting to figure out where we were headed based on the road signs we passed. As I waited for the next sign, I looked up at the sky. It still looked clear, though the weather report had threatened some clouds and even showers. I was hoping that it would stop with the clouds; no matter how many times Roman told me, I still wasn't convinced that he wouldn't run if he saw me caught in a storm again. I laughed and turned my gaze to the road straight ahead; it occurred to me that perhaps I ought to be wishing for the storm, it would give me an answer.

Moments later Roman turned on the signal to turn into a parking lot that suddenly loomed just off the street we were driving down. I still had no idea where we were; and hoped he'd give me a clue soon. He pulled in and parked, but I still didn't see a restaurant. Surrounded by trees, it was hard to see past the perimeter and made it clear we'd driven just past the edge of the Chicago suburbs. I heard Roman chuckle softly behind me at my confused expression as I got out of the truck.

"Why don't you follow me?" He wrapped an arm around my shoulders. I just looked up at him, still not sure I understood, and followed his lead.

We walked towards the edge of the lot right by where Roman had parked. I felt my nerves start to flutter as we walked along it's edge; we'd gone about ten or fifteen feet when I saw a little path that jutted off from the blacktop. I couldn't see where it went because of the trees and undergrowth so I started to walk past it, but Roman pulled me onto it. It cut through the dense plant life, leading us out onto a more manicured scene, and I finally understood where the restaurant was.

"Like it?" Roman whispered into my ear, making me jump slightly.

"It's perfect." I whispered back.

The restaurant was small; I thought it might have been a remodeled home. We'd walked into the back corner of the property so we had to cut our way across the lawn to get to the front door; when we got closer I was able to read the sign that stood a short distance away from the front steps. The information shown there confirmed my guess that it used to be an old house, though the details of who lived there and when didn't mean much to me. The name looked Italian, but I wasn't sure.

"How do you know this place?" I asked quietly as Roman continued to lead me by the shoulders up the stairs to the entrance.

"I have some connections; and of course I used to live out this way, we're not far from the track." I made a face and nudged him in the ribs with my elbow; he just laughed and spoke to the hostess.

"Still, how…" I asked again as we were seated at our table. He didn't answer. "I don't understand -" I broke off; a tall, darkly featured woman was walking swiftly, arms wide, in Roman's direction, and he didn't look the least bit surprised to see her.

"Bonjour, Roman!" She proceeded to speak some French that I couldn't even come close to understanding.

"Ah! Bonjour!" He returned as they hugged; I got the impression this was the answer to my question. Connections indeed.

"Aunt, this is Lisbeth Moore. Lisbeth, this is my aunt, Sophia." He introduced us before taking his own seat.

"It's nice to meet you Lisbeth." Sophia held out her hand for mine. I heard traces of a French accent.

"Its nice to meet you too." I returned, a bit timid in my surprise. We grasped hands briefly before we both turned back to Roman.

"So?" She looked expectantly at Roman.

"So what?" His face appeared too perfectly innocent.

"You know what I mean, so what." She swatted his shoulder half-heartedly. "I haven't seen you in months! What have you been up to?" She shot a sly look in my direction that had me stifling a giggle. Just as she finished speaking a yell came from somewhere in back that sounded like her name.

"Ah, we'll catch up later. You two enjoy your meal. It was wonderful meeting you Lisbeth." With that Sophia walked in the direction the yell had sounded from, and I found myself a bit envious as I watched her glide across the floor. I'd never managed, and still couldn't manage, that kind of grace.

"So. Connections, hunh?" I asked after she'd left.

"Connections are connections."

"Yours just happen to be family ones." I smiled.

"Yes." He returned the smile.

We were interrupted by our waiter with menus, and Roman picked out a bottle of wine. I took advantage of his preoccupation with the wine list to look around the restaurant. Our table was situated in the middle of the back wall of the main room; the tables around us were empty, a fact that surprised me for a Friday night. The lighting was low, mostly candles and a handful of lamps near the hostess' stand. The warmth of the lighting and deep colors of the décor gave me a strong feeling of comfort; it was obviously family owned and run. I smiled softly to myself as the thought occurred to me.

"What?" Roman asked as the waiter walked away to fill our order.

"Oh nothing. I was just taking in all this." I gestured vaguely at the room. "Seems a little empty for a Friday night though."

"Well…" He suddenly looked sheepish. I took another look around the room, wondering what I'd missed.

"You didn't?" I whispered, mouth agape. "You didn't ask them to book the entire restaurant, just for us, did you?"

"Well…"

"Well, did you?" I insisted more firmly this time.

"Yes." His voice was low. "And no." I raised my eyebrows, not quite convinced; he sighed and gave in. "It wasn't my initial plan, but… Sophia got wind of my having booked the private room, and well it kind of got out of control."

"So this was your aunt's idea? Not yours?"

"The romantic dinner was my idea, but yes the 'empty the whole restaurant just for us' was definitely her idea." He was eyeing me cautiously as he spoke.

"What am I missing here? I mean we've talked about pretty much everything there is to talk about all week, and yet somehow I missed the little detail of your having an aunt that owned a restaurant anywhere let alone just outside the city." My voice rose a little.

"I don't know why I didn't tell you." He shrugged. "I guess I already wanted to bring you here, I just wanted it to be a surprise." His eyes were apologetic as they met mine.

"Well it was definitely a surprise. That's for sure." I muttered, still a bit miffed. To avoid conversation I looked down at the menu in front of me, trying to decide what I wanted to eat. Roman copied me a moment later.

It didn't take me very long to decide what I was having, but I continued to peruse the neatly printed menu while I waited for the waiter to return. I'd realized now that the name of the restaurant I'd seen on the sign must be French, not Italian, but the items on the menu I held were of a wide range of origins. I saw a little Italian, the traditional American burger, and various other dishes of mixed origin; I realized then why Roman hadn't thought me underdressed: this really was a family place, not fancy cuisine. I smiled, the thought of someone in Roman's family owning and running a family restaurant with a French name made me want to laugh at the contradiction. I saw Roman look up, a question on his face when the waiter returned, conveniently, to take our orders. I ordered a salad and a pasta dish that looked like it would be good; Roman skipped the salad but ordered a pasta dish as well, though different from mine.

"Alright." He said after the waiter had left us. "You want to know about me? About my family?" He stretched his arms out a bit as he did.

"Yes I do." I folded my hands and leaned towards him. "If you're willing to tell me, that is." I amended. He chuckled.

"I'll tell you. Not that there's much to tell, anyway, but I will." He paused for a moment, eyes on mine. "I already told you that my parents immigrated, right after their marriage."

"I've gotten the impression that they aren't the only ones that did."

"And that would be correct. My aunt and her then husband followed only a few months later, shortly after their own wedding in fact. My own parents were never much for cooking or small business. They both worked at various positions at businesses in the city; my aunt and uncle did the same for a while, working mostly in restaurants since they both had experience in the kitchen. A long story short, they finally saved up enough to start this place. They live in the very top floor, and they remodeled it all themselves, with the help of my cousins of course, who at the point were of an age to be of some use."

"They've done a wonderful job with the place."

"Yes, they have." Roman said, swelling family pride. "Their story rather explains itself; the restaurant has been a great success, and is well known and liked in this neighborhood. My parents' story isn't quite so self-explanatory." He continued, his eyes on his hands, folded on the edge of the table, instead of my own.

"You told me about your mother, that she died about ten years ago." I tried to help by telling him what I already knew, so he wouldn't have to repeat it. "And your father passed away when you were a teenager."

"Yes. That was the end of it all though, not the beginning." He sighed, and looked back up at my face. "My parents never had a healthy relationship. Not abusive." He corrected quickly when he saw the look on my face. "Never abusive in any way. They simply fought, and fought nasty. By the time I came along I think that what was left of the relationship that had led to their marriage had finally started to give way. After that, I don't have the faintest idea what kept them together." He looked back at his hands now. "They fought over every single thing they possibly could. It was like there was never anything that they could just let go. It made life a bit like walking through a minefield. Never knowing when something was going to set them off. That's how I got into horses; needed to get out of the house and started going to the track, and hanging around the track eventually led to me wanting to be a vet." He shrugged again.

"And also explains why you're so driven to stay focused on your work."

"Does it?"

"Well it would be the one thing that could prevent your getting into the same situation as they did. Or almost the only thing."

"I know that not every marriage ends up like my parents' did." He sighed. "I could never understand why they didn't just get a divorce. They weren't religious, and they both knew that they weren't in any way beholden to each other, monetarily or otherwise."

"Sounds like they were just sadistic, or something like that." I said, mind blown by the picture he'd just painted of his family life. "Wait, which side of the family is Sophia from? Mother's or father's?"

"Her husband was my father's brother."

"So, how did they manage to have this," I gestured to the room. "And your parents end up the way they did?" The potential for such a difference had always been a source of amazement for me.

"I don't really know."

"How did you really cope, Roman? The track could hardly have been your first resource. You could hardly have lived close to it, living in the city."

"You're right." He admitted on a sigh. "The track, was a suggestion of my aunt's, Sophia's. She'd always known that I loved animals, especially horses. When she and her husband moved out here to start the restaurant, and of course get my cousins out of the city, she learned about the track. I think she went by and asked about what I might be able to do there, you know like as a job." He smiled a little now, and I returned it when I realized what he was saying. "The next thing I knew I had a job and was taking the train out on the weekends. The job just managed to pay the train fairs and leave a little left over to start saving."

"That explains a lot more than anything else you've told me so far." I could feel things start to slide into place about him.

"How?"

"Well, for starters it explains the way that Mr. Kennedy acted around you."

"What do you mean, how he acted around me?"

"He always listened to you. Didn't seem happy about it of course, but he listened. He also seemed be treating you like you were in a position with a lot more power than you are. Does that make sense?"

"I think it does."

"Now I can sort of understand; you clearly had a longer standing reputation at Arlington than the few years you spent there as a veterinarian." I gave him a look and he ducked; I'd ratted him out.

"Yeah, I guess I do."

"It also explains to me how you could burn out so fast once you started working there as a vet. I mean, most people don't burn out on their job in the first few years. Not to mention the fact that someone as deeply invested as you are in your work... it doesn't make sense to me. Maybe to some people it would, but from my point of view you seem the kind of person who's designed to be in whatever spot you're in for the long haul." I paused. "But you didn't burn out on the track just because of those few years. No you burned out because you'd been there almost half your life. Am I right?"

"Yeah. You're right."

"And of course then there's the fact that you became a partner so fast -" I started to continue.

At that moment, our food arrived, effectively cutting me off, and I realized just how hungry I was. Neither of us spoke for the next twenty minutes or so as we ate and enjoyed our meals. My salad came with my meal, so I quickly picked through it before I moved on to the main course. Judging from the smell I was quite pleased with my choice, a thought confirmed by my first bite. I wondered who the chef was as I savored the various spices in the sauce, and the other flavors from the vegetables and chicken that made up the dish, aside from the pasta. I ate more slowly now than I had at first, still hungry, but wanting to really enjoy the meal. It wasn't very often that I found food at restaurants as good as what I could get at home; Kaya's cooking was more than a little difficult to beat.

When we had both finished our meals, and two completely clean bowls sat before of us, the waiter returned and asked if we would like dessert. We both looked at each other, at our empty plates and declined. Asking instead for the bill.

"My aunt will want to know why we haven't had any dessert." Roman said when the waiter had left, glancing at his watch. "I think, though, she will have to forgive us because we're going to be cutting it quite close if we want to make it to the movie on time."

"Oh!" I looked at my own watch. "Wait, is there even a showing this late? It's after nine."

"I checked before making plans for coming here. The theatre right near here has a late showing."

"Oh. Sounds like you've got things covered."

"I guess you could say that." He replied and handed the waiter a credit card without even looking at the bill. We sat in a comfortable quiet while we waited for him to return with the receipt; both of us lost in thought, so it felt like no time at all before he returned and Roman had signed off on the bill. When we got up to leave I got the impression that Roman wanted to avoid being caught by his aunt. We were also running a bit late.

"No dessert, Roman?" Too late, she'd caught us.

"No, sorry Sophia." Roman said before going off in French for a moment.

"Ah, well I guess I can understand your not eating it here, but why not for later?" She walked to where we were, almost to the door, with her hands outstretched, holding a white Styrofoam take away box.

"I didn't even think of that." Roman said, grinning. "Thank you." He took the box, and bent to kiss both her cheeks.

"You're welcome. Now enjoy your movie. Lisbeth, I look forward to seeing you again. Hopefully next time we will have more of a chance to talk, as well." She shot Roman a sideways glance.

"I'm sure we will." She enveloped me in a hug before I finished my response.

"Alright, Sophia. We need to go, or we're going to miss the whole show." Roman's voice was sarcastic. She shot him another look as she let me go, and I tried to move quickly towards the door without making it look too much like I was running away. I really was looking forward to getting to know more about his interesting French-aunt, but at the moment I was also interested in talking to Roman more before we got to the cinema.

Five minutes later we were in the truck and on the road to the theatre. Roman hadn't been joking when he'd said the local theatre. It was a mere ten-minute drive before we were parked once again in front of a mall with the cinema's name emblazoned in neon letters across part of it. The lot was full so it took a moment to find a spot, but eventually we managed to find one big enough for the truck. We'd stayed quiet as we drove, and for some reason or other, kept it up as we stood in line for tickets and made our way to seats once we were in the cinema. Thankfully we weren't actually late, so we didn't have to wind our way through the aisles in total darkness.

The previews started just as we found seats, and we spent the time deciding whether or not we'd actually want to see the movies advertised. When they were done we'd pretty much decided to see most of them, though we both acknowledged that there was a slim chance we'd ever actually go and see them. By the time the film had reach about a third of the way through, it had more than lived up to its reputation as a comedy. The cinema theatre was filled with laughter from the twenty odd people who had come out this Friday night.

We'd about reached the halfway point of the film, when I suddenly picked up a distant peel of thunder. The sound made me break off mid-laugh, frozen with shock; I hadn't checked the sky before coming into the cinema. A moment later I heard the crack of the lightning before another peel of thunder, closer this time.

"Hey." Roman whispered. "You okay?"

"Yeah, I'm fine." I whispered back, forcing myself to refocus on the film by making a half-hearted attempt to laugh at the antics of the actors on the screen.

I managed for about five minutes before I heard yet another crack of lightning and thunder. This time they were too close for me to ignore easily; another crack following closely on it's heals. This time I froze motionless in my seat, not even responding when Roman asked again if I was all right. The thunder and lightning continued to sound in my head; for some reason, still not sounding like music. The longer I sat frozen in place there in the theatre, the more acutely I was able to hear the storm as it raced towards us. Then, it changed; the music was there now, taking over the sounds of the storm so that my mind was filled with it instead. The next thing I knew, I could feel a pair of arms circling around my shoulders, under my knees, and lifting me up out of my seat. I didn't fight them; drawn instead back into the music of the raging storm.

Then I was in it, the heavy drops soaked through my clothes to meet my skin, and the thunder sounded even louder now that it wasn't filtered through the building walls. As soon as I felt the changes my eyes flew open, not even aware that they had been closed. The first thing I saw was Roman, standing directly in front of me, hands on my shoulders. He didn't speak, simply watched me anxiously, waiting for me to come out of it. Before I could give him any sign that I was aware again, the storm swept me back in, and the music gripped me once again. This time its grip was more complete and I felt my own voice join in with it as it raged with increasing intensity around me. For I don't know how long, I stood with Roman in the parking lot, lost in my own mind and refusing to go to the truck. Then, with a suddenness I wasn't prepared for, the storm released me; letting me fall suddenly, almost hitting the ground before Roman caught me.

"Let's get in the truck." He said, carrying me. "You're soaked."

"So are you." I whispered in reply. Out of the storm, I was now very aware of my body, and of his.

"You okay?" He asked as he carried me to the passenger side door.

"Yes, I'll live." I replied with a laugh. "Its been a while since I've been caught so off guard. I'm sorry."

"Don't apologize. It's fine." He mumbled. "Here, do you think you can stand up now?"

"I think so." He started to set me down. We'd reached the truck. "I can manage, Roman." He still hovered anxiously as I moved to open the passenger door and get in. "Get in before you get any wetter."

"Oh, right." He moved grudgingly to do as I suggested.

The moment we were in the cab of the truck he started it and turned on the heat; the radio came on with it. With the sound of new music, I began to relax at last; the new melody allowing me to grasp onto something other than the one playing round and round in my head. It couldn't completely drown it out, but it came close enough that I could finally get my breathing and heart rate back under control; focused again on what was in front of me, instead of what I could feel, or sense.

"Are you sure you're okay?" Roman pressed.

"I'm fine, Roman. Really, I am." I took a deep breath as I paused a moment. "Thank you for getting me out of the theatre."

"No problem." He put the truck in gear to drive out of the lot.

The drive back to my house seemed shorter than before; I figured because I'd been so caught up in the music, from both the storm and the radio, that I hadn't really taken notice of the time. When Roman pulled into the driveway and turned off the truck though, I became incredibly aware of the tension emanating from him; I tensed in response. Neither of us spoke nor moved, just sitting there in the cab of the truck.

I caved and broke the silence. "I think I should go in. Tom and Kaya will be wondering why I haven't gone inside yet." I was becoming increasingly aware of both his silence, and the enormity of what had just happened.

"I can walk you to the door, at least." He reached for his own door as I did for mine.

"No, you don't have to do that." I said hurriedly. "I'll be fine. Seriously, I can walk on my own now." I shot him a half-smile in an effort to convince him. He didn't reply, but he did take his hand away from the door. I continued to open mine, and get out of the cab.

"Lisbeth?" He said softly as I was about to close the door.

"Hmmm?" I faced him, surprised. "What is it Roman?" I prompted when he didn't continue.

"You'll write the music tonight, won't you?" The question took me completely by surprise. "Am I right?" He prodded when I didn't reply immediately.

"Probably." I answered. "Depends."

"On what?"

"A few things. How tired I am, for one." I gave a small smile. His voice didn't sound the way I'd anticipated. "Why do you ask?"

"Oh, no real reason." He replied vaguely.

"There's always a reason, Roman. Why do you want to know?" I replied sarcastically; turning my body so that I faced him completely, leaning on one leg as I relaxed a little about talking to him.

"Yeah I guess there usually is." He sighed. "Can I watch?" I blinked, blindsided. "Watch you write, I mean." He repeated, sounding unsure of his request. It took me a moment to process his request.

"Come inside." The confidence of my answer surprised me, but I didn't waste time second-guessing it.

"You sure?" He reached for his door again.

"Would I be saying that if I wasn't?" I said, sarcastic again. "Just come inside, and we'll see whether I'm up to writing this down tonight or not." With that I turned, slamming the door of the truck in the process, and walked to the front of the house; he wasn't far behind me.

As I opened the door, and walked into the house, it struck me how quiet it was. I'd expected Tom and Kaya to be awake; their cars were in the driveway. I walked further into the house, going through the living room and into the kitchen where I found the answer to my question. They had left a note on the table, telling me that they had both gone to bed and would see me in the morning. Confused, I looked over at Roman, and as I did the clock caught my eye. It read 12:00 midnight.

"Wow, I didn't realize it was this late. How long did we spend in the parking lot?"

"A while."

"I think that might be an understatement. Though it does explain why we're both so soaking wet." We giggled.

"Shhh!" I hissed out after a moment. "They're sleeping."

"Sorry." He said, laughing more softly now. I looked at him for a moment, as I got my own laughter under control, and made a decision.

"I'm going to go grab a couple towels from upstairs so we can dry off." I motioned in the direction of the stairs. "I'll just be a second, then we can go downstairs. I think you might luck out about my writing the music tonight." I smiled before ducking my head and walking quickly towards the stairs. A few minutes later I'd returned, towels in hand, in a clean pair of sweats and an old t-shirt. I'd realized that I would be sitting in my wet clothes as I'd gotten the towels and made a speedy trip to my own room to change into something dry.

I handed him one of the towels. "Thank you." The other one was around my shoulders, under my still dripping hair.

"You're welcome." I smiled at him. "Come on, let's go down to the music room. We'll wake them up if we stay in here."

"Where is the music room?" He asked from behind me as I walked towards the stairs to the basement.

"Down in the basement." I explained as I walked. "The three of us each have our 'personal sanctuaries', if you will. Mine is the music room."

"Then I'm guessing the garden is Tom's, and Kaya's is the kitchen?"

"That would be correct. You're good."

We stopped talking as we headed down the stairs, and turned to the right, into my music room. I switched on the light as we walked in, illuminating the room. I tried hard not to feel anxious for his reaction as I walked in, lifting the lid from the piano keys, and shifting paper around so I would be organized for writing the melody still locked into my brain. That done, and Roman still not having said anything, I turned to close the door to the room. The act was an unfamiliar one. Although the room was sound proof, I usually left the door open when I played so that Tom and Kaya would be able to listen. It was only on rare occasions that I actually shut the world out of my music making.

"Would you like to sit?" I motioned towards the one chair that stood on the other side of the room. He still didn't speak, simply moving to the chair I'd indicated and seating himself. "Right." I swallowed hard to clear the nervous lump building there. This wasn't something I'd done before.

Following his example, and maintaining the silence, I moved to sit on the piano bench. As I sat, I started to even my breathing, letting myself focus in on the melody and the rest of the storm's music that was burned into my brain. I remembered to flip on my recording device just as my hands reached for the keys, and the song began to find its way out of my head onto the tape and paper. I gradually forgot all about Roman, sitting across the room from me, and became entirely involved in the music that my hand at least was writing; the music coming out of me in a torrent as I became absorbed, again, by it.

The song ended before I expected it to, leaving me seated in a rather dazed frame of mind. After a few minutes, I started to pull myself back into the present moment; I looked over at Roman as soon as I did. He was staring at me again, like he had last Saturday, at Jason's; the same intense look in his eyes.

"So?" I asked thickly, unable to stand the silence any longer.

"That..." He trailed off, making me lean towards him, anxious to hear what he would say. "That was, amazing." he finished simply. "You're amazing."

"Oh." I replied, surprised yet again. He seemed to be doing that to me a lot tonight.

"May I see?" He nodded at the paper in front of me.

"Sure." I choked out, still stunned. "Why don't you come sit over here." I patted the space next to me on the bench.

"Okay." He stood up from the chair and walked, unhurriedly, to sit next to me. I'd expected to feel anxious about his seeing the music, after having watched me write it. Somehow though I skipped the nerves, and was simply comfortable. As ridiculous as it seemed to me that I would feel that way, it felt right.

"So, all of this came from those couple of hours in the storm?" He sounded amazed.

"Yes." I reached over to take back the stack of staff paper covered in my scratched out notes and measures.

His eyes flicked up to mine as our hands touched lightly where we both gripped the paper. His eyes were intense as they locked on mine, the melted chocolate color of the irises ringed with black. We paused, bodies motionless for a few moments as we sat holding the music between us. He moved first, reaching the hand that wasn't holding the music up to cup my cheek. I leaned into the touch, shivering a little as he ran his thumb over my bottom lip, his eyes following the motion. Wanting to return the gesture, I tried to pull the music out of his hand to return it to the piano. The instant he realized what I was trying to do he pulled his hand away from my face, making me pout involuntarily for a second. He then proceeded to remove the music from my hands to sit, frowning at it. The puzzled look on his face made me smile, and laugh lightly to myself.

"What? Looking for the storm on the paper?" He didn't look up. "Roman? You okay?" I reached out, concerned.

"What? Yeah, I'm good. I'm just thinking." He shot me a half smile, looking up a little now. "So much to sort out, I'm still feeling a little confused." He shrugged one shoulder.

"So...getting anywhere?"

"Sort of, well, not really." He looked up sheepishly. "There's something that isn't making sense to me."

"And what would that be?" He looked like he wasn't even sure of that.

"C'mon, shoot. Just ask and I'll see if I can answer the question. Okay?" I tried to look at him encouragingly while hiding my own nerves about what he would ask.

"Why is it that you have so little control over your talent?" I blushed, ducking my head in mortification; I should have guessed. "I just mean that it seems like Kaya can control hers so that she doesn't just start healing random people and animals; and Tom seems to have a similar level of control, otherwise I suppose plants would be reaching out for him when he walked down the street." He smiled at the image that last created. "I'm not questioning your ability. I don't think anyone could after witnessing as much as I have. I'm just… wondering. It doesn't seem to fit that you would have so little control compared to them. Especially when you all live together, and clearly are incredibly close." He finally stopped trying to explain himself, and I took a moment to take a breath before giving him some sort of answer.

"I wish I had a solid reason to give you."

"But you don't?"

"No. I don't." I sighed and shifted my weight so that I wasn't leaning towards him anymore. "Control like Kaya's is mostly a result of necessity; you've already heard her reasons so I don't need to explain that. Tom's is for exactly the reason you mentioned. When we were awakened, the first thing that happened to him was having the ivy in the back garden wind itself around him from head to toe. Kaya and I had to talk it into letting him go." I laughed at the memory.

"I thought you didn't have a talent with plants." Roman looked perplexed.

"Neither of us does. Well Kaya does with whatever she cooks with, but not with the rest of the garden plants, so I can understand your confusion. We think that it's simply a result of who we are: we're connected to everything living and are for that reason capable of communicating with everything living, plants included."

"I guess that makes sense."

"Yeah, I guess."

"But, what you said about Kaya and Tom's control doesn't make sense to me. Storms are capable of great destruction. Then there's the added fact of how thoroughly they incapacitate you when they're happening. It seems like you have an equally good reason to develop a similar level of control. So I don't think that really explains it."

"Wow, you're quick." I bobbed my head approvingly. "So, have you figured out the real reason then?"

"I'm not sure. Why don't you tell me and we can see if I'm right?"

"I'd rather hear what you're thinking first."

"Really?" He sighed as I nodded. "Well, I'm guessing that it has something to do with the nature of the weather, how unpredictable it is. I mean I know that the weathermen try their best but honestly, how often are they ever right?" He shrugged. "So that must make it difficult for you to develop any real control, I think anyway."

"Wow. Maybe you're too quick." I choked out after staring at him. "How...?"

"I don't know. Am I that close?" His voice sounded almost incredulous.

"Yeah, you're damn close." At least I thought he was. I stared at him, stunned.

"Are you going to tell me what I missed?"

"Oh, right, yeah." I stammered out, scrambling to pull together some kind of answer. "You got the part about the weather's unpredictability, but that's not the only part of the weather that makes it overpower me to such an extent." I paused for a moment. "It's the music. I'm, some sort of vehicle for it, you know, a kind of outlet. The storms, well they basically give me no choice in the matter."

"So you write it down, but for what purpose?"

"I don't really know the answer to that. I just know that when I write it, I lose control again, just not to the same extent. Its like the music is fighting its way out of me, onto the page, and I have to direct it there. Like I'm just an outlet, again."

"But why? I don't understand why this music is fighting its way through you if its not intended for something. Last week was the first time you'd actually replayed any of it, and look what happened. Why?"

"I wish I could tell you. I have no idea; been looking for one, too." I chuckled and smiled at the dead end we'd reached. Then I saw his facial expression shift, and for some reason I tensed. "What? Have an idea for me?" I prodded.

"Maybe." He replied slowly. "Lisbeth, were you able to control the storm when you recreated it?"

"I don't really know." I stammered a little over the words. "I was able to regain control of myself, but not necessarily control the storm. Although..." I paused as I remembered events of last Saturday.

"What? What're you remembering?"

"I regained control of myself and I was able to make subtle changes to the music. You know, things like skipping repeats to shorten it, and the tempo I played at. It was odd, the storm didn't fight me, or try and make me play the music the way that it was intended."

"Hmmm."

"What?"

117

"I'm wondering again, about your control."

"Oh?"

"What you're saying about the whole outlet thing seems right. It would explain why you can't control an actual storm, and why they're able to get such a firm hold on you. I just feel like there has to be some reason that these storms are seeking you out, giving you their music, so to speak, besides simply for the sake of preservation. If that were the case it seems like there wouldn't been any result from playing it again. It would want to remain dormant, or at least I think it would."

"So, you think there's a reason?"

"Yes."

"But what?"

"That, I don't know." He said with a smile; I smiled back. He sounded like me now.

"So what exactly are you suggesting?"

"I'm not really sure." He stood up suddenly to pace the room. I sat and watched him for a few minutes, biting back my curiosity as I waited for him to continue.

"I think you might be able to control the storms when you recreate them. I think they're seeking you out for some reason that we don't understand." He'd suddenly stopped pacing directly in front of me, turning around to look me in the eye as he spoke. "You just need to practice."

"Wait, practice what?" I shook my head in confusion.

"Playing the music, controlling the storms that it creates; you need to practice that."

I sat, stunned for a moment, without speaking, as I struggled to comprehend what he was suggesting. Then something else occurred to me, part of what Mom had said, about Roman. Though I didn't quite have the grasp of what he'd suggested that he seemed to have, the memory made my decision for me. I took a deep breath, trying to settle my nerves before I spoke. My mind was moving a million miles a minute and winding me up as it went.

"Ok..." Was all I managed.

"Ok, what?"

"Ok, I'll practice. What did you have in mind?" I asked, finally gaining some kind of control over my brain. "For a first session, I mean."

"I'm not sure. We'll need a piano, right?" He stood in front of me, hands in pockets with his feet spread a bit.

"Not necessarily. There are some that I could manage on the violin, instead." I suggested.

"Oh, ok. Maybe I do have an idea then."

"And that would be?" I asked archly. I was getting a little tired of having to pull every answer from him.

"How about we make it a surprise. I can pick you up on Sunday morning, would ten work again? You'll just need to bring one of the songs and your violin. And yourself, of course." He added the last as if it were an after thought on a chuckle.

"Why not today?" I asked then remembered how late it was.

"Band practice."

"Oh. Right."

"Besides, I thought you would want a day to rest up. I've noticed how draining these storms seem to be for you."

"Oh, yeah, that's true." I murmured, pleasantly surprised he'd noticed. "You guys meeting up at the same time as last week then?"

"Yeah, its when we usually meet."

"Jason's place again?"

"Yup, as usual." We smiled at each other. I had a feeling Jason wouldn't have let it be anywhere else.

"Play for me?" I asked abruptly.

"Sorry?"

"Play for me? Something on the piano; you said you played." I stood up, directing him to take my place on the bench.

"Oh, ah, what would you like to hear?"

"Surprise me. Roman, there's no way I'm going to sleep just now. This way I can relax and finally hear you play." I grinned as I walked over to the chair he'd occupied earlier.

"All right." He said on a sigh as he sat down.

I watched as he played a few chords, testing the keys, then sighed and relaxed into the chair as he started playing a soothing jazz piece. I recognized it, but couldn't quite put a finger on the name. I didn't try very long to remember though, losing myself in the music as he played.

Chapter 12

I was in a church, standing at the end of the center aisle; I could see the crucifix where it hung on the wall behind the altar. The benches on either side of the aisle were filled with people, some of whom I vaguely recognized. Everywhere there were flowers, whites and light blues, in impeccably arranged bouquets placed at strategic points around the church. I saw the priest first, dressed in the traditional pastoral garments. I noticed the man who stood just below the priest, beside the altar, at the same time that I became aware of a woman standing beside me. She was dressed in a white flowing gown, a bouquet in her hands of the same flowers in a larger and slightly altered arrangement from those that I'd already noticed. Her hair was flame red and stood in stark contrast with the pure white of her dress.

The scene vanished, suddenly replaced with unending darkness. It was peaceful at first, and I relaxed after the initial shock of the change, but then panic hit - heart racing and breath ragged in my lungs as if I'd been running from something. I clawed at the darkness with hands I couldn't see and legs I could only feel. I knew that I was lying on something because I was rolling around, getting myself even more entangled in the darkness; I could almost feel it pressing against my face, my body, and finally, down my throat as I opened my mouth in a silent scream.

Just as suddenly as the darkness had begun it ended and I was left to thrash at random pulses of color and light. The pure panic dulled, but was replaced by emotions that alternated with the colors that splashed across my vision. These, instead of pressing against me like the darkness, seemed to shine right through me; my now visible limbs changing color with them. My heart and lungs continued to labor throughout; the intensity of the emotions and the dramatic differences between them almost stressed my body more than the panic of the darkness. Red pulsed with fury, and then green flashed with an equally brilliant tranquility, followed by an obnoxiously happy yellow and tear wrenching blue. Other colors flashed as well, in various shades and brilliancies; each with their own intense emotion, sensation or feeling.

Then everything went white, and a new image flashed across my mind. This time my eyes flew open with a combination of fear and surprise; the image burned into my mind with exquisite detail. It was of Roman and I, present lifetime, in the middle of a farm field somewhere as a storm raged around us. I was seated on the bench of a grand piano while he stood, eyes locked on mine as I played, both of us oblivious to the rain that soaked us. My hair was loose, whipping around my face with the wind; my eyes dark with an intense energy I recognized. I couldn't see Roman's face, but I knew that it would be mirrored there. We were dressed in earthy colors; my dress the color of soil, clinging to my body as the rain soaked it, and his shirt a rust color while his corduroy pants matched my dress. He was holding his guitar, playing with me.

Awake, I dragged my focus away from the picture painted in my mind and suddenly became aware of how tangled I was in my sheets. I had somehow managed to get them tied tight around my waist and legs. I also realized that I was no longer lying in my bed, but rather on the floor, just beside it. I looked up at the mattress, about a foot above my face, and wondered how on earth I had slept through that. Not coming up with an immediate answer, I shook myself mentally and started to sit up and untangle the sheet so that I could stand up. As I moved to do so, sheets finally untangled and sitting in a pile around me, I was surprised to find that my whole body protested the movement. I made it to a standing position, only to tip back so that I was sitting on the edge of my bed instead. Then I remembered a different part of the dream, the colors and the intensity of the emotion that accompanied them. My head swam slightly as the memory filled my mind with fresh intensity. I was no longer surprised at my body's exhaustion; it had just had a workout equivalent to sprinting the majority of a marathon. My heart rate and breathing were settling, in time with pulling myself out of the memory of the dream.

As I settled, I began to wonder at the time. Roman had finally left at around three in the morning and I had crashed into bed not long after. I remembered being glad I hadn't asked to tag along to the band practice today after such a late night. I didn't think I'd been asleep that long; the room was still dark no light coming in through the window. I was just turning to look at my alarm clock when it started to beep incessantly: time to get up. I sighed, and tried to stand again, successful at remaining upright this time. There was no point in going back to sleep now, I'd never manage to get any rest;

so I picked up the towel I'd left on my floor and walked slowly over to the bathroom. I decided to start the day with a shower and go from there.

The phone rang in the kitchen, pulling me from the world of the book I'd been reading for the last couple of hours. I tried to refocus on the story, but when the phone rang a third time, I gave up and went to answer it.

"Would someone answer that? I'm in the shower!" Kaya yelled from upstairs as I was walking into the kitchen.

"I've got it, Kaya!" I yelled back before picking up. "Hello?"

"Lisbeth is that you?" A familiar voice asked from the other end.

"Yes, it is. Is that you, Mom?" Only my biological mother would call on the one day I'd had too little sleep to focus on a conversation.

"Yes it is," my mom answered before setting off on her many greetings and even more questions she expected me to answer, not to mention the various anecdotes she had to tell me of home.

"That's great, Mom." I laughed. "How's Dad?"

"He's good. Still workin' of course, but he's good. If you want to say hello, he's right here."

"That'd be great. I'll talk to you more after, ok?"

"Okay honey. Here's Dad."

"That my Lisbeth?" I heard my father's voice on the other end of the line.

"Yes, it's me daddy." I grinned broadly.

"So. How you been? Not going too crazy down there in the city I hope?" He asked with a chuckle.

"No, not too crazy. I've just been workin' pretty much. We had a call last week from the track, and I got sent on that but otherwise nothing special."

"What'd you get sent on a call at the track for? I thought you were working in the small animal clinic?" My dad asked, sharp as ever.

"Your guess would be as good as mine. It all went well though. There'd been a big stallion fight, four from one barn, so we just had to go through and check them over, patch them up, that kind of thing." I explained.

"Ah, well, as long as everything was all right in the end." He let it drop.

"Exactly. So, how are things at the shop?" I asked, redirecting the conversation.

"Oh, same as ever. Nothing new there I'm afraid."

"No interesting orders, or anything like that?" I asked, a little disappointed. He usually had great stories from the store to tell me whenever we talked.

"No, not really, sorry. I guess people just aren't feeling like doing any home repairs at the moment. Though we did have a big rush for the usual tools and such a few weeks ago. People getting their homes all prepared for Labor Day Weekend, I suppose."

"Yeah, I guess they've just gotten things all taken care of now."

"Next run will be for winterizing their homes, I suppose." He continued rather unenthusiastically.

"Hey, you alright dad?" It wasn't like him to sound so odd on the phone. "You sound different than usual."

"What? Me? I'm fine. Just been a little tired lately, honey, having a hard time sleeping, that kind of thing. Nothing worse than that though."

"Promise?"

"Promise. Now, I'm going to hand you back over to your mother. She's been dying to talk to you for weeks now, so you just let her talk herself out." He whispered that last so only I would be able to make it out. I guessed my mom was standing right there.

"Okay, dad, I'll talk to you more another time. Love you."

"Love you too, babe." He replied and handed the phone to my mother. I had to stop myself from cringing when she came on the line. I loved my mother dearly, but she just had the worst timing.

"Hey again, Mom."

"Hey, honey. Right, so tell me. How has work been? How are Kaya and Tom? Give me the details, how have you been?" Of course she would start with the questions for me instead of the stories. I thought about what the honest answer would mean revealing to her, and did some fast thinking to come up with a more plausible story for my sleep deprived state.

"Well work has been pretty much the same. You probably guessed from what dad was saying that we had one odd call last week from the track that I got sent along for."

"Yes, I caught that. Sounded like things worked out with that though."

"They did, thankfully. Other than that though there hasn't really been anything interesting going on. Tom and Kaya are both doing well. You know Kaya's been working at a restaurant in town since she'd graduated, and now she's considering doing some more classes or something. I guess I'll let you how it turns out when she decides."

"Yeah, I guess." My mom said with a laugh.

"Tom is still working at the police station, so nothing much to tell there. You already know what his job usually is like." I heard her laugh again. "Though I think he said something the other day about an opening coming up for a detective position so maybe I'll have some fresh news about him for you to pass on to his family sometime soon."

"Oh, that would be good. I hope he does that, it would be good for him."

"Mom, you know he won't do it unless he wants to."

"Yeah, I know."

"And recently it hasn't seemed like he's wanted to. So I wouldn't get your hopes up. Not yet at least, anyway."

"Oh, well, I can still hope. I just won't pass the word on to his folks about it."

"They still upset about his not staying home?" I asked, surprised.

"Well, you could say that." She answered vaguely.

"Argh! When will they get over that? Seriously, it's not like he's an only child!" I said furiously. Tom's parents had a misplaced sense of how things worked.

"I know honey, I know it's frustrating." My mother crooned, trying to calm me down before I went off in a fury. "Now I've got to tell you…" I smiled; she was off, now all I had to do was listen. I pulled a chair over from the table and settled into it. I would probably be here for a while.

"Alright Mom. I'll talk to you again soon, promise." I stifled yet another yawn a few hours later. "Yup. Love you too. Hug, kiss." I repeated after her, before I hung up at last. I put a hand up to cover yet another yawn when Kaya walked into the kitchen.

"You finally get a call from home?" She walked towards the sink.

"Yeah." I smiled weakly.

"What time did you guys get in last night? You look like you've barely had any sleep." She failed to hide her amused smile.

"If I look like it, its because I haven't had more than three hours of sleep." I said sarcastically. "We got back at around midnight last night."

"So, how'd you end up with about three hours of sleep then?" Her eyebrow arched.

"Storm." Was all I needed to say for understanding to dawn on her face.

"You were writing music last night then I take it?"

"You would be right." I stared at the floor as parts of last night flicked through my mind. The dinner, the movie, then the storm and sitting in my music room after we'd gotten back; the fact that he still hadn't run away from me, but had in fact watched me write the music after getting caught in a storm and was even going to try and help me with controlling my gift with storms.

"He stayed, didn't he?" Kaya said softly.

"What?"

"He stayed while you wrote, didn't he?" She repeated.

"Yes. He did stay."

Kaya put down the bag of rice she'd just taken out of a bottom cupboard and walked over to where I was, still seated in the chair by the phone. She stopped in front of me, placing one hand on my shoulder and the other reaching to lift my chin. She stood like that for a moment, just looking at my face, studying.

"Are you going to tell me what really kept you up last night?"

"I just did, Kaya."

"I mean are you going to tell me why you've had no sleep instead of just a few hours. Why you're curled up on the couch instead of going for a run or helping Tom in the garden like you do most weekends." I got her point and sighed as I was forced to remember my dreams.

"I...had bad dreams."

"Oh really? In what way?"

"It started as a dream but then it shifted. It was colors with emotions. First I was in pitch-blackness, unable to see anything but feel everything. Then it was flashes of color with extreme emotion, so much so that I felt like my heart and lungs would burst from the stress." I paused for a moment, trying not to fallback into it. "Then it was about the future, the present one I mean. I could see myself, and Roman, but I couldn't recognize the place or understand what was going on."

"Oh my." Kaya dropped her hand from my face. "Well that certainly explains the way you're looking right now."

"Thanks." My voice was icy.

"Oh, don't be so cranky. I'm going to start on dinner now, I want to practice a dish we're going to be putting on the menu at the restaurant so I need more time. Why don't you go lie down on the sofa with your book again and I will call you when it's ready, okay?" She turned back to where she'd set the bag of rice.

Seated again on the sofa, book in hand; I forced myself to focus on the story, reading each word on every page as if I needed to memorize it. In reality I was just fighting hard to keep my mind from getting lost in itself. My dreams this morning had left me with a few too many unanswered questions that I was still unprepared to address, so I was avoiding them as long as possible.

I sat on the floor of my music room, storm music scattered around me, twenty minutes before Roman was to pick me up. My violin was already packed and sat, waiting, by the door. I'd been sorting through my two year collection of storm music, trying to find the right one for a practice piece. I still hadn't made a choice. None of them were grabbing me quite the way the one from last week had, and I had no idea which would be the least harmful to wherever we were going, which of course would have been easier to know if I actually knew where we were going. The only thing helping narrow down my choices

125

was the fact that I would be playing it on the violin instead of the piano. That meant I could only play the storms with an easily condensed score.

"Lisbeth, Roman just pulled into the driveway." I heard Tom yell from the top of the stairs about fifteen minutes later.

"I'll be right up, Tom." I yelled back.

I finally just closed my eyes and randomly picked one of the five I'd narrowed it down to. They were all scores to minor thunderstorms that had occurred in the last two years, and the shortest of those. I chuckled to myself as I left the rest of the music where it was and went to grab my violin; none of the scores could really be called short, these were simply the shortest of the bunch, though still at least five pages of music, and that wasn't including any repeats.

"All set?" Roman asked as I walked into the living room. It seemed Tom had invited him in, making me wonder if he'd just pulled in, or just gotten in the house. I smiled, not really minding either way.

"Yup, all set to go." I held up my violin case and music in one hand.

"Okay, let's go." He stood up and headed for the door.

"Hey, Roman." Tom called after us. "Bring her back in one piece, will ya please?" Roman just laughed.

"I'll do my best, Tom."

"Mind you do. Oh, and if you'd like you can stay for dinner when you get back. Provided, of course, that you bring my little sister here back uninjured."

"That'd be great, Tom." Roman said, still laughing.

"Thanks for that, Tom." I growled under my breath at him. He just smiled, he knew I wasn't really angry, just annoyed.

"C'mon, Lisbeth."

"Coming." I hurried out the door to catch up with Roman at the truck.

I didn't bother asking where we were going as he pulled out of the driveway. He'd never given me the most helpful answers when I'd asked before so I just left it alone this time. It struck me again as Roman started driving down the road, that we had settled into a routine whenever driving anywhere. Roman always drove; the music was generally my choice and usually something bluesy, or at least relaxing, and I just let him get us wherever we were going, not offering directions, just trusting his sense of direction. Thankfully, thus far, it had proved correct.

I sat in the passenger seat, eyes watching the houses, cars, and various people pass by as we made our way onto the highway. At that point I started to watch the sky, a habit I'd developed in the last two years as a way of staying aware of the weather. Today the sky looked clear, nothing hovering on the edge of the horizon.

"You sleep okay? Yesterday I mean."

"Yeah, I slept fine. Not for very long though, so I had an early night last night." I smiled tightly at my white lie.

"That's good. You didn't miss much at the jam sesh. We just played around with that song Jason had us working on last week, and then just had some fun with our old favorites." He was grinning as he told me. "Jason was sad you didn't come though."

"Missing my mad violin skills?" I teased.

"I guess. He almost made Billy play the part."

"Does he play?"

"A little, but not nearly as well as you do. Needless to say, Billy was relieved when he didn't have to play it."

"Oh."

"Yeah. Jason asked me to invite you for next week."

"Cool. I'd like that."

"Really?"

"Yeah, I liked the guys. Plus it's fun to play in a group for once." I shot him a half-smile. "It gets a bit redundant playing alone. No one to collaborate with, you know what I mean?"

"Yeah, I get your point."

We lapsed back into silence after that, both of us just listening to the radio as we traveled along the highway. I kept my eyes on the sky, watching the clouds as we passed alternately with the various neighborhoods and other buildings we passed. After a little while things started to look bit familiar, and I remembered an entirely irrelevant detail from the night before.

"Roman?"

"Hm?"

"What happened to that dessert your aunt gave us on our way out of the restaurant?" I turned in my seat to look at him.

"I took it home with me. It's in my refrigerator. Why?"

"Was I ever going to get to have some of that?" I teased.

"Well, sure if you want some."

"When though?" I pushed, an idea forming.

"Well. Would you like to come over to my place after this? Then we can eat it together and you can see my place for once."

"Mmm...I like that idea. Deal." I grinned like a small child. He looked over at me, and, laughing, returned the grin.

"So. Where exactly are we going?" I broke down and asked.

"Haven't you guessed yet?"

"No. I haven't." I answered sarcastically.

"Well, why don't you think about that for a second and get back to me."

I shot him a look meant to make him answer, but he just laughed. "Think for a moment."

"Oh." I said a moment later. "We're not going to the restaurant again are we?" I felt a bit scared; that area was pretty well developed.

"Not exactly, but you're close. We're going to a place near there, on the edge of Arlington Park. Well away from the track, promise." He added at the look on my face.

"You sure?"

"Lisbeth, think who you're talking to here. Yes, I'm sure."

"Okay, then." I gave in slowly.

He pulled off the highway at a familiar exit a few minutes later, and I started to feel more comfortable with his assertion; it was the exit we'd taken to get to the track. I watched as we drove past the turn off to the entrance to the track grounds, and continued for several miles down the road before turning off. I was caught completely off guard when, ten minutes later, we pulled into a private driveway. I glared at Roman as he turned off the truck; this didn't look like a park to me.

"What?" He asked after I'd glared at him for a while.

"You know what. I thought we were going to the park." My voice was low.

"We are. This is my Aunt Sophia's place; we're just parking here. Her property directly boarders the park so we can walk from here." He opened his door and got out of the truck.

"Oh."

"Come on." He stood at the edge of a path I hadn't noticed before. I just laughed at his sudden impatience and got out of the truck to join him, remembering to grab my violin and music in the process.

The path that Roman had chosen was surprisingly well worn, a solid dirt track between the trees. The woods we were walking through weren't thick, most of the trees young, so the undergrowth was thicker than it might have been otherwise. We didn't have to go very far, proving that Roman's aunt's property did in fact border the park. The path ended when we reached a campsite, one of several that happened to be unoccupied in that area. Roman walked over to a picnic table that stood in a secluded corner of the site, and stopped.

"Here we are." He motioned broadly to the site.

"This'll work." I nodded my head in approval and walked over to join him at the picnic table, setting my violin case down on top of it to open it. I took my time, focusing on breathing and settling my mind. My nerves had built up as we'd walked through the woods, winding tighter with anticipation the closer we came to the place he'd decided on for my first official practice round.

I hadn't been nervous at Jason's, having no idea what would happen when I played those first chords. Knowing what was coming, I felt my stomach knot tighter with worry.

"You sure there isn't anyone around here?" I asked as I prepped my bow and tuned the strings.

"Yes, I'm sure. There isn't anyone within about a mile of here."

"But your aunt's house is just that way." I was confused.

"She's not home though, and neither are any of her neighbors. They're at church, or at least the neighbors are. Sophia is at the restaurant."

"Oh. Well I guess that works then. No one home from church sick then?" I tested.

"Not that I'm aware of. Besides, anyone sick isn't really going to put things together when it starts storming, and besides that, they won't be able to hear you playing. So they won't put that together with the storm. That's the really important part right?"

"I guess." I agreed grudgingly. A small part of me had still been holding on to that small chance that this wouldn't work. Finally my violin was ready to go, bow waxed and strings tuned. I arranged the music on the picnic table so that I could read it, using various rocks to keep it in place when the wind picked up. I took a deep breath, settling myself again.

"You ready?" Roman had positioned himself a short distance away from me, poised so that he could get to me quickly if needed. I smiled at the thought; there shouldn't be any reason for a rescue today.

"As ready as I can be for this. So what's the plan here? Am I just going to play or do you want me to try and make something specific happen?"

"Good question." He answered before pausing to think for a moment. "Why don't we mess with changing the tempo; keep it simple for today. Would that be okay?"

"So speed it up and slow it down at various points?" I clarified

"Yeah."

"All right. That shouldn't be too difficult. If that works, should I try and do anything else?"

"No, I don't think so. Unless you think of something while you're playing, I mean."

"Okay."

I lifted the violin and settled it onto my shoulder, taking my time so that I wouldn't be tense or rushed when I started. I continued to focus on my breath, keeping it steady and consistent to settle the nerves in my stomach. After a moment, I looked at the music score, and, lifting my bow, I played the first notes on the page. Two things happened simultaneously: I felt a pull in my core, and a clap of thunder sounded in the distance. The storm proceeded to build as I continued with the music, building in intensity at the same rate. After the initial tug, I didn't feel any other draw on my energy source. Instead I simply felt myself become fully absorbed in the music, unable to notice anything else. I was, however, able to completely control my playing.

As I continued to play I toyed with the tempo of the music; slowing dramatically at one point, and then speeding up suddenly at another. The difference in the storm was subtle, changing only the time between claps of thunder and flashes of lightning, and the rate at which the rain fell from the sky. I realized, as I noted this effect, that there was no way to change what happened during the storm, except by altering the music itself, as if each note was a drop of rain, clap of thunder or flash of lightning. The idea intrigued me, and I began to play with it, skipping notes here and there and, when this had the desired effect, attempting to cut whole bars of notes. I was amazed when there was no pull on my core, to tell me to stop.

I glanced up at Roman for the first time as I was doing this and locked my eyes on his. That was when I felt the strongest pull on my core energy yet, but somehow it felt different, there was something mixed with it. Something pure and raw that had me tearing my eyes from his and going back to the music in front of me. I was nearly done now, the whole process having moved much faster with me dropping bars here and there. Then, suddenly, it was over; I'd played the final note of the last page. I stood there, breath heavy with the exertion of playing, staring at the paper that sat, soaked and stuck to the top of the table.

As I gradually got my breathing back under control I started to set my violin back in its case. I was silently grateful for having thought to close it before the storm had started. I looked sadly at the music. I would have to think of a way to move it to a place it could dry before I put it away; it was all but ruined thanks to the rain from the storm. A stray thought reminded me suddenly that Roman had yet to say anything since I had stopped playing, and I turned to see why that was.

The moment that I met his eyes I felt the same intense pull on my core as when I'd been playing. He was looking at me, watching every little movement I made, but hadn't moved an inch himself. Standing there in the middle of the campsite, simply staring at me, hands hanging useless by his sides and feet slightly apart. As I looked at him, I was suddenly overwhelmed with the enormity of what I had just done; and as I walked slowly towards him, I felt silent tears start to trickle down my cheeks.

"It worked." I said when I was about a foot away from him.

"It did." He agreed.

"Thank you."

"What are you thanking me for?"

"This was your idea, so thank you. For helping me, helping me start to control a part of my gift. I…" My throat thickened with more tears.

"What's the matter? Why are you crying?" Roman moved forward to close the short gap between us and lifted a hand to wipe the tears from my face in the process. "Aren't you happy?"

"Of course I'm happy. I don't know why I'm crying. Roman?" I looked up at him and leaned my face into the hand now cupping my cheek.

"Yeah?" His voice sounded even thicker than before.

"What are you? Why do I feel this way with you? How?"

"I wish I knew." His gaze dropped to my lips. "I wish I knew."

As soon as these words passed his lips his hand slid from my cheek into my hair, lifting my face to his as he leaned down to kiss me. I didn't move at first, as his lips slowly moved against mine, savoring the feel and the texture of the kiss. I felt the heat begin to build in my body, and lifted my arms to wrap around him, running my hands over his back and shoulders as we deepened the kiss. Uninterrupted this time, the kiss swiftly deepened so that he was the center of my focus. As my hands explored his body over his shirt I felt his explore mine, a fire in their wake. I barely reacted when he reached down over my legs and lifted me suddenly so that I could wrap them around his waist. A moment later I felt my back connect with tree bark, and I was forced to break the kiss as surprise momentarily overpowered me.

Roman had me leaned against a tree. I hadn't even been aware that we'd been moving, but somehow we'd maneuvered, or rather he'd maneuvered, ourselves so that we were now on the edge of the clearing, the opposite side of the picnic table. As I absorbed this, I felt Roman's hands slide underneath my shirt and fresh heat and shivers coursed through me at his hands on my skin. At that moment I felt another pull on my core, but this time it had the opposite effect as before. I leaned in to kiss his mouth again, while simultaneously reaching for his hands and pulling them away from me.

"Too fast. Too fast." I panted out.

"I'm sorry. I'm sorry." He said between breaths. "This isn't the place anyway." He leaned his forehead against mine and smiled. "Wow."

"Wow, indeed." I smiled against his cheek. "May I get down now?"

"Oh! Of course." I laughed as he pulled me away from the tree and then lifted me even higher before setting me feet first on the ground. I felt a little thrill at the feeling of being lifted like that, I wasn't a lightweight; it occurred to me he was stronger than he looked.

"Ready to go then?" He asked a few minutes later.

"Sure. I just need to figure out how to move the music." I turned to walk back over to the table. I had to move slowly, my limbs not quite cooperating. I poked at the music with a finger, testing how wet it was while trying not to tear it. I was pleased to see that it didn't just fall apart, but I still wasn't very hopeful about rescuing it since it was still thoroughly saturated.

"Is it salvageable?" Roman asked as he came up behind me, resting his hands on my shoulders.

"I'm not sure." I didn't look up. "It's pretty soaked."

"Hmmm…" He mumbled as he reached out to touch the paper himself. "Wow, yeah that's… that's soaked alright."

"Ah, yeah, I already said that." I said sarcastically.

"Grab your violin and let's go back to my aunt's house." He grabbed my hand to pull me along behind him.

"Wait. What?" I stammered as I snagged the case with my free hand before being pulled gently back to the path. "What about the music?"

"It's not going anywhere, don't worry."

"Yeah, but what're we going to do about it? I can't just leave it there!"

"Don't worry, we won't." He sounded much calmer about it than I felt. "We can get something from my aunt's to put it on. A cookie sheet or something, then we can leave it at her place to dry."

"And how do I get it back precisely?"

"Don't be silly Lisbeth. I can get it for you easily." He kept moving but turned his head to glare at me.

"Sorry. I just don't want to lose it. Its kind of an original copy you know." I half-ducked my head with embarrassment.

"Yeah, I understand." We came out by his aunt's house, right where the truck was parked.

We found exactly what Roman had suggested in the kitchen of his aunt's house and after some very careful maneuvering of the paper, managed to lay it out on the kitchen counter to dry. Roman wrote his aunt a brief note explaining its presence, and directing her not to move it. Once that was done, we both went back outside to the truck, careful not to track mud all over the house. It was easy to forget how wet you got in these storms when they were happening, but once they were over it seemed to be the one thing you were strikingly aware of.

"What would you say to going over to my place to eat that dessert and dry off?" Roman asked as we got into the truck.

"That sounds like a good plan to me." Settled into the seat; I'd started to get a little chill, and my body was finally reminding me that I hadn't had the most sleep in the last couple days. I closed my eyes and let my mind drift as Roman drove, not bothering to talk, waiting instead for when we got to his place to start picking the days events to pieces.

My eyes fluttered open when I realized that the truck was no longer running, the air quiet now that the truck engine was off. I yawned, and rolled my neck to stretch; I'd managed to fall asleep for the time it took to get here. I looked around me then, wondering exactly where here was.

"This your place?" I asked after a moment. Roman was still in the driver's side seat, waiting for me to notice where we were.

"Yeah, this is it. Shall we go in?"

"Sure." I undid my seat belt and opened the door. He was already out of the truck by the time I had my violin and had walked around to his side of the truck. I would have to lay the instrument out so that it, and its case, could dry out a bit while we were here.

As I walked to meet Roman by the head of the truck, I took a look around. Judging from the amount of foliage at the back I guessed we were still near the park, but I was pleasantly surprised to see we'd pulled into a private driveway.

"Do you live here alone?" I asked when I stood next to him.

"Sadly, yes." He turned to lead me up to the front door of the little house. We were in a small neighborhood; I could see the next houses down were of a similar style: small backyard, with a neatly manicured lawn that suited the architecture of the house. He hadn't done much by way of a garden but there were a few trees planted in a cluster near where the property line bordered the park.

"Well, here we are." He gestured to the interior of the house as we walked in.

"Nice." We were standing in a foyer that opened into a small living area on one side, and a kitchen on the other. He was watching me as I took it all in, his brow raised in comic anxiety as he waited for me to elaborate on my reaction. "Really, Roman, I like it. Now where can I put my violin? It needs to dry out a little."

"Oh, you can put it over here." He walked in the direction of the kitchen. I followed, trying to contain my laughter. He led me through to a small mudroom that appeared to lead either to the backyard or the garage, and it contained the washer and dryer. "You can set it out on top of here if you want." He patted the top of one of the machines.

"Okay, that works." I said as I went to do just that. I tried to figure out just how water logged the instrument and case actually were; getting a little nervous that I'd managed to ruin both.

Roman left me to it and walked back into the kitchen. I heard him open the refrigerator and pull something out, and then something clicked and a moment or two later I heard boiling water. I smiled, something hot would feel good right about now; I was starting to feel more of a chill now that I had been sitting still for a while.

"Why don't you put your wet clothes in the dryer? They can dry while we eat that dessert." I jumped, not having heard him come up behind me. "Sorry."

"That's okay." I had a hand on my chest as I turned to face him.

"You can put this on instead if you want." He held out a sweatshirt and sweatpants. "I know they're going to be a bit big, but I didn't think you'd want to sit around in what you have on." He nodded at my still saturated clothes.

"That would be great. Thanks." I smiled at him, recovering my composure. I reached out and took the clothes he held. "Why don't you go put something else on, too? You're just as soaked as I am."

"Don't worry, I intend to. You go ahead and change first though, I'm going to make some tea."

"Mmm, that would be lovely." He returned my smile before turning to go back into the kitchen. As soon as I knew he was out of sight, I stripped off my wet clothes and slid into the ones he had brought. I was swimming in them, but after I'd rolled the waistband down several times and rolled up the sleeves, I made it work. I left my shoes in the mudroom and threw my socks, with the rest of my clothes, into the dryer. I didn't turn it on though, waiting for Roman to put his own things in to do that.

That taken care of, I went to take a look at the rest of the house. Roman wasn't in the kitchen anymore, so I guessed he had gone to change. The kitchen, like the house itself, was small and basic. Everything was neat, clean and orderly; I had a feeling he didn't exactly spend much time in it. I saw two mugs of steaming tea on the counter beside the sink, steeping while they waited for us to drink them. The colors of the room were warm, though I had a feeling I should give credit for them to the previous owner, not Roman. I walked through into the living room, and found it much like the kitchen: small, neat, and orderly. The color scheme was also like that of the kitchen, warm browns and creams. The furniture was sparse: a sofa and a lazy boy chair positioned precisely for watching the TV that sat across the room. The window behind it looked out on the lawn and the park beyond. I wrapped my arms around myself as I stood in the middle of the room, taking it all in; so different from my own place with Tom and Kaya. It felt so empty, like something vital was missing; I wasn't sure what, but it left me cold inside.

"Those really are too big for you, aren't they?" Roman commented as he came up behind me. This time his footsteps preceded his voice so I didn't jump.

"Yeah, you could say that." I laughed as I looked down at the rolled-to-fit sweats I wore.

"You want your tea?" He held out one of the mugs I realized he'd been carrying. I nodded and reached for it, inhaling the steam as I cupped it close in my hands.

"Thanks." I felt the warmth of the mug finish heating my hands as we stood in silence for a few minutes. "So." I said then. "How about that dessert you promised me?"

"That would be in the kitchen." His smile was teasing. "Would you like to have it now?"

"Yes, please." I batted my eyelashes and did my best to look like a five year old. He laughed and I broke out of it in a grin.

"Okay, then." He turned to lead me back into the kitchen.

As we walked, I wondered about what it was I felt was missing from this house. It clearly looked lived in, there were stacks of various magazines on the coffee table, and everything was worn with use. As Roman opened the to go box, I started to realize what it was. Instead of saying anything I took the fork he offered after setting the dessert out between us on a plate. My mouth started to water when I saw a massive slice of cheesecake smothered in cherries.

"Ladies first." Roman grinned as I ogled the dessert.

"Is this for real?" I murmured as I reached out to take the first bite.

"Quite real." He laughed.

"And quite delicious." I added after thoroughly savoring my first bite. I didn't hesitate to take another, making Roman laugh again.

"I suppose I can tell Sophia you liked it then?" He teased.

"What do you think?"

"I think that's a yes."

"Yes it is." I paused to let him get some before going for a third forkful. Silent as we continued to eat and enjoy.

"I think that next time, we need to pick a location where we can be inside." I said as we at the last bites of the cake.

"What, you don't like the idea of getting soaked to the bone every time?" He asked.

"No, not particularly."

"Okay, we'll keep that in mind then." He set his fork down on the plate and leaned back against the edge of the counter. "So."

"So?"

"Are you going to tell me how it worked this time?" He asked, looking expectant.

"You couldn't tell?"

"No. I could barely make out the fact that it didn't take control of you like it usually does."

"Well that would be true." I picked up my mug while I organized my thoughts. "It never got that kind of control over me this time; I felt a pull at the beginning, like it was going to try, but then it didn't."

"So were you able to play with the tempo?"

"Easily. I tried that for a little while, but it didn't seem to really affect the storm. You know, as if each note made up a part of the storm and you'd have to cut the note in order to cut that part of the storm." He nodded as I continued. "So when I realized that I decided to try cutting pieces out; notes, rests, whole bars of music. That's what finally made a difference. Things like the lightning would stop happening if I didn't play the notes that were their part, and the rain would lighten if I did that with theirs; then it got shorter if I cut whole bars."

"So if you played a part from the middle of the music, would it just create that part of the storm? Not the whole thing?"

"I think so. I'm not sure." I paused to consider the idea. "I suppose that would be something to try at another practice round."

"But on a piano next time?" He asked with a half-smile.

"Yes. I don't think my violin can handle another bout with a rainstorm, Roman. Seriously."

"Okay, I get, I get it." He raised his arms in a submissive gesture. "We'll go somewhere with a piano next time."

"So when is the next practice session anyway? I mean this was your idea after all."

"So that means I get to do all the planning, huh?"

"Yeah. Basically."

"Then I think I'm going to have to get back to you tomorrow because I haven't got a clue."

"Okay." I took another sip of my tea as I tried to think of what to talk about next. I wasn't ready to leave yet.

"You know your clothes won't be out of the drier for a while yet. Do you want to see the rest of the house?" Roman asked after we'd been standing there for a few minutes without talking.

"Sure."

Roman walked ahead of me, leaving his tea behind, over to a short hallway that opened up off the kitchen and foyer. I sipped my tea as I followed, watching as he led me past a door he pointed out as leading to the basement stairs, and another that went into the master bedroom. He opened that door for me to look in, and I found it much the same as the rest of the house in style and color, though his comforter was a burst of burgundy; I remembered he'd said it was his favorite. We turned around not going in, and I led the way back to the foyer, where he directed me to a set of stairs that were started on the same side of the foyer as the hallway, disappearing into the second floor.

"Roman, don't you have a piano? I thought you said you played." I asked tentatively as we reached the top of the stairs.

"Why don't you open that door there and see?"

I did as he'd directed, and opened the door on my right. Against the opposite wall, below the window, stood a mahogany colored upright that gleamed in the sunlight filtering through the light curtains. The room was set up much like my own music room, with stacks of music organized near the piano, and shelves of CDs and records lining one of the walls perpendicular to the piano. It was small, just like the rest of the house, but here nothing was missing. I turned to look at Roman where he hovered just behind my shoulder and back at the room.

"You can go in if you want." He nudged my back with his hand to get me to move.

I didn't say anything, simply following his direction as I took a couple of steps past the door. When I did, I noticed there was a row of about three guitars in their stands against the wall the door opened up against. The walls were the same cream color as the rest of the house, and the carpet matched, giving an odd sensation of walking into a room larger than it was. I walked over to his collection of CDs and records and took it all in, taking my time as I flipped through them, making various noises of approval, surprise and shock, or disgust, as applied.

"Its not quite as extensive as yours." Roman said after he'd let me sift through them for a while.

"You have such different music though." I countered, not looking up from the CD I held. "It hardly matters."

"I started in college, collecting I mean." He explained. "I couldn't afford music lessons so I started teaching myself by ear. When I had some spare cash I'd pick up an album and listen to it until I could play it myself."

"That's impressive." I finally looking up. "I started in high school, which would explain why I have the larger collection, but I bought it to listen."

We let it drop then, and I went back to combing through his collection, feeling like a kid in a candy shop. As I looked at the CDs and envied the records, which he had more of than I did, I began to understand why nothing was missing here, while the rest of the house felt so odd to me. This was where he really lived, where he was really himself. The rest of the house was merely a place to live, prepare food and hang out. This was where he really let himself be himself. My hand tightened on the case I held as I remembered the pull I'd felt at the park. It had been something more than a simple draw on my core; it had been a connection to it, an old one. I shook myself gently and forced myself to back away from that very dangerous territory. It had barely been two weeks, no point in getting myself in over my head. I relaxed my hand on the case and put it back where it'd come from.

"Ready to see the rest?" Roman asked before I could.

"Yeah, let's go." I turned away from the shelves towards the door. My eye caught the guitars as I did, making me smile. "My dad would love those."

"He play?"

"No. He's always wanted to though. I keep telling him I'm going to buy him a guitar for his birthday one year so he has to."

"Are you going to?"

"Maybe. One day. Maybe as a retirement present. That is if he ever retires." I rolled my eyes as I thought about my dad.

"Workaholic?"

"No, just likes his job is all. My parents own a hardware shop in my hometown that's been in the family for generations." I explained as we walked through another door into an office.

"That sounds cool." The desk was covered with papers, a telephone and a desktop computer that clearly explained that this was where work overlapped with home for him.

We lapsed into a comfortable silence after that as we walked back down the stairs to the kitchen. I still held my mug, though I'd already finished the tea, so I ditched it in the kitchen before he led me to the door down to the basement. As we made our way down the steps, he grabbed a pull-tab for the light to turn it on. I was surprised, when the light flickered on, to find that the basement was actually mostly finished off. There was carpeting in most of the giant space, but it was clearly used mostly as storage. There were several heavy-duty snow shovels stashed in a corner, next to various other bits of winter gear that lay in a semi-organized fashion in and around a basket next to them. When I looked over to the other side of the room I saw what looked like a stack of random boxes of things. Curious, I walked towards them.

"What's in here?" I asked as I made my way over to them. The boxes were fairly small, but there were a lot of them, and coated with enough dust to tell me they'd been there for a while. "May I?" I asked before reaching to pull one open. They weren't sealed, the tops simply folded into themselves so they weren't open.

"Go ahead." He from a little ways behind me.

I lifted the one closest to me open, and gasped when I saw what was inside: pictures, it was full of perfectly filed packets of old photos from decades ago. I pulled one out, marking carefully where I'd gotten it from, and opened it. They were old Polaroid's, black and whites, of a couple on a beach somewhere. I could all but feel the happiness on their faces, and I felt myself tear up at the pure simplicity of it.

"Hey, you okay?" Roman asked, when I sniffed softly. I felt his hand on my shoulder, and turned into him, the picture still in my hands.

"These are your parents aren't they? When they were still in France?"

"Let me see." He reached for the picture. "Yeah, it is." He barely glanced at it before handing it back to me.

"It's, so beautiful." I explained through my tears. "I just…its such a shame knowing how their relationship ended up." I looked up at him, hoping he would understand.

"I know." He said almost too softly for me to hear. He took the photo then, and set it back in the box, not bothering to see where I'd marked its spot. He pulled me close then, wrapping his arms around me to squeeze me tight. It felt good, being held like that, and I relaxed into the embrace. As my tears started to slow and I felt my emotions level out again, I didn't pull back from him. He seemed to sense how I felt, and I felt one of his arms loosen its hold, his hand sliding between us to cup my face, and pull it up to his.

The kiss was sweet and brief, meant only to comfort. When we pulled away it was only to rest our foreheads together, still trying to stay close to one another. We stood like that until I heard a buzzer sound upstairs.

"I think my clothes are dry now." I grudgingly broke the silence.

"They can wait." He didn't move. I sighed, knowing it must be getting late.

"Roman, I think we need to get going." I started to pull away from him to put some space between us.

"It's not that late yet." He sighed.

"Yeah, but I still need to change back into my clothes, and we need to get back to my place pretty soon. They're expecting us for dinner." I explained slowly; I didn't really want to leave.

"Well, if you say so." He gave in.

"I do." I started to nudge him back towards the stairs. "Besides, I think Tom has something big planned for dinner since you're coming. The least we can do is be on time."

Chapter 13

As I sat in the living room to wait for Roman, the routine we had formed over the past weeks made me smile. Had anyone told me, or asked me, about having such a close relationship in August I'd have denied it all as impossible. Instead, as I waited for him, my eyes studying the fall leaf colors through the front window, it felt natural. The runs, the drives to work, all of it, felt like it had been routine for several years instead of several weeks. I heard Romans' truck pull into the drive, for once right on time. Eleven o'clock. I didn't wait for him to get out of the truck, but left the house and opened the passenger-side door before he could get out.

"You're in a hurry today." Roman observed as he restarted the truck.

"No, not really." I buckled myself in. "I guess I'm just in a good mood, or something."

"Or something indeed." He let it go as he started to back out into the road. I reached out to adjust the radio station, settling on something soothing and jazzy as he drove.

"So, are you going to tell me where we're going this time? Or do I have to guess, again?" I asked when the song changed.

"Why don't you guess?"

"I don't want to. Tell me." I pretended to whine and pouted a little.

"Oh, come on. It's not that hard. Think for a minute, you'll figure it out."

"Oh, all right." I recognized the exit we were taking, and it clicked. "Are we going to Jason's?"

"Nice."

"Am I right?"

"Yup. We're going to Jason's."

"But I thought he'd left to go home? Has he not left yet, or what? I'm confused." I made a face, making him laugh.

"He left last night on a redeye flight, so his place is empty. I asked him yesterday though if he'd mind me bringing you over." He shrugged, but I wasn't quite ready to leave it at that.

"What did you tell him, Roman? What does he know now?"

"He doesn't know anything, Lisbeth."

"Then how on earth did you explain this to him?" I was still confused.

"I didn't really." He shrugged again, irritating me.

"So, what you called in a favor or something?"

"Lisbeth. Chill out okay? I didn't tell him anything about you; I just asked him if we could use his piano. If you want to say he owes me, then fine, that's what it was. But don't worry about it, okay?"

"Fine." I let it drop. We were driving through the city now; so I turned to look out the window instead of talking. I relaxed again as I listened to the music from the radio and watched the people hurrying down the sidewalk. It wasn't quite as sunny as yesterday, but it was still enough to have people out and about. I was going to feel a little bad, bringing a storm into their day. We pulled into the parking garage and wound our way around until we were on the level of Jason's apartment, and found an empty spot big enough for the truck to fit in. I was glad, now, as always, that I hadn't driven. I would have felt out of place amongst all these shiny imports. The truck was at least fairly new.

"You have the key, right?" I picked up my bag and started to get out of the car.

"Yeah, I got it from him yesterday."

We met up on the other side of the truck, and walked side by side to the door to the building. When we got to the door of Jason's apartment, Roman fished out the key from his pocket to unlock it. It felt odd, walking into the place, not having everyone there. It seemed much bigger to me now than before; I wondered how Jason could live here by himself. We both slid out of our shoes, knowing Jason wouldn't appreciate us leaving mud all over the place, and made our way to the door of the music room. I followed behind Roman, carrying my bag with the music in it. I'd brought a couple of pieces to choose from, having not been able to decide between three of them before; I figured I would get Roman's opinion, he knew what we were going to try and work on today anyway, not me.

"I brought three storms to choose from." I told him once we were in the room.

"Oh! Had trouble choosing?" He teased as I pulled them out of my bag and sat them on top of the piano for him to look through.

"You could say that. Choose one." He picked one up and flipped loosely through the pages.

"Right. Well…" He mumbled, picking up the next one. "I guess we're going to want the longest one, since we need to work on picking out notes for what they represent."

"Is that what we're going to work on this time then?" I asked from behind the piano.

"Yeah, I think so. We seem to have a handle on what you can do with the music, and the effect it will have on the storm. Now we have to figure out how much you can manipulate it."

"Basically, you want to find out if you have to play the notes together or if they'll have the same effect played on their own.

"We're certain that you can cut whole sections of notes, but not if you can cut simply the ones you don't want. So, yes that's what I want to know, or we want to know, rather."

"Oh, right, we want to know." I rolled my eyes at him.

"Why don't we use this one?" Roman said as he held out the second of the three pieces to me. "That okay?"

"Sure, I said it was your choice." I took it from him and arranged the pages in front of me on the piano.

The music began to play in my head as I looked at the page, making me want to play it. I waited for Roman to pull up one of the chairs so that he was sitting close to the opposite side of the piano, and then played a couple of random chords, re-familiarizing myself with the keys.

"Ready?" He asked softly when I'd finished.

"Ready as I'll ever be."

I took a deep breath and began. Throughout the practice sessions over the last several weeks, I had developed a kind of pattern in the way that I worked through the music: always starting with the full chords, and then progressively breaking it down so that I was no longer playing all of what was written, but only what I chose to. This time, no different from any other, I felt the pull on my core as the opening chords sounded in the silent room. I barely registered the appearance of storm clouds in the sky outside the window, but I heard the rain when it began to pour outside.

The piece that Roman had chosen, I had written down as only played by piano, but as I played the opening bars, I started to recognize the instruments intended for each note, and with them the part of the storm they belonged to. I didn't feel any other pulls on my core after the initial tug, and for once I remained in control of the music from the start. To test that, I started to mess with the tempo of the next several bars, wanting to make sure it was responsive to my playing. Once that had proven successful, I started to pick and choose the chords to play; noting the results of every note. By the time that I had done all of this I had gotten through about a third of the whole piece; apparently Roman had chosen the longest of the three, so I would have plenty of time to keep playing with it. I could hear the thunder and lighting crash and flash outside, and had an idea for how to test my control.

Now able to recognize which notes created the lightning and thunder, and which created rain, or wind; I began the next two thirds of the piece by cutting every bit of lightning and thunder out of the storm. The change was immediate, and without any protest from the storm itself. Apparently it didn't mind being cut into pieces. Then I added them back in, playing them for only half their note value or longer, depending on what fit better. Resulting in lengthened and shortened flashes of lightning and claps of thunder. I came to a line then that consisted of nearly all flashes of lightning, and, forgetting where we were, I cut the rain instead. I barely registered the fact that it had stopped raining, but I did recognize its sound when I started to play those notes again a few lines later, finishing the piece with full chords.

Lifting my hands from the final chord, I became immediately aware of the silence that filled the room. The clouds were dissipating rapidly from the sky, and a moment later the room lit with sunlight again. As it came streaming back into the room, I lifted my eyes to meet Roman's. I knew that he had been watching me the whole time, he always did, but I had learned, after our first attempt at these practice sessions, not to look at him until I had finished. As I did now, I felt the familiar jolt, the pull on my core that no longer overwhelmed me during the music, but now seemed to wait for him. Keeping my eyes on his, I stood and walked around the piano to where he still sat in the chair. His eyes were dark in a way that had begun to feel familiar, melted-chocolate-brown ringed with black. He reached up with one hand, when I stood in front of him, to slide his fingers into my hair and pull my mouth down to his.

The jolt I felt when his lips met mine, never failed to overwhelm me; it always seemed to me that it was intensifying rather than weakening. Deepening the kiss I swung my leg over his lap so that I was straddled him; his hands moving to pull me closer, mine moving up to thread through his hair. The heat that coursed through it spiked as my body pressed against his, hands racing over each other, frustrated with the barrier of clothing. Then I felt his hands on my skin, and something like an alarm went off in my mind, forcing me to pull reluctantly away from him. He froze instantly.

"I'm sorry." I whispered; feeling a little embarrassed as I rested my head against his shoulder.

"It's okay, you're not ready; I'm not going to push that." He rested his hands lightly against my back. "Lisbeth." He pulled my head up so that I looked him in the eye. "What's the matter? You know I'm not going to push you. How many times do I have to say that?" His eyes seemed concerned, making me feel guilty all over again.

"I believe you, trust me, its not that that has me apologizing." I tried to drop my eyes, but he caught my chin and pulled them back up to his.

"Then what exactly is it? Spit it out. Let's get this figured out. I don't like you feeling like this. Whatever it is you are feeling like."

"Um." I stalled. I had no idea how to say this. "I…its not because I'm not ready. I…I just don't know what I'm doing. I mean…you know…I've never done this before." I ducked my head as heat flooded my face; he didn't try and stop me this time. "I want to…just, not here and… yeah…" I finished lamely.

"Oh." I held back a smile at his response, secretly pleased to have at least surprised him with my answer.

He didn't say anything else, so I sat back so that I was perched almost on his knees, putting at least that much space between us. I wasn't feeling quite as embarrassed anymore, though I couldn't help wondering what he was thinking, how he was really reacting to my words. I watched his face closely, waiting for him to say something, but after a few minutes of that I gave up.

"We should probably leave. I mean, we've done what we planned, so…" I mumbled as I stood up completely, and started walking back to the piano. I felt his eyes on my back as I started to collect the music and put it back in my bag. Slinging it over my shoulder, I turned to face him. "Well?" I asked, starting to get uncomfortably frustrated. I resisted tapping my foot or drumming my fingers on something, but barely.

"I guess you're right." I frowned at the tone of his voice, my whole body going a little tense; he didn't exactly sound pleased. My eyes locked onto his once again as he stood, walking slowly towards me. A shiver ran up my spine as he closed in on me; he seemed so predator-like. He smiled then, and I felt the breath go out of my body. This kiss was light, sweet, nothing like the way he looked. When he backed away from me only a moment later, I found myself looking longingly at his mouth, pouting a bit at not being able to continue the kiss. "We should go." He whispered, and turned away to lead the way out of the room.

"Okay." The word was hardly a whisper on my lips as I scrambled to catch up with him, my body struggling to follow direction.

We didn't speak as we locked the apartment, and walked out to the truck. As we drove out of the garage, I occupied myself by flipping through the radio stations in search of the perfect one to listen to. I knew that it was uncharacteristic of me, but I couldn't resist, I needed something to occupy my mind, the thoughts filling it at present didn't appeal to me. I had paused on a news station, not having had much luck finding a music station I liked, when I caught a random word from the weatherman and immediately cranked the volume.

"The freak storms that have been making appearances all around the outskirts of the city, seem to have made an appearance directly in the city today. As you all might have noticed, there was a serious thunderstorm that came seemingly out of nowhere this morning, to empty approximately an inch of rain on the city." The man paused for a moment, and then continued. "This storm lasted almost two hours, and seemed to behave in some bizarre patterns that our meteorologists have been struggling to understand. It isn't exactly normal for thunder and lightning storms to stop raining momentarily, and then return full force with no break in the cloud cover." Roman hit the power button suddenly, almost making me jump with surprise.

"Fuck. How could I have been so stupid; of course they would notice a storm in the city." He slammed his hands against the steering wheel as he cursed again.

"Roman?" I watched him carefully. "Hey! You can't think of everything. I'm the one with the gift here, I should have thought of that. Hell, I should have thought of that weeks and weeks ago." My voice rose as I spoke, starting to feel a little scared; my mind dreaming up ways that they would be able to connect the storms to me, most of which were impossible, or all of them really.

"Well, at least we know now. Besides, its not like they can connect any of this to us." He looked at me, a small smile on his face. I tried to return it, but failed miserably.

"I guess that's true." I mumbled, looking away.

"Hey." I turned to look back at him. "I'm sorry. I know attention is the last thing you want, even if it's in a way they can't connect with you."

"Its okay, really. I mean its like you said, they can't connect it to us, or me rather."

We lapsed into silence after that, not even bothering to turn the radio back on and finding a music station to listen to. I forced myself to look out the window, not liking the turn my thoughts were taking as I continued to stare at the dashboard instead. The sun still shone, though it had moved further down the horizon since it was now after one in the afternoon. I glanced at the clock; it was almost two, actually. It would be dark in a few hours. With my thoughts occupied, it wasn't long before we were pulled into the driveway of my house. I saw Tom and Kaya's cars parked ahead of us, and winced. They had probably heard something about the storm; I wondered how they would react.

"Do you want me to come in?" Roman asked after he'd turned off the truck.

"No, I don't think so today. I think it'll be better if it's just me explaining the news report."

"Oh, right."

"I'll see you tomorrow morning though, okay?" I turned towards him. I felt bad not inviting him in. I knew that he was probably feeling pretty rotten after that radio report, though I wasn't really sure why. It wasn't his fault. As I sat looking at him now though, I had to suppress a smile; it was just the way he was, and part of the reason we worked so well together. He always seemed to forget I was the only one who should take on the burden of the results of my gift.

"Yeah, I'll see you tomorrow morning."

"Okay." I leaned over to kiss his cheek before getting out of the truck. I moved quickly, not wanting to give him the chance to snag me and draw me into a longer kiss; I needed a little more time before I did that again.

Walking up to the house, I heard him put the truck in reverse and back out of the drive. Drawing in a deep breath, I opened the door and stepped into the house. I closed my eyes as the anticipated reaction hit me full force.

"Lisbeth Moore!" Kaya had known the second I'd opened the door, and her voice reached me at that exact moment, closely followed by her. "What the hell did you think you were doing? I know that storm was you! Don't you try and tell me it wasn't. What the fucking hell do you think you were doing, playing storm music in the city. Where the hell did you go that you could play anyway?"

"Kaya. Can I please get into the house at least, please?" My voice was tired. I'd known she'd react this way, she always did.

"Fine." She bit off, turning to march into the living room and stand, feet spread, in the middle of it.

"Thank you." I followed her in the process of taking off my shoes and setting my bag down by the door. Tom leaned against the wall just a little ways beyond Kaya. He didn't look very happy, though he was thankfully keeping it to himself, unlike Kaya.

"Well?" Kaya demanded once I'd walked into the room. "What do you have to say?"

"Not much." I said tiredly. I hated fighting with people; it was always so stressful. "We had one of our practice sessions, like I explained to you already."

"And I thought you said that they weren't able to be linked with us." She cut me off.

"They can't be, Kaya, of course they can't. No one knows the source of the storm."

"Oh, right." Her voice sounded flat now and I knew I'd given her something else to consider.

"Yeah, now are you going to let me talk or not?" My voice finally sounded sharp. "We were having a practice session; at a friend's place in the city. He's not home and he let us use his piano. Roman pulled a favor I think; he swears he didn't say anything about what we were going to be doing." I gave Kaya a meaningful look when she started to open her mouth. "I wasn't doing anything beyond what we usually do: manipulating the music. I've already explained that to you."

"Lisbeth, don't you think that would be something that would attract attention?" The sound of Tom's voice made me turn. "I mean, it sounds like you managed to cut the rain out of the song, effectively making it a lightning and thunder only storm. Little odd, don't ya think?"

"Neither of us thought about how that would work when we decided to try it. We didn't even know if I could do that."

"Why not, you can cut whole parts of the song, why not individual notes?" The look he gave me made me squirm.

"Tom, I'm already feeling like a major idiot okay? There's no need to heap on the extra helping of 'how dumb are you?' okay?" I felt my eyes well up a little as I spoke, the guilt coming on in full force.

"Yeah well maybe next time you should take the time to think before acting, okay? It's about time you learned to do that." Kaya's voice cut through me like a knife and I felt myself crumble.

"I'm sorry you feel that way, Kaya. Tom." I acknowledged them both, my body stiff with repressed tears, and then turned to walk towards the steps and my room.

"Lisbeth- " My hand whipped out in response, effectively cutting Tom off. He took the hint, looking at Kaya instead. I didn't catch the look on his face, but I had a feeling he wasn't feeling quite so upset anymore. I didn't care now though, I just focused on making it to my room before the tears came.

The colors flashed swiftly from one to the next, emotions shooting through me so fast I couldn't keep them straight. My heart raced so fast I thought for a second that it was going to come right out of my chest if it didn't just give out; my lungs raw with exertion. Then blackness enveloped me, and I all but felt it against my skin as I struggled without seeing. My already maxed out heart and lungs pumped that much harder as terror worked its way into my system, adrenaline flooding my blood. My eyes were open wide as I strained to see something, anything at all in the thick black I was suspended in, and my mouth opened wide in a silent scream so that I even felt it on my throat as it tried to get inside me any way possible.

The blackness began to flicker suddenly, a scene backed in white flipping across my vision in short intervals. I couldn't see what was happening at first, the light blinding me as thoroughly as the darkness until my eyes adjusted. The scene I saw did nothing to settle me; instead it only served to change the tone of the anxiety I felt. It was the same scene from my dream almost two months previous. Roman and I in the middle of a farm field in a place I didn't recognize; me seated on the bench of a grand piano and Roman standing across from me, guitar in hand with the strap across his shoulders.

The sound reached me before I even realized I could hear anything. It was storm music, generating the rain that lashed at us both. It wasn't a storm I recognized, no matter how closely I listened, but as I listened I realized something else: Roman was playing with me, the same music, simply on the guitar instead of the piano. Then something else clicked. My eyes were locked on Roman's, and his on mine; the energy threading between us palpable even to me on the outside.

This time I woke up when my head cracked against the floor, shooting into a sitting position the second I did. It took me a minute to pull myself back into my body and start to settle into a healthier rhythm. I didn't move, just continued to sit there on the floor, eyes closed, focusing on my breathing until my heart no longer felt like it was going to come out of my chest; my lungs were still raw, but they slowly calmed down too once I was no longer panting with exertion. Calmed, I reached a hand up to check the back of my head, wincing at the bruise forming beneath my fingers.

"Yikes." I muttered into the empty room. "That's going to hurt for a while." I tried to stand, but just like the time before, I fell back onto my bed once I made it to vertical.

As I sat there, re-gathering myself to try and stand again, my dream came flooding back to me. As I began to connect the things I'd seen, my breathing spiked again and I had to focus fast so that I didn't start hyperventilating. Settled again, I waited a minute before trying to stand. I needed to talk to someone, and the only person who would probably understand had screamed at me the last time I'd talked to her. I took a deep breath and managed to stay on my feet, when I made it there, this time. Quietly, I pulled on a pair of pajama bottoms and walked softly over to Kaya's room. I didn't knock, knowing it wouldn't wake her up, but carefully turned the knob on the door and walked in so that I stood right next to her in her bed.

"Kaya." I whispered harshly, shaking her gently at the same time.

"Mmm, what?" She moaned without opening her eyes. I shook her gently again.

"It's me, wake up."

"Lisbeth? What's the matter?" She shot upright, looking around wildly.

"Hey, calm down, it's just me." I motioned for her to quiet down. I didn't want to wake Tom.

"What do you want?" She mumbled, wiping sleep out of her eyes as I sat down on the foot of her bed.

"Can we talk?"

"Dream?" Her voice was thick with sleep, but she looked awake now.

"Yeah, but not a memory dream."

"Oh." She looked at me blankly. "Then, what kind of dream was it?"

"It was about my present lifetime, not a past one. It was about the storm music."

"I thought Mom said you wouldn't have dream help with that though?"

"That's what I thought too, which is why I wanted to talk."

"Okay, shoot. What was it about?" She settled so that she leaned back against her headboard.

"It's a single image, Roman and I in the middle of a hay field somewhere I didn't recognize. I was sitting at a grand piano, playing storm music. The odd thing is, that Roman is there with me, playing the same music on his guitar. The first time I had the dream-"

"You've had this dream before?" Kaya interrupted.

"Last time was a couple of months ago, after the first practice session we did."

"So, there was a change in the dream this time?" I knew she'd pick this up fast.

"Yeah, last time it was just a silent image, no sound, just a flash in the pan picture before I woke up. This time, not only could I hear the music, but it lasted longer."

"Long enough for you to realize what it was trying to tell you." It wasn't a question.

"I could feel the energy between the two of us, even in the dream. It was like we were connected, you know in my core. But...I...I don't understand how. I mean, he's not one of us, so how is that possible?" I stuttered lamely.

"Hmmm...I'm not sure either." She stared at me intensely. "Lisbeth, was there anything else you dreamt of tonight?" I looked at her blankly for a moment before ducking my head and blushing. "Was there?" She asked again, raising an eyebrow in amusement."

"Yes, but its silly."

"Spit it out."

"There were colors, every one you could possibly imagine, flashing from one to the next, never repeating. Then with them were pure emotions, shooting through my body with enough force that they were almost painful; at the very least they had my heart and lungs working on overtime. Then…then there was just black. Thick, black darkness; you know the kind where you can't see anything, but you can all but feel it against your skin? It came with terror for an emotion, and it stayed the longest." I shuddered at the memory and kept talking so I could forget about it. "Then white light started flickering, like an old film real, across my eyes until it stayed long enough for that scene to be visible to me."

"And then you woke up?"

"Yes, then I woke up, and here I am. With a very large bump on the back of my head I might add." Kaya smiled at my sarcasm.

"Fall out of bed?" She teased.

"You could say that."

Neither of us spoke for a while; I could tell by the look on her face that Kaya was thinking hard about what I'd told her. I wondered if she would have any ideas about what it was all going to mean, or if it was even a dream that I needed to worry about, a figment of my own overactive imagination. Part of me hoped that was what it was, but a bigger part hoped it wasn't.

"What do you think?" I asked after about ten minutes.

"I'm thinking a lot of things, and I don't know if you're going to like all of them."

"Shoot." My eyes focused on her to show I was listening.

"Okay, here's my theory." She looked me dead in the eye as she spoke. "As to what the dream means, I think it means you stumbled across your soul mate. You're connected in your core because your core is your soul, and your soul is how you are connected to the earth, which is your core's source of energy. As to the source of this dream, I think this is a direction directly from the Earth. It's teaching you first hand about your newest talent with your gift. Mom said your memory dreams wouldn't be of any use, but she never said to disregard your dreams. The colors only serve to confirm my idea; they're representative of the purity of the dream's source: Earth."

"You sound so certain." I still couldn't quite wrap my mind around what she was saying.

"Well I'm not, but whatever." She laughed lightly. "The soul mate part I've been thinking about for a while. I mean, you went from zero to sixty with this whole dating thing, and then you said Mom even mentioned Roman when you talked to her that time so…" I smiled at the sheepish look on her face.

"Been wondering about it for quite a while then haven't you?"

"Yeah; kinda." She grinned.

"Well at least one of us doesn't have tunnel vision."

"Yes, indeed. Wouldn't we be in trouble?"

"Indeed." We just sat there again for a few minutes, both staring off into space in thought. "The color thing really does make sense when you look at it that way." I said into the silence. Kaya just smiled.

"Of course I could be wrong."

"But you know you're not." I shot back.

"Well I don't know, but that's what I feel."

"Well." I sighed and looked out her bedroom window. "Looks like I've got something new to talk to Roman about, about my gift." My voice was full of the resignation I felt; this wasn't something I was one hundred percent comfortable with. Even with Roman.

I took my time gathering my things and walking to my car after work, knowing that Roman would be waiting for me like he does always these days. The sun had only made a brief appearance sometime in the morning, so I still needed the coat I'd thrown on against the chill morning air; it hadn't exactly had a chance to warm up. It wasn't quite dark, though it was close, so Roman looked more like a tall shadow than a person as I walked towards him. I never had figured out exactly how tall he was, the fact always seemed to slip out of my mind when we were together.

"Hey." I said by way of greeting when I was close enough to be heard.

"Hey yourself." He was leaning against his truck, but on the passenger side so my driver's side.

I pulled out my keys from my pocket as I kept walking; not stopping until I stood right in front of him. He leaned down when I'd stopped, and pulled me up so that he could kiss me. It was relaxed, a greeting; though I still had to stop myself from trying to take it in a different direction. I sighed when he let me go, settling back onto my feet.

"Have a good day?" I asked sleepily. His kiss had reminded my body that it hadn't gotten much rest last night.

"As good as they can be." He replied vaguely. "Nothing dramatic but nothing too boring."

"I can sympathize. The only dramatic thing happening on our end was the girls speculating over our love life." He winced. "Yeah, they reverted back to that again."

"I wish they would let it go." He whined.

"Hey, at least you don't have to actually listen to it."

"You wish. What makes you think I don't hear it, too?"

"Oh really? So the girls harass you and me. How did I miss that?"

"No, not the girls."

"What? Who then?" I was a little confused. It hadn't occurred to me that anyone else at the clinic was speculating about us.

"Ah…"

"Who Roman? C'mon…"

"The other partners have been giving me a hard time, you could say." I couldn't quite see his face in the growing darkness, but I had the feeling he was blushing a bit.

"What!? Dr. Halle?" I couldn't get any of the other names out.

"Yeah…"

"Oh man! What're we like the only thing interesting going on around here or what? I can't believe this."

"Well I think we have to. At least we can be thankful we didn't have to field questions about the storm yesterday. Or at least fudge our way talking about." That pulled me up short; he was right.

"That's true. Hey, are you free after work tomorrow?" I asked after a few minutes of silence.

"I think so. Why?" I didn't have to see his face to know I'd caught him off guard. Usually we didn't meet up after work, it was when we both did what we couldn't get done during the workday.

"I was just thinking; would you want to come over for a little while? Maybe stay for dinner?"

"Whose night is it to cook?"

"Kaya's. Interested?"

"Sure. I can do that." I could tell he wanted to ask something else, so I waited for him to continue. "What do you want to do Lis?"

"I have two ideas. One I'm not telling you until tomorrow, but the other I can share."

"Which is?"

"I want to try writing something with you. You know write music?" My uncertainty as to his response made my voice timid as I spoke.

"Oh. Sure. That would be great." My head shot up at the excitement in his voice. "I'd love to do that."

"Really?" I couldn't suppress the disbelief; though it didn't belong there.

"Really." He tapped my cheek with a finger, and I smiled. Definitely should've known.

"Cool. So I'll see you tomorrow then?" I moved to unlock my car.

"See you tomorrow." He leaned over to kiss my cheek goodbye, and then walked around to get into his truck. I got into my car as soon as he'd left me room enough to open the door. I took a deep breath before starting the car to back out of my space, waving to Cassie as I passed her, on the way to her car.

As I pulled onto the road leading to the house my cell phone beeped: text message. I reached over to where I'd thrown my bag onto the passenger seat and dug out my cell. Flipping it open, I read the text. It was from Roman.

Can we change location? You come to my place instead?

I pulled into the driveway and parked before replying.

That'd be fine. We'll leave right from the clinic.

It looked like Kaya was going to have to wait to cook for Roman again.

Thanks to a head start, I got to his music room first, claiming the piano bench before he'd even entered the room. I rested my music bag against the side of the bench, I leaned over to sift through its contents. I'd picked out a handful of my favorites; songs I knew would be fun to play around with to figure out what we wanted to write ourselves. I pulled one of them out, arranged it in front of me, and dove in.

"Okay, you first." I heard Roman mutter behind me; I just smiled and played on. The next thing I heard his office chair being pulled into the room and positioned behind me to watch me play.

"Here." Finished, I scooted over to one side of the bench, and patted the other side in an invitation for him to join me. "Sit next to me."

"What're we playing?"

"What do you want to play?" I looked up at him, feeling small even seated next to him. We always seemed to be standing around each other, when we weren't in a car; it brought home his size even more to sit right next to him.

"Did you bring any duets?"

"One or two. How about one of these?" I held out the two options; both classical duets I'd played with friends over the years.

"That one." He pointed to the one in my left hand.

"Okay." Returning the other to my bag, I spread the music out in front of us. "One, two, three, four..."

We played the six-paged duet through more smoothly than I'd anticipated; I suspected he'd played it before, but didn't bother to ask. Instead we slipped back into no-talking mode, anticipating and motioning at each other. When we had finished the duet, I didn't bother pulling out the other one. Roman slid smoothly from the written music into something he knew by heart, and I followed his lead. By the time I looked at my watch again, it had been over an hour.

"What?" Roman asked when I went bug eyed in response to the time on my watch.

"Nothing. Just didn't realize we'd been playing that long. That's all."

"Oh. Yeah, we've been playing for a while." He just shrugged. "Did you happen to bring any staff paper? I forgot I didn't have any when I suggested coming over here."

"You would." I rolled my eyes and reached for my bag yet again. "Luckily I figured as much, so yes, I do happen to have brought some with me." I waved the staff paper in front of his face.

"Nice." He laughed and pulled it out of my hand. I stuck out my tongue, but didn't try to take it back.

Roman opened the book of staff paper to a clean page, and set in front of us. I set the pencils I'd brought within easy reaching distance. We exchanged a look before both resting our hands on the keys, and, without a word, we began to play. This time the time didn't seem to pass quite so rapidly. Instead everything seemed slowed down: the notes we played and then scratched out on the paper; the melody that eventually formed on the page; the harmonies that surrounded it. Everything. The music came to us as if it had been waiting in the wings for its debut. It didn't have the same violent effect on my faculties as the storms, but it did seem to have a mutual source.

As the song progressed it began to take on a somewhat familiar shape I'd never had quite this level of connection to music I'd composed. Not even since my awakening, and that he was with me when it did told me more than even I realized.

"So what's the working title?" I teased.

"Seriously?"

"Seriously."

"Earth Song." I stared at him. He just stared back.

"Why?"

"You know why." His eyes darkened as he spoke, going from amber flecked to black rimmed.

"Us." I croaked.

"Yes." I could feel his eyes as they raked over my face. "Haven't you figured it out yet Lisbeth?" His voice pitched low.

"Figured what out?" I knew, but I asked anyway.

"Soul mates." Our bodies had leaned towards each other, closing the small gap between us on the bench. His words had me sitting back again in shock.

"How is it that you figured that out already when I only just figured it out two days ago?" I fought to keep my voice level, but lost the battle as my voice slowly rose in volume.

"Is there another explanation?" He asked simply. I didn't answer, turning back to face the piano as I ordered my scrambled thoughts. Stalling, I skimmed my fingers lightly over the keys, never playing a note, simply touching for the sake of touching. I didn't notice until a tear splashed on my hand that I was crying, and then I realized my whole body was trembling with emotion. Just as I became aware of the tears soaking my face, Roman turned me into his chest, enveloping me in his arms so that I was cradled against his body.

At first I simply pressed my face into his shirt, letting the tears soak it, not trying to say anything. He didn't talk either, just held me.

"You okay?" I heard him whisper in my ear after we'd been sitting that way for a few minutes. I'd turned my face to the side to breath easier, and talk.

"Yeah." I whispered. When I felt him start to move, I pressed against him, making him stop.

"What is it?" I could hear the concern in his voice.

"Nothing. I just don't want you to let go of me just yet." His arms tightened, making me smile.

"Do you like the title?"

"You know I do."

"Good." We fell silent.

As we sat there in front of the piano, my mind raced. I remembered the conversation with Kaya after my dream; the fact that both she and Roman had come to the same conclusion; and the strongest proof to me: the song we'd just written. He'd dubbed it "Earth Song"; I thought "Our Song" might be the more appropriate choice. It was our earth song; straight from the source. I pulled back then, steady now that things were fitting together. I shushed him when he opened his mouth to speak, pressing a finger to his lips. Moving slowly in smooth movements I swung my leg over his lap so that I straddled him. His lips were on mine before I could even lean in to kiss him, his hand in my hair and mine in his. Faster than ever the kiss deepened, and before I was even aware of it happening both our shirts were on the floor and we were touching, skin to skin.

No alarm went off this time. Nothing was stopping me, and nothing could, except myself, and I didn't. Instead, it was Roman who pulled away first. He didn't say a word. Simply looked at me, with the question in his eyes. I grinned slowly, a cat with the cream, and leaned in.

Chapter 14

The weatherman was miming his way through the forecast as I went through the motions with free weights in front of the basement TV. I had it on mute, since anything important would be displayed on the screen anyway, and had substituted the monotone voice of the meteorologist with some rock'n'roll. It was my third weight workout this week alone, and about my twentieth indoor workout in the month since Christmas. I was developing cabin fever, but the deep freeze that had taken over the northern Midwest didn't allow for anything outdoors beyond driving to and from work, if that.

I set the free weights aside and pulled out a yoga mat. I left the music on as I started stretching, not in the mood to listen to them repeat the same speculations as the day before the day before. Global Warming this, the end of the world that; after the first time let alone the second it got old. It amused Tom that I got so annoyed with it; he had more patience with human idiocies than I did. We both knew the reason I worked at an animal hospital instead of a human one, was because I'd probably end up decking someone in the first week. I didn't mix well with stupid people, or at least people that did stupid things; though the two often went hand in hand.

I paused to read the day's forecast when it flashed across the screen. The high was still below freezing, and the current temperature was closer to the low than the high with the wind chill. I shivered, silently giving thanks to whoever invented the furnace. As I continued to stretch, I wondered how folks were managing if they couldn't find shelter. I felt a chill run up my spine as an image flashed in my head of the mice we had found frozen to death in the garage the other day. Kaya had been devastated. I just hoped that people weren't finding worse in the city. It hadn't made the news just yet, but I knew that it was only a matter of time, and a miracle it hadn't happened already.

I switched off the TV, rolled up the yoga mat and stashed it, before heading upstairs for a shower and some lunch. It was Wednesday, but Dr. Halle had given me the day off. With the weather the way it was, there had been more techs than animals to take care of. He hadn't seen the point of having us all come in every day and so now we were on a rotating schedule until the weather broke. Of course I hadn't missed the fact that he had put Roman and I on the same schedule. Knowing it was on purpose annoyed me, but I didn't complain. It was nice, just irksome knowing your boss was trying to promote your love life.

Roman was walking out of the bathroom when I reached the top of the stairs. I smiled at the image of him in just a towel; not the least bit surprised to find him so. Though it still bothered Tom that he sometimes spent the night, he was getting over it, and nothing made me happier. We'd limited the sleepovers to his place at first, not wanting to push Kaya and Tom's comfort zones, but since the deep freeze had started, it was easier for us to sleep here, so Roman had basically moved in. That he helped with the heating bill was the way I'd explained it to Tom. He'd just laughed, but I knew he understood my point, or at least I hoped he did. In the end the deciding factor had been the simple fact that I wanted him to move in, and they'd both left it at that. It held more weight than the heating consideration, anyway.

I caught the towel Roman threw me from my room, and walked directly into the bathroom. Twenty minutes later, I walked, wrapped in my own towel and pink cheeked, into my room to change and join Roman for lunch. I could already smell whatever it was he was cooking; it made my stomach growl. Smiling, I threw on sweats and a wool sweater, and ran down the stairs to the kitchen.

"Smells amazing." He laughed, pointing at the already set table.

"It'll be ready in just a second. Hungry?"

"Famished." I slid into my seat at the table as he picked up a steaming pan of something and followed me over. My stomach growled again as he set it on the table and we both smiled. Then I heard his and burst out laughing.

"What?" He feigned insult.

"Hungry?"

"Famished."

"Well join the club, we've got t-shirts."

"Already got one." I laughed at the childish grin on his face as he slid into his seat across from me. "Dig in." I didn't need to be told twice.

"Have you heard from Jason recently?" I scooped food onto my plate as I talked.

"Yeah, I talked to him yesterday. Sounds like they're experiencing the same slump in business we are." I handed him the spatula. "He said they had all their appointments cancel for the rest of this week so he's closed up. He and the other vets are rotating a call schedule in case anyone needs them, but otherwise they have no reason to even stay open."

"Yikes." I blew on my steaming forkful before putting it in my mouth. "At least we're not closing."

"That's for sure."

"Heard anything from any of the other guys?"

"No, not this week anyway. They're all holed up in their own homes pretty much." We both shrugged, it wasn't new news. "So, what do you want to do this afternoon?"

"Well I was thinking-"

"Another board game?" Roman interrupted with a whine.

"No. Not another board game, Mr. five-year-old." He laughed. "I had another idea."

"Which is?"

I bit my lip nervously.

"Practice session."

Silence. No response until, "You want to do what?" We hadn't done a practice session since the time at Jason's apartment that had gotten attention on the radio.

"Not a full one. I just had an idea that I wanted to try. Nothing that is going to get us into any trouble or anything." I floundered in my explanation.

"Promise?"

"I promise." I tried to look insulted, though I really understood his concern. Usually that was my line.

By this time we'd both finished eating I'd decided to take the initiative and start cleaning up. I was hoping that he wouldn't see how nervous I was about my idea. I still wasn't sure about it, no matter how many times Kaya had tried to convince me otherwise. I still hadn't told Tom about my dream; after his reaction to Roman moving in, I didn't feel like giving him another excuse to act like the big brother he technically wasn't. The information the dream had intended to convey had been at the front of my mind without exception for the last three months, and I'd been playing with ways to test it for weeks now. When the rotational schedule had been put in place at the clinic, I knew it was time to just suck it up and try.

"All set." I declared when the kitchen was clean. Roman had watched me from the table, as I'd scurried about, washing up. "Shall we?"

"I believe we shall." He led the way back downstairs to my music room.

"No, you sit at the piano." I directed him when he started to walk over to his usual chair on the other side of the room.

"Wait. I thought you just said…practice session?" He stuttered.

"I did say that. I also said it wouldn't get us in trouble." I explained as I picked a piece of storm music out of the pile on the table and handed it to him.

"What are you doing?" He was making me feel bad for springing this on him.

"It's something that came to me in a dream, months ago. I've been waiting for the right time to try it. Today seemed as good as any day."

"You dreamed what, precisely?"

"Sit." I pointed at the bench. "I'll explain." I walked over to the chair, and pulled it closer to him, sitting down before I kept talking. "I dreamt that you could play the storm music and recreate it, the same way that I do, just through me rather than through any power of your own." I blurted out. Silence. No response.

"Soul mates." My eyes flew to his at the whispered words. "Of course."

"You're scary. The way you pick up on things like that." I whispered.

"I'm dating you. It comes with the territory." I laughed when he just shrugged.

"So are you willing to try?"

"Of course. What do you want me to do?"

"Well, I want to keep it simple. Nothing that's going to attract notice in this weather, or time of year; plus I'm confident if we just prove this right, that you'll be capable of playing whole arrangements with me."

"So, what do you want to do to test it?" I stuck my tongue out at him, perturbed by his nonchalance.

"I want you to do this." I launched into an explanation of the notes, what they represented, and what I wanted him to play. I figured that by simply having him play the wind parts we could effectively test the truth of my dream, and without creating a rainstorm in January, or rather an ice storm, considering the temperature. When I'd finished with my explanation, I leaned back into the chair; it was up to him now.

I felt the pull on the first note, the same tug I felt when I began a piece myself, except this time it didn't stop, but continued, increasing slightly the more he played. It was paralyzing at first, not giving me the chance to say no. As the connection grew stronger I felt my control grow. It occurred to me, when I was fully in control again, that it was as if it were ensuring something; perhaps ensuring that it would happen, the music. Either way the results were the same: winds rushed outside the house, changing as he played and stopping when he did.

"Play those last couple of lines one more time, I'm going to try something." He didn't hesitate, but followed my directions so that the wind almost never stopped. This time I tried to refuse the connection; trying to effectively cut off the connection and essentially test my control of it. I was thrilled to find I was able to. The winds stopped though he continued to play, and began again when I allowed the connection. This time when he stopped, I was beaming at him.

"Did it work? What you were trying to do?" I nodded, speechless with amazement at what we'd managed to do.

"I can control the connection." My voice was almost a whisper when I finally managed to speak.

"So it worked? The test? Your dream was right?" I nodded again. This time we were both speechless.

"Soul mates, indeed." Was all I had to say, and the next thing I knew, he had pulled me into a passionate kiss. Laughing a little I shifted so that I was seated on his lap. We stayed like that, happy simply to caress each other for a while. I wasn't sure how long we'd been in the basement, let alone kissing, when we finally came up for air. Then he pulled me around so that I was cuddled against him, and we sat, basking in the glory of our discovery.

The cold had my teeth chattering violently and shivers wracking my body. I couldn't see; everything had been whited out with what I guessed to be snow. I was forcing my body to move, slowly, forward to I knew not where. The only thing that I knew was that I had to get somewhere, and fast; and those were the two things that didn't seem to be happening. Anxiety had adrenaline pumping in my veins alongside the knowledge that something was happening without me that I was meant to be a part of, or not be a part of as much as prevent from happening at all. Suddenly I felt my legs slip out from underneath me and I was in a free fall.

I flew upright, almost flying out of the bed with the exertion. My breath was ragged, making my throat and lungs raw with the force behind it; my heart was racing alongside my lungs. The darkness was a shock after the white out of my dream, and the confusion it caused my brain, helped calm me. When I had finally settled, my breath and heart rates lulled back into a healthier rhythm, I tried to lie back down and sleep; thankful as I did that Roman hadn't woken up.

My alarm hadn't gone off yet, so I slid out from underneath the quilt so Roman could keep sleeping. I'd barely been able to doze since I'd woken from my dream, and had given up. My mind was too full of questions there was only one person to ask, and it was a meeting I needed to have alone.

I crept slowly down the stairs so I wouldn't wake Tom, whose bedroom was on the ground floor, and into the living room. The sky was turning grey now, the sun a faint glimmer of yellow on the horizon. Standing in the middle of the room, I somehow felt peaceful, like something had clicked together. With the very first rays of the dawn light filtering in through the window, I closed my eyes and folded my body down into a cross-legged position. My eyes stayed closed as I took a deep breath, letting it out slowly as I carefully settled into meditation.

"Good morning, daughter." Came the familiar voice in my head. "I see you have been busy since last we spoke." I felt the smile in her voice before I saw her, an image on the backs of my eyelids. Her dress was a light shade of turquoise this time, though in the same style as before; her features the usual blend of the oddly familiar. I didn't waste time, not wanting to be interrupted by everyone when they woke up soon, and started to go through the events of the last five months in my head. Beginning directly after our last meeting and ending with the questions piling up inside my head.

"My goodness you have been a busy girl." She spoke slowly while rubbing her hands over her face in a tired gesture. Then, in a sudden motion, she folded her arms across her chest and turned to pace, her normally serene face intensely thoughtful. I watched her for I don't know how long; doubt growing in the back of my mind, the longer that she remained silent. "I'm sorry to stress you my dear, I just needed to think some things over." She came to stand in front of me again; her face returned to its previously calm state. I waited for her to continue, my whole body tensed, wired with the anxiety of insecurity as to what she would say. She took a deep breath to begin to speak, and paused briefly as if uncertain of how to continue before finally speaking. "So, to answer your first question: no, I still don't know what the trigger is for the development in your gift. We both know that something did, but I can't help you to know what that is. Lots of things have been changing lately." Her face went briefly dark, but she quickly recovered herself. "Then again, when aren't things changing? Still." Somehow that didn't make me feel better.

"I am quite surprised to see how quickly your relationship with Roman has progressed." Her voice lightened with the change of subject. "I don't quite know how much your dreams have shown you, regarding your past relationships, but normally it is the one thing that does not continue to get smoother which each progressive lifetime. It's as if someone has hit the fast-forward button on this one." Her mouth curved into a smile at those words, clearly amused by the idea. "I wish I knew what the catalyst was; or perhaps I don't." She seemed to pick up then on the fact that I had yet to relax. In fact, I was quite the contrary; parts of the words she was saying ringing a little too true for my comfort. Memories from bits and pieces of the last several months, couple of years even, popping up in my mind as she spoke.

I felt, her sigh; the resignation it held palpable. A tremor ran through me as I watched her face change, shifting into an expression of such sadness I felt my own chest ache with her. "You're sharper than the others give you credit for. Even more so than Kaya." Her voice was flat, not quite monotone; her eyes dull now rather than warm, the edge they might have had dulled by the pain I saw in them. I knew then that she had seen in my thoughts the conclusion I was reaching. "My child, I cannot tell you the answers to your questions. Yes, I know the answers, and I hope you can forgive the fact that I cannot tell you them. This is your journey, and you must find your own way now." She stopped, but didn't leave, continuing to watch me despite the finality of her words. "Put the pieces of the puzzle together, and you will find the key. The problem and its solution are within your grasp, all you have to do is reach out and grab them." She started to reach out to me, her hand trembling slightly, the sadness and the pain growing clearer in her face; I barely saw the tear slide down her cheek when she vanished, the ghostly whisper of her final words echoing in my mind.

I opened my eyes and stood as if in slow motion. My mind struggling to keep up with my body as I rose to stand in the middle of the room once again. The sun shone more brightly now, as the sun rose higher above the horizon. The peaceful silence that had filled the room when I'd entered it had become too quiet now. The kind of eerie calm before the storm that sets your teeth on edge; waiting for what you knew was coming and could do nothing to prevent. I didn't move a muscle. Waiting for something to happen, to break through the silence and be the switch that would set things back in motion. My body was wired with an odd kind of electricity threading its way through my nerves as I stood there in the silence. I had no idea what I was waiting for; I only knew that I was waiting.

Two things happened then in progression. My vision blurred, the images from my dream suddenly taking the place of the living room; and then something cracked. Like a whip snapping through the air, but louder, not as crisp. It resonated to fill the entire room with an ominous rumbling that had me steadying myself even though nothing actually moved. The images stopped as suddenly as it had started; the silence was over. I heard my alarm start to sound upstairs and moved unconsciously to walk upstairs and turn it off. I was also conscious of something much more instinctive: it was beginning. Whatever it was; I wasn't sure whether that was a good thing or not.

PART 3

Purpose

Chapter 15 — Figuring

"So she knows all the answers, but can't tell us?" We were all seated around the kitchen table, tea steaming in untouched mugs in front of us. At the moment Kaya was venting her frustration and finding it all a little hard to believe. "Well then how is she supposed to ever help us?"

"I don't know Kaya." I had my hands pressed against my face. "She seemed to think that we could figure this out on our own."

"Yet she couldn't even give us some direction?" She demanded.

"If you thought for a second, I think you would realize how untrue that statement is. Kaya." I looked her straight in the eye as I waited for my words to connect.

"Oh."

"You figure it out?"

"Your dreams directly from the earth. They're from her; she's earth." Her eyes bugged out of her head. "I'm such an idiot!"

"You could say that." She glared at me. I'd already spent the last hour or so thinking through what had happened with Mom that morning and was waiting for them to catch up.

"Lisbeth?" I turned to face Tom. "What dreams?"

"I'm sorry Tom."

"Why don't you just tell me now?"

"Okay. There have been two, both related to my new gift in some way, but neither of them memories. Hang on let me explain." I held up a finger to cut Tom off. "Kaya's the one who figured it out. They're dreams sent directly from the earth. Lessons straight from Mom."

"She can't just tell them to you? How does that work?"

"I don't know. That doesn't make sense to me either. But I don't think that that's what we need to focus on. The first dream came to me twice; first after a small clip of memory dreams, but the second time without. Both times it began with color flashes and blackness before it showed me the same image, a clip from the present lifetime; something that hasn't happened yet, if it ever does." I paused to let the information sink in. I glanced briefly at Roman before continuing. "The image was the same each time, just a little longer and with sound the second time around. It was of Roman and I in the middle of a hay field I didn't recognize. I was seated at a grand piano and you were across from me with your guitar. We…we were playing storm music; together."

"That's where you got the idea for the practice session. Isn't it?" Roman asked after a momentary silence.

"Yes." I sighed heavily with relief. "And it's an idea I wouldn't have had if it weren't for the dream."

"What about the second dream? If the first one was how you learned that I was capable of creating storms through you, then what did the second one teach you?"

"I don't actually know what it means. It's a white out, like snow; and I'm trying to move through it. There's this incredible sense of urgency that had me completely freaking out; physically and mentally. It was as if I were missing something, something vitally important. I just don't know what."

"Blizzard." The word was ominous in its simplicity as it hung in the air between us. Tom had had first hand experience with blizzards when we were growing up and it hadn't exactly left a good impression.

"The weather we've been having has been pretty odd for Chicago, even at this time of year." That came from Roman.

"But a blizzard?" Kaya asked.

"Its not impossible."

"He's right." Tom chipped in. "This weather is definitely out of the ordinary. A blizzard would simply take it to the next level."

"Well, then why doesn't one of you tell me what you think my dream means? Since you both seem to know so much." I asked sarcastically.

"I think I can do that." Kaya interrupted; I waited for her to continue. "It's coming."

"The storm?"

"Yes; and soon." She looked at me with a frown as she continued. "Lisbeth, how did Mom look when you talked to her? Were there any serious changes?"

"Nothing that I could tell at first. She just seemed more serious than usual, but at the end there was something, something very different." I stopped, unsure of how to describe what I'd noticed. Kaya watched me as she waited. "She looked ragged, like someone being worn slowly down by something. When she finally told me there was nothing she could do, her face was so sad and full of a pain I couldn't understand. Kaya, something's hurting her; killing her even. Do you think this storm could be the key to saving her?"

"I think you're half right. I think the storm is just a result of what is killing her. Come with me." She stood suddenly and walk into the living room before the rest of us were even out of our chairs.

"What?"

"I want to see something, and I want you to watch with me." She turned on the TV and flipped through the channels to the news. It didn't take long; we don't have cable.

"Kaya, I've seen the news at least a hundred times in the last few weeks. What are you getting at?"

"You'll see." The weatherman came on, and I winced as he started to give the report. Two things connected in my mind as I watched him wave his arms around in front of the blue screen.

"Kaya, I've got it!" I jumped up, excitement bubbling up in my chest. "Oh my God I'm so stupid. How can I not have seen it before? It makes so much sense!"

"What does? What did you figure out?" Kaya demanded.

"Kaya, it's global warming. The trigger for my gift, the catalyst for my relationship and bond with Roman, and…" I trailed off as sadness took the place of the excitement. "It's killing Mom."

"Oh no!" I whirled around to face Tom where he stood in the doorway to the kitchen. "No, no, no, no, no." He chanted out. "This isn't happening."

"What isn't?" His face was pale, and concern flooded me as I wondered what had scared him so much. All he did was point at the now silent television. The weather map for the whole of the Midwest was currently on the screen. It took me a minute to see what he was getting at, but the blood drained from my face, too, when I did.

"Warm front." We all said simultaneously in disbelief.

"Blizzard indeed. Roman, get your keys. I'm going to want your Internet." I turned then and walked swiftly out of the room to get my coat and pull on some shoes.

"Lisbeth, what're you going to do?" Tom called after me.

"I'm going to do what I should have done to begin with. I'm going to do some research." It was all I had time to say. Roman was already at the door, keys in hand, coat and shoes on. We exchanged a look before he opened the door and ran for the truck. I didn't take the time to worry about whether or not Tom and Kaya would understand. I could explain it to them later. Right now all that mattered was getting as much information as possible about the current global weather situation. This wasn't just about Chicago anymore, this was far bigger than that; I had a feeling I had yet to realize how big.

When we pulled into Roman's driveway, I jumped out before he could even put the truck in park. I knew where the spare key was kept, so I let myself in. I moved quickly, not wanting to waste time, and all but ran up the stairs to his office to switch on the computer. The house was freezing, considering it had essentially been uninhabited for at least the past three weeks. So while I waited for the computer to boot up I went to get blankets from his room downstairs.

"Hey Lis!" Roman was in the foyer, taking off his own shoes and jacket more slowly than I had.

"Yeah?" I spun to face him, as I backed down the hallway to his bedroom door.

"Can I talk to you a minute?" He walked towards me.

"Ah, sure. Just let me grab some blankets from your room ok? It's freezing up there!" I spun back around and disappeared into his room; two minutes later I stood in the doorway of his office again, a duvet and various other blankets in hand. "So. What's up?" I wrapped myself in blankets as I talked, throwing a few at Roman for him to do the same.

"Hey! Are you going to tell me what's going on here? Why do you need my Internet? Not like you don't have it at your own place." He spat out the question as he wound a blanket around his waist, another draped over his shoulders the same way I had.

"Yeah, I'll tell you." I shuffled my way over to the rolly-chair in front of the freshly booted-up computer.

"So?"

"Yours is faster."

"Oh come on Lis, what do you think I am? Stupid?" He walked over so he stood behind me, watching as I tapped away at the keyboard.

"Okay, fine. Though that was part of the incentive." I looked at him over my shoulder as I brought up the Internet. "I didn't want to be around Kaya and Tom while I did some research. I mean, you're okay because you're part of this." I paused and typed in a search engine's web address then turned around to face him as I waited for it to load. "It was just the way Mom was talking to me; the dreams, the inconclusive answers, just… everything." I groaned and raked my hands through my loosely bound hair in frustration. "I need to find these answers myself, and with Kaya around…" I looked up at him instead of saying more.

"Your test?" He rested the hand not holding the blanket on my shoulder. I nodded slowly. "Okay then." He crouched down so that he was at eye level with me. "Our test." He held up a finger to cut me off when I tried to protest. "Hey! Think about that for a minute. As corny as it may sound, we both know that we're in this together, in more ways than one. I'm in those dreams too, and I don't think-" He broke off for a second. "I don't think that I would have been there, been here even, if I wasn't supposed to be a part of this."

"Soul mates?" I whispered.

"Soul mates." He repeated, moving his hand from my shoulder to my cheek. I leaned into it, raising my own hand to rest on top of his. I felt tears begin to well up in my eyes with the sweetness of the moment. I didn't want to relinquish this feeling, but I also couldn't afford to waste any more time.

"Have I ever told you I love you, Roman Fournier?" The words were out of my mouth before I even realized what I was saying, but I didn't take them back.

"I love you, too. Miss Lisbeth Moore." We kissed briefly before I turned back to the computer screen. As I rode on that high, I started to search the web.

I started with the major periodicals of the globe, searching for any hints of environmental occurrences of the necessary magnitude. I still wasn't completely sure what exactly I was searching for, but, as I explained to Roman when he asked me after the first twenty minutes of searching, I knew I'd recognize it when I saw it. When I'd exhausted that resource and found nothing, I started looking for articles in science periodicals. There wasn't much recent there, but the one detail I was confident in was that I was looking for something that had happened, at most, in the last month. Potentially something too recent to turn up in a journal. Then, in a brief and obscure news article, I found what I'd been looking for.

"Roman, look at this." I pointed at the text on the screen.

"Whoa! Part of the artic shelf broke off again; a chunk they estimate weighed nearly one-hundred tons!" He stared at the screen, my mouth agape. "Would you please explain to me why this is not in the mainstream periodicals? I would have thought this would make the news. That is a ton of ice!"

"I'm not going to try and understand that part of it. All I know is that this might be the catalyst I'm looking for."

"For the storm you mean?"

"Yup." I hit the print button so I'd have a hardcopy of the article. "How of course I don't know, I'm no scientist, but this is what I was looking for."

"Now what?"

"Now." I started typing into the search engine again. "Now, I need to start looking for weather patterns. Globally."

"Looking for your storm?" He chuckled.

"You could say that." I scrolled my way through the list of results, searching. "I need to find a map that will show me the fronts moving across the globe, not just for Chicago."

"Ah...got it."

"I want to see if there's a way to predict the timing of this thing. I mean, we know we've got a ridiculous warm front hitting us today or tomorrow. The blizzard would be caused, most likely, by another deep freeze kind of cold front coming in behind it."

"So we're trying to find out where that's coming from?"

"Exactly." I looked back at the screen. "Aha! Found it." I clicked on the link to bring up the map I'd been looking for.

"And?" I ignored him as I scanned the map, looking closest at the Wisconsin and Canadian areas that were north of us.

"Give me a chance to look at it." I muttered, my attention on the computer.

At first glance the weather patterns looked completely normal for the region at this time of year: cold and snowy. I could see the warm front moving up from the south, towards Chicago; standing out to me against the frigid state of the rest of the Wisconsin and Northern Illinois region.

"I don't really see anything drastic heading this way." My murmur broke the hushed silence that had filled the room.

"I know what you mean. I can't see anything in that either." He joked.

"You would if it were there." I'd had quite a bit of practice in reading the radar and various other forecasting maps over the last few years. It came in handy to know when there would be storms coming through; particularly when they have the kind of effect that they have on me.

"That's true. But why can't we see anything there then? Did we miss something?"

"I don't know. I know that that ice chunk was the start of it all. It would have caused just enough of an alteration in the Atlantic current, you know in the ocean, to shift the weather patterns here."

"Really?"

"Well that's a theory anyway. I had this science teacher back in high school - obsessed with environmentalism, even back then - he kind of filled my class in on some stuff. Never thought it would come in this handy."

"Ah. Well maybe we should write him a thank you note."

"Ha. That would be difficult considering he died about four years ago." I pulled up a new tab for a new search. "Heart attack."

I turned back to the computer and scrolled through the search results. There were plenty of simplified sites that would have answered my question, but I wanted something more official. I didn't feel like cutting corners with this.

"What're we looking at the city records for?" Roman asked after I clicked on the link.

"You'll see." I scanned the site for a link and clicked on it when I found it.

"I'm still lost. Why are you looking at record snow falls and temperatures in January?"

"Well, have you thought about how we're going to stop this thing? This storm, I mean." I stopped scrolling down the list of measurements and turned to look at him.

"Not really, why?"

"Think. How would this help us?"

"Uh?" He looked so clueless it almost made me smile. It was nice to see him stumped for once.

"Okay, think about it this way." I turned my body to face him. "I can't control this storm. I can't just stand up in the middle of the city and force it to break up and spread across the region. It's far more likely that this storm is going to take control of me; orchestral style like most snow storms, no doubt." We both laughed at the image. "So if I manage to do anything at all, how do you think I'm going to do that, hm?"

"The storm music you already have? Of course! Connect pieces of them so that you can break up the system as it comes into town."

"Now you're getting it. Any idea how this information would be of help?"

"Not really. Explain it to me."

"How am I supposed to pass this off as a typical storm if I don't know what would be considered typical and what would be considered extraordinary?" I answered in an exaggerated tone.

"Wow. Yeah. Good point. How did I miss that?" He pretended to scratch his head in bewilderment.

"I'm not sure. Make sense though?"

"Totally. So, how are we going to do this?" He looked at me expectantly.

"Do what?"

"Now who's slow? How are you proposing that we prepare for this? How do we know which songs to use? Which parts? Do we even know where we can go to do this?"

"Whoa, slow down." I interrupted him. "I'm not that far yet. Give me a second." I turned back to the computer, tapping at the keyboard again as I bookmarked the sites I'd found useful. Finished, I shut down the computer.

"Are we done?" He asked when I turned back to him.

"Here, yes." I pulled my blankets tighter around me; they'd slipped as I'd typed.

"Cold?" His eyes darted to where my hands clutched at the edge of the blanket.

"A little." I smiled. "I'm fine though. Just couldn't keep this close enough while I was typing." He didn't look convinced but let it go.

"Oh my God!" I suddenly sat bolt upright.

"What?" Roman asked, doing the same. "What's wrong?"

"We were supposed to have work today!" I moaned and glared at him when he just laughed.

"Actually..."

"Actually what?" I demanded, voice sharp at his sheepish tone.

"Dan called while you were running around for blankets and such." I glared at him again. "He said we didn't need to come in. He said more people had canceled, and there was no point in having even half of us there."

"You didn't think I needed to know that?" I asked, insulted.

"It slipped my mind. Not like there wasn't enough on your mind. I just figured it could wait an hour or so." He looked meaningfully at the computer.

"Well, next time tell me." I settled sulkily back into my chair.

"Right, I'll remember that. In the mean time, why don't we go back to your place, if we're done with the computer?"

"Cold?" I teased.

"You could say that." He said with a slow smile.

"Okay, then. Let's go." I unwrapped my blankets as I stood and shivered as my warm skin hit the cool air. Roman did the same.

It didn't take us long to lock up the house; sprinting to the truck to avoid spending excess time in the cold. Of course it took a little while for the truck to warm up, but that wasn't the point. Roman took his time driving as we listened closely to the radio, which was tuned, for once, to a news station instead of music. When we pulled into the driveway we saw that both Tom and Kaya's cars were missing; they still had to work today. It occurred to me as we ran from the truck to the house that I might have to talk to Tom about borrowing some of his warm clothes for when this storm hit. I had a feeling I was going to be outside for at least some part of my interaction with it; regardless of whether or not I was effective, there didn't seem to be any point in freezing to death. I already knew that Roman had gear, his job meant going outside in all temperatures as well.

Knowing we couldn't really do anything until either my housemates returned from work or the cold front made an appearance on the radar, we both made our way into the kitchen. Getting there first, I flipped on the hot water pot and pulled out our mugs. Roman had been with us long enough now to have his own favorite amongt our collection.

"What would you say if I suggested curling up on the sofa in the living room and watching a movie on our under-used TV?" I pulled teabags out of their boxes and stuck them in the mugs.

171

"I think I would say you're looking for a distraction." He leaned against the counter next to me.

"Well you would be right." I picked up the hot water pot once it'd clicked off. "I do want one." I murmured as I poured the hot water. I felt his hand on my hair and looked up to find he had slid so that he was almost on top of me, his other hand moving to turn my body towards him from my waist. I complied, hot water pot still in hand.

"You so sure a movie is the best distraction?" He leaned down so that his forehead pressed gently against mine. When I didn't respond he just smiled. "I think we can find of something better." Moving slowly he pressed his lips against mine.

"Mmm...I'm sure we can." I agreed between kisses. "I'm sure you can."

I felt him lift the water pot out of my hand, setting it next to the mugs on the counter. The next thing I knew, he'd scooped me up into his arms, and was walking quickly towards the stairs as he kissed me. I didn't protest, but threw myself into it, thankful once again that he knew me so well. Besides, tea was better after steeping for a while anyway.

I could hear their voices, echoing in the empty space and filled with an emotion I couldn't put a name to. I tried to move, go to them, help them somehow; but my feet wouldn't move. I couldn't go anywhere. I felt something sharp cutting into the skin around my wrists and ankles when I tried to move. The voices grew louder as I struggled, adrenaline kicking in as panic took over. I still couldn't make out what they were saying, but subconsciously I understood. I needed to get to them, to get there - whoever and wherever they were.

Abruptly the multitude of screaming voices became one, and it rose into a bloodcurdling scream. I felt my body go cold, numb even to the panic. I forgot about the pain around my wrists and ankles where my bonds chaffed, and started to struggle all over again. I knew who that scream was coming from now and I knew where. I just couldn't move. Something gave, and a crack sounded that muffled even the scream, as I fell forward in a free fall, I recognized my own scream as it joined the other.

Without a sound the whole scene changed, and I no longer fell, but stood; the bark of a tree branch cutting into my bare feet as I looked out at mountains from the top of a pine tree. I heard a hawk screech and whipped around to see it soar through the air in my direction. It landed in the branches beside me, but didn't seem to see me, so I looked back out to the sky. That's when I saw it. The clouds - banked miles high and wide in a near-black mass - moved slowly in my direction. I watched as lightning flickered briefly from within it and smiled at the ominous roll of thunder that pounded through the air several seconds later.

Just as the storm was about to reach the mountain where my tree stood, things started to flicker, images flashing in front of my eyes briefly before they vanished again. The feeling of serenity that had filled me as I'd watched the storm approach was gone. Now dread and fear built on each other as they filled me; escalating towards a climax only I could hardly predict. The screaming had returned, painful but no longer high pitched as much as thick and full of intense pain. It was the scream of someone dying, and dying hideously. I started to struggle again, but couldn't seem to move my body. It was as if I moved through thick syrup, stickiness grasping and clawing at me as it tried to stop me.

A shape loomed up out of the flickering images, clearly separate yet indistinguishable in shape. The only thing that set it apart was its color: a dark shade of violet that stood out against the darker shades of the other images. Then they stopped altogether and I was left in blackness as the violet thing got closer and closer, and more and more clear. It was about a hundred yards away when I realized what it was; a scream escaping my lips before I realized it, and the next thing I knew I was choking on cold water and cursing as I struggled against the arms holding me under it.

"What the fucking hell do you thinking you're doing? You maniac!" I all but screamed. "That's fucking cold!" Finally my hand connected with a body and I heard someone grunt.

"Hey calm down, it's just me." I froze as I recognized the voice. It was Roman; tears joined the water streaming down my face as the dream flooded back into my memory.

"I'm sorry." I sobbed as he lifted me out of the shower in a towel. I stood, limp, as he turned off the shower and started to gently towel dry me when I didn't do so myself.

"Lisbeth? Roman?" I heard Tom and Kaya yell from downstairs, and groaned. Perfect. "Hey! What's going on? What happened?" They both sputtered out when they'd reached the bathroom door.

"Lisbeth we could hear you screaming outside, what was it?" Tom demanded.

"Another dream." I was surprised at how steady my voice sounded; far steadier than I felt at the moment. The scream from my dream still resonated in my head.

"What happened?" Kaya asked.

"I don't know." I stopped, struggling for something to say. "Someone was screaming, and I couldn't move, couldn't help them. Then it was a memory dream, of a storm in the mountains. Probably somewhere out west, but then the screaming came back, and it wasn't a memory anymore, or rather it was a blur of memories. You know like someone had put a slideshow on rapid speed." I stopped again to catch my breath.

"Who was it, Lis? You saw them, didn't you?" It wasn't really a question. I sighed; of all people, Kaya would be the one to realize there was more to this than I was saying.

"It was Mom." I felt everyone freeze.

"Why?" Kaya's voice sounded rough, as if she were trying not to cry. "Why was she screaming?"

"I think I have an idea." Tom cut in. We all looked at him. "Lisbeth, we know now that global warming was the trigger for the change in your talent, right? But why the change? Why did the changes in the environment trigger changes in you?"

"I don't see what that has to do with Mom."

"Let me keep going. What I'm saying, is that I think it changed you because the adaptation in your gift is needed for something more than this one storm. I mean, sure it's a good thing you're maybe going to be able to divert, or do whatever, with this storm and prevent a huge mess. Whatever. What is it that is really being hurt by this?" None of us answered so he continued. "Mom."

"You think that I'm supposed to be trying to save Mom by stopping global warming by controlling the storms I recreate?" I shook my head. "You're out of your mind." I shook off Roman's hand and stalked out of the bathroom in my towel.

"Do you have a better idea?" He added. I stopped in front of my bedroom door.

"I tell you what then." I turned around to face them. "I'll make a deal with you."

"Okay."

"I'm going to have my hands full just trying to deal with this storm, when it finally comes anyway. While I'm dealing with that, you and Kaya can start to research the extent of the situation with Mom. Look up reports and stuff like that on global warming."

"What about Roman?" Tom asked.

"Roman's with me on this." I said less sharply. Tom frowned but didn't say anything.

"Deal."

"Deal." Kaya echoed.

"Alrighty then. I'm going to get some clothes on. We've all got some work to do." I turned around and walked quickly into my room; I was getting a chill from the freezing water Roman had decided to shove me under. I hoped I wouldn't have these dreams too often in future. I didn't feel like having to go through the cold shower routine all the time.

Chapter 16 — Prep

I smiled at Cassie as I dropped off my last client's folder, pausing before rushing off to the next one since their appointment wasn't for another hour. The day was still oddly slow despite the spike in the temperature. Though the phone had been ringing off the hook with people rescheduling appointments all day.

"Hey Cassie. More re-scheduling?" I leaned against the edge of the counter to chat.

"That's pretty much been the theme of the day. It would appear that people have found their courage to venture out of doors now that the temperature is above zero." We laughed.

"That does seem like what's been going on. I guess it'll be nice to go back to full time, though. It's been weird working so few days these past couple of weeks."

"I know what you mean. I don't think I've gotten that much time off in my life." She turned to answer the phone. I waited for her to finish with the call to keep talking.

"How long do you think it will last?" I asked when she'd hung up. "This wonderful heat wave?"

"Who knows? I'm no weatherwoman, that's for sure. I just hope it lasts." We both chuckled a little and I beat back my ever-present nerves. "Hey, check that out!" Cassie pointed out the window at the front of the waiting room and I moved behind her to see. "God is he crazy? Walking around in a t-shirt like that when it's still below freezing!" She looked up at me before hurriedly rearranging her features into a more welcoming expression when he walked through the door.

"Good afternoon, sir." Cassie greeted him as he led a graceful German Shepherd up to her receptionist's desk.

"Good afternoon to you, too. We're here for our appointment, my apologies, we're rather early." The man's accent was strong, southern and made me even more curious as to what he was doing in a t-shirt in this weather.

"That's fine. We've had a lot of cancellations anyway, so we can see you now, if that's all right?" Cassie responded smoothly.

"That would be great." I realized as he smiled that there weren't any goose bumps on his arm and he wasn't shivering. I looked back out the window and realized that the sun was blazing fiercely and the little snow we'd had had vanished.

"Wow." I said to no one in particular.

"Sorry, what was that?" The man asked thinking I'd spoken to him.

"The weather. What happened? Everything's melted. What's the temperature?" I turned to face Cassie.

"It just hit 70°F." The man cut Cassie off before she could speak. "Amazing isn't it? After that deep freeze?"

"Amazing, indeed." I murmured. "That makes it a record, doesn't it?" I said more clearly.

"That's what they're saying on the radio, anyway." He replied.

"That really is amazing." I reached for what must be his dog's folder, and took a peak at the name on it. "Ben? Is that your dog's name?"

"That's us."

"Right, why don't we take a look at him now then, since you're here?" I motioned for him to meet me at the door from the waiting room, and went to walk around.

The rest of the afternoon I anxiously waited for a chance to talk to Roman about the conversation. I hadn't expected such a spike in the temperature from the heat wave I'd seen on the map and wondered what it would mean when the cold front finally hit. Then another thought occurred to me: it must be how the storm would be formed. My nerves settled a little at that thought, but still nagged at the back of my mind for the rest of the day. I was getting sick of waiting.

The little CD player I kept in the music room gently pumped out classical piano as I sat on the floor, storm music scattered all around me. I'd been sitting like this for almost an hour, going through each score with a fine-toothed comb; picking out the ones I thought I could utilize with the most force and effect against the blizzard. I knew I needed to have the sharpest tools I could find; I focused particularly on winds. Warm ones that would both help to turn some of the snow to rain, and others that were strong enough to break up the blizzard's central structure. Those I found were in tornadoes, which made me nervous; to create a tornado in January would do more than dissipate the blizzard, it would make history and that was what I was trying to avoid.

"Hey, I made tea." Roman said from the door.

"Thanks." I smiled up from the ground as he crouched to hand me the mug.

"Any success?" He asked when he was on my level.

"Some." I inhaled the steam from my tea. "It's difficult determining which will have the strongest winds, you know?"

"I can believe that." He reached out to pick up one of the scores I'd already set in a pile. "You're not planning on breaking out a tornado are you?"

"No. No. I'll have to pick out the strongest winds from the whole and break it up, you know what I mean?"

"Oh right, yeah, that makes sense. Like what you had me do to test our bond?"

"Exactly like that."

"So..."

"So, what?"

"So..." He looked up at the ceiling, then at me. "So do we know where we're facing this thing?"

"No." I said flatly. "We don't know that yet."

"Because I have a suggestion to make."

"By all means, suggest away." I gestured widely to make my point.

"There's this place I know, on the northern end of the city suburbs. A place I used to go with my friends during my undergraduate." I pursed my lips and nodded as I thought it over. "It's respectable, and they have a good piano. Also, it's an ideal point to be at."

"How's that?"

"Well we know the cold front is coming from the north so we'll be able to get at it sooner than later. Then there's the fact that it's easily accessible, so even if we get caught in the snow, we'll be able to get there; provided we get there before the full storm hit anyways. What do you think?"

"I think that this place would be as good as any other. Though I like that it'll be in the northern part of town." I paused to think. "Sure. If you can get us there and in, then I'm game."

"Great. I'll call the owners once we know the cold front is on its way." He kissed my forehead. "I'll leave you to it again. Let me know if I can help though, okay?"

"You already know there isn't anything you could do so don't worry about it." I smiled up at him. "I'll be up for dinner, I promise."

"Okay." He took an exaggerated sniff of the air. "Smells like Kaya's already cooking."

"She's stress cooking." I commented flatly and turned back to the score I'd been looking over.

"Well, it smells delicious, whatever she's doing." He muttered on his way up the stairs. I was glad I had him with me in this; knowing I wasn't alone was helping to keep my brain inside my head despite the stress. He was so good at keeping the mood light.

It was almost a full three full hours before Tom yelled down the stairs that dinner was ready and waiting. My body creaked as I forced it to stand up and rubbed the back of my hand over my eyes, which were dry and tired from reading scores. I was pleased, however, with the fact that I'd actually found several potentially useful ones, and they weren't all tornadoes. The useable stack was actually slightly larger than the discard one.

"I'm coming." I called back from the base of the stairs. I could smell whatever Kaya had made, the scent getting stronger as I climbed the steps to the kitchen. "Smells delicious, Kaya. What did you make?" The answer lay on the table in front of me.

"Well, there's a curry, and then I made pakoras to go with." She pointed things out on the table as she spoke. "Then there're the egg rolls and some sauces for them, but I didn't make those. And there's salsa, guacamole, and nachos that I did make." She turned to smile at me.

"Stress cooking?" It looked amazing.

"You could say that." She replied, her smile fell slightly.

"Well it looks, and smells, stunning. When do we get to eat?"

"As soon as we're all seated." She motioned for us all to take our seats. I hadn't noticed Roman and Tom standing off to the side, so they surprised me when they walked over to take their seats.

"Hey, I didn't see you there."

"You just zoned in on the food." Tom teased. "One track mind. Tsk tsk."

"Ha ha ha." I retorted. "So what did you guys do today?"

"We had a crazy day at the restaurant. The heat wave had everyone out of their houses. Sick of cooking for themselves, I suspect. It was nice though; had something to do the whole day, which was refreshing after the last few weeks." Kaya offered for conversation.

"I know what you mean, though I have to say I preferred my job when it was cold. No one wanted to do anything outside, which meant fewer issues for us to deal with. Today everything was crazy. People everywhere. There were dozens of calls to report thefts, and various other petty crimes. At least during the deep freeze we were mostly following up on trespassing calls; you know homeless people looking for a warm place to sleep?"

"Sounds like you all had a busy day."

"You could say that." Kaya smiled at Tom.

"I guess that makes me happy I was at the clinic. We didn't have a rush for today. More like we had a rush on the phone for rescheduling all the canceled appointments."

"Well that's lucky. Did you enjoy the heat wave, Roman?" Kaya asked.

"Well it was certainly nice to get rid of a few layers. I was getting kind of sick of resembling the Michelin man." He shot me a lopsided smile.

"I can understand that." I returned the smile. "I had a funny moment with Cassie, this afternoon."

"Oh, really." Roman said.

"Yeah, really." I smirked. "See we weren't exactly aware of the heat wave. So when Cassie and I saw one of the owners walk into the clinic in a t-shirt, we kindda flipped. Then we found out what the temperature was and it made sense, but it was still mind boggling."

"Suppose that was a shock." Roman's response was sarcastic.

"Shock would be an understatement. Its been bothering me all day. Since when does a heat wave cause quite that dramatic a spike in temperature at this time of year?"

"Could be another part of the global warming impact." Tom murmured. We all went quiet as we remembered the scene with the shower the other day.

"Have you guys been able to find out much?" I asked.

"Haven't really had time to do much of anything that resembles looking. So that would be a negative." Tom answered.

"Same here." Kaya sounded regretful.

"That's okay, we'll have more time once this storm passes through. Then I'll be able to help." I took a bite of the food I'd scooped onto my plate while we talked. I tried the curry first. "Wow, Kaya, this is amazing."

"Thanks. It's a new recipe I found."

"Well, it's worth keeping." We ate in silence, once we'd started as if there'd been an unspoken mutual agreement to simply enjoy each other's company without the additional stress of words.

"Has anyone checked the news tonight?" Kaya pushed her empty plate slightly away from her.

"Not that I know of." I finished the last bite of nachos. "Should we turn on the TV?"

"Sure, we can have it on while I wash up." She said, about to push back her chair and rise.

"We're washing up, not you." Tom cut her off, by grabbing her plate out of her grasp as he stood. "You've done enough tonight. It's our turn." He turned to look at Roman.

"Right." Roman stood suddenly. "Our turn." He reached over to pick up my empty plate.

"Thanks." I smiled at him, thankful to be spared clean up duty after having spent hours in the basement with music scores. I could feel the headache brewing behind my eyes. "I'll go turn on the TV." I jumped up to leave the kitchen.

They were giving the local news report when I switched it on and saw the weather channel was already on. I sat cross-legged in front of the screen to wait for the weather report to begin. The anxiety I'd felt most of the day anticipating what was coming was less now, though I wasn't sure why. I'd learned nothing that would calm me, but somehow I was as I waited to see the answer to the question of the last two days: when the cold front was coming.

I sat up straighter when the weatherman came on and began to go through his usual routine in front of the blue-screen, essentially repeating what was on the map behind him. When they switched to the radar screen there, just above the Illinois border, was a cold front heading straight for Chicago was indicated in bold blue lettering. At first I watched the weatherman's blather in silence. Finally I heard something useful.

"The cold front you see here, is moving quickly slightly southeast towards the city of Chicago." He continued, but I zoned out. Instead I'd stood and walked slowly back into the kitchen; I didn't have to say a word. My expression seemed to say it for me.

"It's on its way, isn't it?" Roman asked when he looked over to where I stood by the table. "The cold front you've been waiting for. It's coming now, isn't it?"

"Yes and fast." It was all I could manage to say. I was in shock; stunned by the fact that things were finally happening. I hadn't dreamed this up.

Everything was white. Everything, confusing the mind as to up or down, right or left. Nothing was distinguishable, as if the world had suddenly turned into a blank sheet of white paper. I felt my feet move forward, or at least I thought it was forward, but I was barely conscious of it. It felt peaceful in a way that was foreign to my body. I lost track of time. The concept seemed unimportant in the blank space stretched out before me.

The change was almost imperceptible at first; it was so gradual, the incremental addition of grey to the picture, until the previously pure white was gone. Like an artist adding layers of paint to a canvas, thin lines of grey shades appeared in my vision. Shapes became roughly visible in them as they connected. I had stopped moving by this time, concentrated on the lines, and distinguishing the shapes. They became sharper under scrutiny, distinguishing themselves from the white foreground. They were buildings, I didn't know where, but I recognized their general structure as that of city buildings. It was as if I were looking out a window without having lifted the blinds.

A sudden shift in the foreground grabbed my attention. The white lines that had remained while the scene had grown up behind them broke up, but didn't disappear. Instead they shifted from lines into a series of tiny dots; making the image appear more like a high school art project than a window view. The dots continued to shift, not even remaining for a short while, just like the lines. Their shape morphed again into snowflake shaped specks; the subtle shape shifts continued without pause as I watched. The peace that had filled me until now fled; slowly emptying me of any sense of comfort as an intense feeling of foreboding took its place.

The shapes began to fall noiselessly in a continual stream, never accumulating anywhere, but still falling steadily from the top of my vision to the bottom. I looked down at my feet and was pleasantly surprised to find that I could actually see a pair of boots where my feet should be. I tried lifting them; first the right, then the left and then jumped straight up with both. They moved as I directed; so did the legs I saw were attached to the booted feet. Essentially, I could see my entire body. The white out was over.

The instant I realized the thought, everything went blank again. This time the peace that had filled the initial white out was nowhere to be found, and the sense of foreboding gave way to full on fear. I started to move again as if I were running both to and from something. I didn't know what I was afraid of yet. Just that there was something to be afraid of. I could feel the snow now as it fell; it accumulated around me as I ran, crunching under my boots. I didn't know where I was going, darting in and out of alleyways from road to road. Not stopping until I began to wonder if I was running in circles; finding my way more by sense of feel than sight, which only made me doubt my way even more.

I stopped, in the middle of what I thought was a street, my fear escalating to terror. It was accompanied by the nagging feeling I needed to be somewhere; that I was trying to get to a specific place, and needed to be there soon, or else something would go incredibly wrong. I started to spin around in circles, almost making myself fall over with dizziness. Finally I stopped and stood still again. The terror ate away at my nerves, making me frazzled and more anxious than ever to find my way to wherever it was I needed to be.

I dropped down on my knees, aware that my face was wet and that my shoulders shook with silent sobs. I couldn't find my way. Something was going to happen without me, and that caused me more pain than ever. It was as if I felt what would result from my inability to find my way. My sobbing intensified as a wind kicked up. It blew lightly at first, just kicking up the snow to let you know it was there, but it intensified with an almost supernatural intensity. Before I was even aware of it, my sobbing choked off, and I knelt in whiteness under the reign of terror.

Chapter 17 — Storm

Locked in the grip of the storm that raged around me, my mind raced. Unable to move my body I fought to figure out just what it was I was supposed to do. Where I was supposed to be. I knew both were important, but I couldn't see how or why. I struggled with it as whispers began to mix in with the wind; growing steadily from inaudible to crystal clear.

"Almost there." The unexpected words shocked me. I tried to whirl around, but my body still wouldn't move. I hadn't recognized the voice; it was bodiless, hollow, and yet full of an almost disgusting joy. I listened hard, trying to hear more over the wind.

"Ready darling?" The voice asked. This time I knew it was talking to me. Panic flooded and sent my heart into overdrive as anxiety and adrenaline pumped through my immobile body. I didn't even try to move this time, knowing it would be useless.

"I'm here." The voice taunted, almost as if a person stood right in front of my face. Now I struggled, the puzzle pieces falling together abruptly so that I suddenly knew exactly what was happening. My arms and legs moved mere millimeters, but I kept fighting, desperate to break loose. Finally I simply took a deep breath and screamed.

I felt my body connect with something hard, and my eyes flew open. I'd fallen out of bed again; Roman was sitting up in the bed, staring at me, a concerned look on his face. I closed my eyes again as the dream came flooding back; focusing on my breathing I fought to relax, organize my thoughts, and be able to speak. All the while I did this, Roman said nothing, just watched. I was pretty sure he had a pretty good idea of what had happened; either way I was glad that he let me be. When I'd settled my breathing, and my heart was back to it's resting rate I started to stand. Now Roman moved; swung smoothly and quickly out of the bed to help me up to sit on the edge of the bed. I didn't try to keep standing, experience had taught me that I wouldn't be able to stay upright after something like that.

"You feeling all right?" Roman asked after a little while.

"I'm getting there." I frowned, unsure anymore of what I should do. I wanted to run out of the house and try to find where my dream had taken place, wait for the voice to come. That brought me up short. I was supposed to be worrying about a storm, why was I suddenly more concerned about a voice in a dream? I shook my head. It didn't make sense.

"Hey? You still with me?" I heard Roman ask.

"I'm here, I'm fine." I mumbled.

"Okay." I felt the bed dip next to me as he sat down, and my eyes flew open - I hadn't even realized I'd closed them; no wonder he'd been asking where I was. I turned a little to look at him. He studied my face silently and I let him, wanting him to be the first one to speak.

"It's here, isn't it? The storm is here." His voice was hushed.

"It's almost here." I corrected. "It'll be here sooner than we thought." I sighed and turned my face back so that I stared straight ahead again. "We need to wake the others. It's time." The terror that had gripped me in the dream nagged at the edges of my consciousness. With an effort I pushed it away and stood; I didn't have time to waste on fear now, I needed to focus.

"Okay, let's go." Roman stood up next to me with his hand rested at the base of my neck in a comforting gesture. Without speaking we walked out of the room, moving quickly to wake Kaya then Tom. Less than five minutes later, the four of us sat in the kitchen yet again, and I was preparing tea.

"So, where do we start?" Tom asked when I brought the mugs over. "What are we going to do?"

"I think it's more a matter of what Roman and I are going to do now." I went to get my mug; I hadn't been able to carry all four at once.

"If you say so. What can we do to help though? I mean, you can't be thinking that we'll just sit around and wait for you two to take care of the situation, are you?" I smiled as I sat and listened to his rapid-fire questions.

"Well, you sound excited." Kaya teased from her seat next to him.

"What?" He raised his hands in a questioning gesture as he looked sideways at her. "This is what we're here for right? Children of the Earth? What good are we if we don't do something? We're hardly meant to just sit on our asses every day of our lives." He picked up his mug and tried taking a sip; he made a face when it burnt his mouth.

"Well that's a fair point for why you three are involved." Roman joked. "Me - I just follow Lisbeth here." He pretended to fade into the background.

"Like hell do you follow her anywhere." Kaya admonished. "You might as well be one of us now." Her voice was so low when she spoke those last words that I had to struggle to hear the whole thing. What I did catch made me smile. It would make sense for the soul mates of the old souls to be a part of their group; otherwise, what was the point?

"I'll second that." Tom said a moment later.

"Same here." I looked over at Roman. His face was beet red as he stared into his mug, steaming on the table.

"Here is what I'm thinking." I turned back to the more pressing topic to take the pressure off Roman. "Roman knows a place in the northern part of the city suburbs. I propose for the two of us to go there, with the music. You two can stay here, watch the weather report, keep us posted, that kind of thing; we'll have cell phones with us."

"That's assuming the storm doesn't manage to take some of the cell towers with it, of course." Roman chipped in.

"Well, we'll be able to use them at the start anyway." He looked less embarrassed now when I glanced over at him. "I don't really think there will be much that either of you will be able to do. I mean, the dreams and everything, have been coming to me; so I'm pretty sure I have to be the one to face it."

"Not alone." Roman said. I smiled and grasped his hand in mine.

"I wish there were something we could do." Kaya muttered. "It'll be hard to sit here while you're out in it. Which reminds me, you'll need to dress warm." She looked at.

"My stuff should fit close enough." He'd gotten the hint. "You know, my stuff I wear for on the job in winter." I nodded. "Roman, you have your own things from work, right?"

"Yeah, I'm all set in that area."

"Just let me know if there's something you need." Tom looked Roman up and down, smirking. "That is of course, if any of it'll fit."

"Hmmm... that might be an issue - pipsqueak." Roman punched Tom playfully on the shoulder. Kaya and I burst out laughing; sometimes they could be such men! It never ceased to entertain; even when I was as stressed as I was right now.

"Right, if you two are finished, why don't we get moving? I don't think we have that much time." I stood, hoping the others would follow my lead.

"What was the dream about, Lisbeth?" Kaya had asked the question. I took a moment to compose myself, hoping she wouldn't see how disconcerted I was on my face, before turning around.

"It was a repeat of the second dream, of the storm." I simplified. "Just a little more detailed." I remembered the snow, the buildings, the voice.

"Oh. Okay." I had a feeling she didn't quite believe me. It didn't surprise me, you couldn't hide much from Kaya; but I was intensely thankful she'd chosen not to push the subject at the moment. I'd tell them what had really happened in the dream after we'd dealt with the storm, maybe by then some things would make more sense.

"Right." Tom stood to follow me, taking a sip from his tea in the process. "Let's go get you suited up."

His enthusiasm made me smile, as I followed him to his room to get the clothes I needed to borrow. We would be inside for as much of the storm as possible, but I was going to bring my violin as well, just in case something made us take things outside. I wasn't sure why I thought that could be a possibility, but I did. My arms full of long underwear and UnderArmor©, I made my way up to my room to change. Tom and I had agreed it would be best to err on the side of too many layers than too few, so I would be wearing what amounted to about three layers, plus my own windproof running pants and heavy winter jacket. Then of course my own hat and gloves, though I would probably need a headband as well to keep my ears from freezing off in the wind, since my hat wasn't the most windproof.

"Oh, hey." I walked into my room to see Roman was changing, too.

"Hey. All set?" He looked at the bundle in my arms.

"I think so." I dumped my load on the bed, and started stripping out of my pajamas, replacing them first with the long underwear, then the UnderArmor. I was already feeling warm by the time I put on the third layer.

"You ready?" He sat on the bed, already finished dressing.

"I think so." I pulled a wool sweater over my head. "You look like you are."

"Yeah, pretty much. I wasn't referring to clothes, Lis." I sighed and looked up at him.

"I know you weren't. I'm...ready, I guess. I think mechanical might be the more fitting adjective, but I guess ready works too."

"You don't have to do this you know."

"Don't I? Don't I have to do this? It's like Tom said, this is what we're here for. What am I here for, with the abilities I have, if I don't use them to help?"

"Yeah, I guess you're right. I guess I'm just...nervous? Scared even?"

"Don't be. What's the worst that could happen?"

"I'm not sure I want to know the answer to that." He touched my cheek gently with his fingers.

"We can handle this. You know we can. Don't stress over it so much." I tried to reassure him, but it was hard to do when you didn't actually feel that way yourself. Something about the voice I'd heard in my dream told me that there was more behind this storm than any of us realized. That knowledge frightened me more than a little.

Roman's truck flew down the highway, oblivious to the 65mph speed limit; his speedometer pushing about ninety. I didn't watch the road, trusting him to get us where we were going, and counting on the fact that it was four in the morning to help us avoid any cops with radar guns. The last thing we needed was to get pulled over just now. I had my eyes glued on the window, watching the sky as we drove. It was remarkably clear given the temperature had dropped considerably from the heat wave we'd had during the day; still no signs of cloud cover to alert us to the pending storm.

My violin and Roman's guitar were in their cases behind our seats with my bag of music: our weapons of choice, if you will. We didn't have music or even the news on the radio this time, both of us too stressed and focused to listen to anything. As we drove my mind raced over my choices for music, trying to sort out where and how to begin. I wasn't quite certain how this was going to work. At first I'd figured it would be a simple matter of picking the right winds at the right times, and blowing the storm to pieces, but after my dream, I wasn't so sure anymore. Now all I was sure of was that this was going to be an extreme test of my abilities, with who knew what results.

"Hey, you all right?" I blinked, surprised by the words after the long silence.

"Yeah, I'm fine. What's up?" It had took me a moment to figure out what he'd asked.

"Good, because we're almost there." I looked back out the window, but at the road this time, noticing for the first time that we weren't on the highway anymore, but in a residential area.

"Hey, where are we?" I was confused.

"It's a small place just down this road. Bar - Restaurant kind of thing; friend of mine from the undergraduate days family owns it."

"Hang on. Did you call and ask them about this?" I remembered we hadn't exactly been to this place before.

"I talked to them as soon as you agreed to work from here. I figured sooner would be better than leaving it 'til later. Now I'm glad we did. I wouldn't exactly fancy calling them up with this request at two in the morning." He made a face that made me laugh.

"No, I wouldn't want to do that either. Its why I asked." We lapsed back into silence as we pulled into the parking lot of the tavern. It looked like a nice place, family oriented. We both took our time getting out of the truck, pulling out our instruments, and making our way to the main entrance to the building.

"Where'd you get that?" I asked when I saw him pull a key out of his pocket to unlock the door.

"I picked it up from them when I was out on a call yesterday."

"But you didn't even ask me about coming here until last night." I was confused again.

"I know." He grinned.

"You didn't call them last night, did you?"

"No. I didn't; but can you blame me?"

"I guess not. Still, it would've been nice to know, you know." I complained as we walked into the building. The piano was easy to find, tucked neatly into the corner beside the bar. We dumped our things on a nearby table and went to lift the lid from the keys and test them out; I was pleased to find it was a well-tuned instrument. That done, I turned to get my violin out of its case. No point in waiting; there might not be time later, and I would regret not having it ready if I needed it.

"We've got clouds starting to darken the northern horizon." Roman said abruptly.

"I know." I said in a dead voice. "I can hear it already."

"That strong, hunh?"

"You could say that. Ugh, I've left the music in the truck." I said in disgust. "I'll be right back."

"Okay." I could tell he wanted to say something, but I didn't give him a chance as I walked out the door to the truck. I was sweating in my layers, but as I walked to the truck I noticed that the temperature had dropped again so that I was barely comfortable in spite of them.

I'd gotten the bag out of the truck and was walking back towards the building when the volume of the storm suddenly cranked up in my head; the sound of the orchestra in the wind stopping me in my tracks as it started to take control. Panicked that I would be paralyzed and unable to help before the storm had even reached us, I looked over at the window, but Roman wasn't standing by it anymore. Then the grip of the storm tightened, and I couldn't even think to yell for him let alone make my way inside. I could still see and understand what was going on, but doing anything about it was impossible. It wasn't until Roman appeared suddenly in the driveway that I realized I was singing.

The look on his face was almost comical; it was so contorted with what I guessed was fear. He all but ran to me across the parking lot. The wind thankfully not strong enough yet to stop him from moving; he reached me quickly, saying nothing as he scooped me up and carried me into the building. I was still unable to speak, or even move, when he set me down in a chair inside. I watched his mind work as I sang, trying to think of something that would give me back control of my own body. He reached for his guitar, strapping it violently over his shoulder as he grabbed a score from the bag he'd taken off my shoulder. I'd stopped singing momentarily at this point, though only because there'd been a change in the music.

The instant that he played the first chord, I felt a change; felt the different pull on my core as he played from the score he'd picked. By the time he'd reached the third chord I could tell my control had returned, though the music still played in the back of my mind, the volume had turned down to a more tolerable level. The instant I detected that change, I stood and all but ran to the piano, grabbing my bag of music as I went. I shook my head violently at Roman when he tried to stop playing. I had a feeling that the instant he did we'd be back where we'd started, and I didn't need to look out the window just now to see that our time had run out. The blizzard was all but on top of us, and moving fast.

"Even if you have to keep playing one chord over and over again, do it. I don't know for sure, but there's a really good chance that the moment you stop, I'll be back in the storm's control. Got it?" I said once I'd reached the piano and started playing.

"Got it." He returned to his own score.

I'd picked a score from the top of my pile, having arranged them in order from smallest to biggest, from top to bottom, so I could start with the least amount of strength and build. No point in starting with the tornadoes, if they didn't work I'd have nothing bigger to try. I listened to the music from the blizzard in an effort to pick up on its movement as well as determine how effective the southern winds I was playing were on it. There was a minimal break in the music, almost inaudible. I tried to keep the break in my own playing to a minimum as I pulled another score from my bag, and began the process again. I listened closely to the storm as I played. The second score had a more discernable effect on the blizzard, but not enough, so I switched again. The third score was the same: more but not enough. I'd reached my fifth score and was getting anxious by the time that I actually felt any kind of break in the storm.

The shift was gradual, barely even noticeable at first, but eventually I could feel it. Of course by now I could see the effect of the storm through the window, the snow from the blizzard creating the white out from my dream in the space outside the building. Happy with the effect that my southern winds were having on the northern ones of the blizzard, I added in eastern and western ones of the same caliber in an attempt to spread out the storm and its massive amounts of snow. I felt the goose bumps on my skin before I heard the voice; my heart nearly skipped a beat at the familiarity of it, sickeningly casual.

"There you are, Lisbeth. I've been looking for you." My head whipped around, the voice had sounded from near the door, and just managed not to stop playing. I could feel the storm react more dramatically now, splitting and spreading slowly away from the city.

"I'm sorry, I didn't realize you were." My voice was too sweet; the woman standing in front of me, snarled, or something like that.

"Like you didn't know." She mocked; her voice malicious. "You going to tell me Mom isn't sending you dreams anymore?" That caught me off guard, and I stopped playing abruptly, stunned. She grinned, but it didn't reach her eyes. Roman had slowed his playing, making me look over at him in concern. He couldn't stop. Catching my eye he picked up the tempo again, and the pull on my core regained strength. I ignored his shocked expression; I'd have time to explain it all to him when this was over, or at least that's what I told myself. I wasn't so sure now that I knew this woman was real.

"Clearly we have some catching up to do, sister." She hissed and I knew I'd guessed right. "Maybe we could start with an introduction, perhaps? Let me start. I'm Lisbeth Moore. Its nice to meet you." I kept my manners light, not wanting to acknowledge the gravity of the situation just yet, though I could feel the storm rebuilding in my head as we talked.

"Ashlin Tiernay. Wish I felt the same way. Can't exactly say I'm all that thrilled to meet you. If I had it my way, neither of you would even exist." She looked Roman and I up and down. I didn't respond, not wanting to rise to the bait. "Surprised? Thought so. Mom has gotten so lax in the last few centuries, then again she never was that huge a help with anything."

"That would depend on how you expect her to help."

"Well if you consider distorted dreams help, then maybe she is. Personally I don't like to think that hard to get my answers. You know what I mean?"

"I think I catch your drift." I shot back sharply, eyes narrowing as I started to get an idea of where this was going. "So what's your specialty then? Clearly something brainless, I mean, if you don't like thinking this job can get a little rough." I watched her face go red at my sneer. Good. I wanted her angry; it might give me an edge. Instead I felt the storm outside pitch faster, more violently; I took the hint.

"See that's where Mom went wrong with you lot; this specialties thing. Don't get me wrong, it can be useful; but don't you ever get sick of watching the others do things you can't?"

"No, I can't say that I do." I said slowly, confused.

"See, I don't have a specialty. I can do everything; everything that all of the rest of you can do, just in one person. You see, I was the first, you know out of all of us. Supposed to be the only one, too. But Mom got nervous; too much power in the hands of one human. So she created you and the others, dividing what she'd given me between the three of you. Let's just say she's been paying for it for millennia." As I watched her face I could almost feel the pleasure she took in that last sentence. It almost made me sick, as I understood.

"What, the spoiled brat can't share?" I said after a moment with hard won smoothness. She hissed softly in response.

"You don't understand." Her voice was low, menacing. I wondered if I'd somehow managed to push her too far. Though I had to laugh a little to myself; her blond, Barbie doll looks were almost comical when she got this pissed off.

"Oh don't I? I think I can understand the words "power hungry bitch" pretty well, don't you, Roman?" A plan fell into place as I pushed her even further.

"I suppose you think you do." Ashlin hissed out, her gloved hands curled into fists. Then, so suddenly it caught me off guard, she smiled. "What was I thinking? Of course you'd understand that. About as well as I suppose you'd understand hundreds of people freezing to death during a record setting blizzard, followed by the deepest freeze to hit the city of Chicago since the Ice Age." Her smile twisted cruelly.

"I understand the words. I'll never understand the motive." I clipped out as I lifted my violin and bow from the table I'd conveniently left it on next to the piano.

"Softie." She snorted out. "No, I guess you wouldn't understand that part. You don't even realize what you're missing."

"Nor would I want to know." I muttered to myself, knowing she'd hear it anyway. I still had the melody from the score I'd been playing from in my head, playing in opposition to that of the blizzard.

Ashlin's face went blank as I lifted the violin to my shoulder, clearly displeased with the action, but unsure how to deal with it. With a deep breath through my nose, on the exhale I began to play with a renewed sense of urgency. The reaction from the blizzard was almost instantaneous as it began to break the way it had been before I'd been interrupted. Ashlin's face became suddenly livid, and I felt resistance in the storm. My instinctive reaction was to step into the pressure, to try and push it away. The result was me walking, with steady and determined strides, directly at Ashlin where she stood in the doorway. Open doorway I now realized as she began to back out of it.

Urgency and stubbornness filled me, drove me to push back at her and the blizzard. They made me oblivious to the white out when I was suddenly through the door in the wind and snow. I could just make out her shape in the white, her black clad figure standing out just enough that I could pinpoint her location. The storm stayed the same for what felt like forever as she and I battled within it. Neither of us gained or lost ground. We were too closely matched.

Two things happened almost simultaneously. First was the scream: the same high-pitched whistle I'd heard in my dream, resounding in my head; I knew she heard it too because I heard her laugh. Something snapped in me just as the second thing happened: Roman stopped playing. The blizzard didn't even have a chance to retake control of me as fury ripped almost painfully through my body. That was Mom's scream. The image of her when we'd last spoken filled my mind so that I could almost see her in front of me; her face full of exhausted pain. It was Ashlin's fault. In my fury my bow and fingers flew over the strings, fueling the music with fresh energy, and burning away any remnants of control the blizzard might have had over me, or been regaining. It was as if the storm had burst, like a balloon or a bubble, it was gone that suddenly. With it went the scream in my head, replaced with a new one: Ashlin's.

"Nikolous!" I finally figured out what she was screaming. The snow was settling, the weak rays of dawn filtering in from the east through the last flakes settling on the ground. "Nikolous!" Ashlin continued to scream, looking at something just beyond me.

Just behind me was what appeared to be a black mass writhing in the couple feet of snow that had fallen. I blinked, trying to figure out what I was seeing. Then it hit, why Roman had stopped playing, he'd been attacked. It was Roman there in the snow, well into a fight with a man I didn't recognize, but guessed to be the Nikolous that Ashlin was screaming about. As we watched, Roman pinned the smaller man to the ground, panting as they stilled.

"Roman!" I yelled when I was sure it was okay to distract him. His head whipped around to look at me. The fury I saw there mirrored what I had felt only seconds before. It made me smile. "It's gone. The storm is gone. Still panting he didn't say anything, just nodded, and turned back to the man he'd pinned.

"So you broke up my blizzard; so what?" She'd walked over to stand next to me, about ten feet to the side. "What? Do you think that that's the end of things? That was one storm, Lisbeth. Don't get your hopes up." The last thing I heard was her laugh before I saw her do something no human should be able to, or at least not that fast. In a matter of seconds she managed to shove Roman to the side, pull Nikolous up into her arms, and vanish. Without thinking I just screamed.

"I'm going to kill you!"

"You've already tried." The words cut me off short with shock, her voice echoing out of nowhere. "See you later Sis." I was speechless, completely lost as to what had just happened. Then I saw Roman, and broke out of the trancelike state as I ran to him, violin in hand.

"Hey, are you okay? You're not hurt are you? What were you doing, fighting with him?" The questions flew messily out of my mouth as my hands flitted over his face, shoulders, arms and chest, checking for injuries and reassuring myself that he was okay. Suddenly he pulled me sharply against him so that I lay on top of him in the snow and I was silenced by his kiss.

"You're ok?" He pulled away a short while later. "The storm, it didn't take control of you again? How? What happened?" He asked as he skimmed his hands gently over my face.

"I don't know. I just, snapped I guess. I heard Mom screaming in my head, and just couldn't handle it anymore, knowing who was doing that to her." I shrugged. "What about you? Why were you fighting with that Nikolous guy?"

"I caught him sneaking up on you when you'd gotten through the door. He had a knife in his hand, so I jumped him. I think the knife is buried in the snow somewhere around here." He started searching the snow around where he'd been fighting.

"It's okay... leave it..." I started to say when I heard my cell phone go off in the restaurant. I'd left it in my jacket pocket, which I'd taken off before starting on the piano. Leaving Roman where he was I went to get it. It was probably Kaya having a heart attack over what was going on. "Hello?" I answered.

"Lisbeth? Lisbeth? Is that you?" As predicted, Kaya was freaking out. I felt a grin slide slowly over my face, and then I started to laugh. "Hey! Lisbeth, you okay? What's so funny? Hey? What's going on?" Kaya asked from the other end, sounding confused.

"I'm fine." I said mid-laugh. "I'm fine, really." I tried to stop laughing, but just started up again. Finally I managed to settle down enough to talk. "Kaya, we're fine. We managed to break up the blizzard, and we're fine." I started to look around us, finally taking in the amount of snow that had accumulated. "I think it's going to take us a while to get home though."

"Oh thank God!" I heard her exclaim. "The weather has stayed on, and they're saying that snow plows are at work already, but that it'll take some time. You know, they're not exactly used to this kind of accumulation." I smirked; no one in Chicago was used to this.

"We'll just sit tight here until they get them cleared enough for us to drive home." I glanced over at the truck where Roman stood scraping snow off the roof. "On second thought I think we'll be spending that time shoveling out the truck."

"Buried?"

"Just kinda. Kaya, I'll keep you updated okay? Everything is okay though, so you can calm down."

"I'll wait for that until I see both of you in front of me with my own eyes, thank you very much." I smiled. Typical Kaya.

"You do that then, and we'll see you when we see you. Call if you hear anything-important okay? We're going to have a lot to talk about when we get back."

"Right. Get back ASAP."

"We'll try. Bye."

"Bye." I closed the phone and turned to walk over to where Roman stood, just looking at the truck. "Hey, you all right?" I wrapped my arms around him from behind.

"Yeah, I'm good." He held out a fisted hand. "I found the knife." He opened the hand to reveal a collapsible hunting knife. I gulped. If he hadn't jumped Nikolous... I didn't complete the thought.

"Thank you."

"You're welcome." He smiled at me over his shoulder, and pulled me around so he could hug me back.

"Let's go inside for a bit." I suggested after a minute. "I'm starting to get cold."

"Ha, ha. Okay. It is a bit chilly, isn't it?" He teased.

"A bit." I smiled up at him. "I love you." I said before we turned to walk inside.

"I love you, too." He said when his eyes met mine, smiling.

We walked the short distance back to the restaurant, wading our way through the snow. When we got inside, we busied ourselves putting our instruments in their cases, returning music to my bag. We worked in silence, neither of us ready to talk about what had happened with Ashlin. So when we'd finished with organizing that, we simply carried it all out to the truck, storing it inside before setting to work on digging it out from it's snow trap. When I checked my watch after we'd dug, with our hands and a small shovel Roman had had in the bed of the truck, it read seven o'clock and the sun had risen. I didn't check it again until we heard snowplows headed our way. It then read 12:37pm, and we'd been sitting, radio on, in the truck for about half that time, after we'd finished digging enough snow out that we'd be able to reverse out of the lot.

We waited until we'd seen, not just heard a plow go by the street the parking lot was adjacent to, before we actually tried to reverse. It took a further twenty minutes to successfully make our way out of the parking lot; once we were on the road, driving slowly, we wound our way through the freshly plowed streets. It was nearly dark by the time we pulled into our own driveway at last; Kaya was running for us the moment we'd parked in the driveway, Tom close on her heals.

Chapter 18 — Inconclusive Answers

"Kaya, I swear we're okay." I said for what felt for the millionth time. "No frostbite. No hidden wounds of any sort."

"Okay, okay, I get your point. I'll back off." She raised her hands in surrender.

"Thank you." I took a sip of the tea in my hands. "So, now we've told you our part of the story, let's hear yours."

"Hang on a second. I have another question." Tom interrupted.

"Okay, shoot. What?"

"I'm still confused. I mean, how is it that she exists and yet none of us know about this? Not from memories, not from Mom, nothing. And yet she appears to be the greatest threat to everyone on this frigin' planet. How does that work?"

"Ah, now that would be the very question that I've been trying to answer myself for the last several hours." I replied. "When you figure it out let me know."

"Right. Have you had any ideas? Any at all?" He pushed.

"No, I actually haven't. Well besides the fact that it's possible it's been shut out. You know, like selective memory or something like that. Probably not on Mom's side, but for us it's possible." I shrugged. "That's been the only theory I've come up with so far."

"Judging from how you described her, I'm pretty sure that's what I've done. Who wants to remember such a bitch?" Kaya muttered over her tea. "Who turns on their own mother?"

"You'd be surprised what some kids will do to their parents." Roman said flatly.

"I'm sure you're right." Kaya conceded. "I just have a hard time imagining it, I guess. I'm so close to my family."

"Hey, I'm not that close with my mom, but I'd never do something like this to her." I burst out.

"None of us would." Tom agreed. "Then again, we're not exactly talking about a human mother here are we? Mom is on another level."

"That doesn't change the relationship." Kaya said petulantly.

"Either way, Miss Barbie is acting this way. So maybe we should just set that down as a fact, no matter what we would do ourselves and move on?" I said loudly.

"Was she really that gorgeous?" Tom asked. "I mean, you keep referring to her as Miss Barbie, so?" He shrugged.

"Try this: tall, golden blond, blue eyes, red lips, perfectly slim and curvy body, and wearing heavy duty winter gear while still looking like a supermodel. Get the picture?" I said bluntly, not taking any pleasure in the memory of Ashlin. It left a sour taste in my mouth.

"Got it." Tom mimed a salute that made me snort. He'd gotten the point all right.

"So, what are we going to do?" Roman asked. "I mean obviously we can't just sit around and wait for Ashlin to strike again. I mean, we've seen some of what she's capable of conjuring up, and judging from what she said herself, I have a feeling it's only gong to get worse." No one answered. "We should probably at least try to think of what we could do. Don't you think?"

"I think you're right." I agreed. "She's not finished with us."

"I'm actually getting the impression that she's got the three of us pegged for some reason." Kaya mussed. "Its like she's not just getting her revenge on Mom, but on us as well. You know what you mean?"

"Yeah, I get what you're saying." I said.

"I'm getting that impression as well, and I haven't even met the woman." Tom said. "Its like we're missing half the story, like it's something we just didn't get told about, but now its becoming important again. Do you know what I mean?"

"You mean like its been omitted from the history books?" Roman tried to clarify.

"Exactly." Tom agreed emphatically. "That's exactly what I mean."

"I have an idea." Kaya stood abruptly to dig a paper and pen out of a drawer by the phone. She scribbled something down quickly before sitting back down and looking around at the rest of us. "Let's make a list. Questions, facts, things we're confused about, that kind of thing. Then we can contact Mom and ask, or at least present them to her, you get what I mean? Maybe now that we already know she'll be able to tell us. You know, like we have to figure out most of it on our own, but she can clarify, maybe?"

"Not a bad idea." Tom and I said simultaneously and smiled.

"Where should we start?" Kaya asked.

"Let's start with listing the things we know about Ashlin." I suggested.

"Okay, that'll be all you, so shoot. I'll write." Kaya agreed.

"She has the combined power of us and the rest of the Children of the Earth. She can move incredibly fast. Is capable of being heard as if in echo when she's not even standing next to you. She has a vendetta against Mom because she wasn't the first and the only one of us; not to mention that she split her powers between the rest of us. Roman, can you think of anything else?" I asked when I came up short. Was there really so little information?

"Well there's the fact that she's eerily beautiful and has a rather homely boyfriend." Roman said sarcastically.

"Whose name is Nikolous." I added.

"Oh wait, they're married not just dating." He corrected.

"How do you know that?"

"I saw the wedding band and engagement ring underneath her glove, and then I saw his when we were wrestling." Roman shrugged. "And yes, his name is Nikolous, but what was the last name? She gave her full name when she introduced herself."

"Ummm...." I tried to remember.

"Started with a T, I think." Roman tried to help.

"Tenay? Treney?" I threw out.

"No those aren't it..."

"Oh, got it. Tiernay!" I snapped my fingers as it hit me. "That's what it was. Tiernay."

"Ashlin and Nikolous Tiernay?" Tom sounded suspicious.

"Yeah, why?"

"I've run across the names before. That's all." He answered vaguely.

"Work?" He nodded. "Can't share?" He nodded again. "Okay."

"So what should we list next?" Kaya asked then. "That is assuming that's all we know about those two." No one said anything more. "Right, so what next?"

"Well let's write down Global Warming; we know she's involved with it somehow. Or at least I think we can know that for sure." I suggested.

"Well that would actually make some sense." Tom chipped in. "I mean, its like what I was saying before, we're here for a reason, right? To help. So if she's causing problems that we have to fix, then isn't she really the trigger? Not the global warming?"

"That does make sense." Kaya agreed.

"But if that's how it works, then why haven't either yours or Kaya's gifts changed?" Roman asked. "Why just Lisbeth's?" The three of us exchanged a look.

"We actually don't know if theirs will change, too, or not." I said softly. "Mine might just be the first one to change. There's still time for theirs to do the same."

"I guess you'll find out, hunh?" He nodded his head.

"I guess we will." Tom muttered.

"Anything else?" Kaya asked again.

"I'm not sure. What else do we need to ask Mom?" Tom and Kaya exchanged a look. "What?" I pushed, curious.

"We took the time you guys were gone to finally get started on some research, you know about the global warming and such, like you asked us to." Tom replied.

"Okay, but what does that have to do with talking to Mom, precisely?"

"What we found didn't completely fit. Like that the ice break you found and thought had caused this storm, wasn't actually big enough to cause a problem." Kaya explained.

"So then why would I connect it with the blizzard?"

"That's what we couldn't figure out, but that was before you told us about Ashlin Tiernay." Tom's eyes were on Kaya.

"It would probably be a good idea to see if she can tell us anything at all about Ashlin in general. No matter how simplistic the information she give us, it might help." Kaya watched Tom, too.

"So you think that Ashlin is the real problem behind all this?" I asked bluntly, making them both look at me.

"Well, not exactly, but in the basic sense, yes." Tom said.

"Okay." I sighed. "Wow. How did life get so complicated suddenly?"

"No kidding. What happened to the days where all that mattered in life was good beer, food, family, and a good woman?" Tom said in an exaggerated wistful tone.

"Is that what used to matter in the old days?" I asked him. "I thought it was all about cleaning up after the men. Didn't realize there was anything pleasant involved with it." He threw a piece of napkin at my head, but I ducked, laughing. "I'm kidding, I'm kidding. Truce." I ducked as more napkins came my way, pretending to try and hide under the table and making everyone crack up. Finally I surfaced, grinning and happy to have lightened the mood.

"Okay, you done being two year olds you two?" Kaya demanded as she struggled to keep a straight face.

"No, but that's okay." I pretended to pout.

"Right, let's go try and get in touch with Mom." She stood, then stopped. "Oh, Roman…" She trailed off as she looked over at him.

"That shower is calling my name." He answered without having to be asked. "I'll be at least as long as it takes you three to have a chat with dear old Mum."

"Thank You." Kaya started to walk around the table again.

"Thanks." I whispered and kissed his cheek as I went to follower her. He squeezed my shoulder quickly before letting me go, the gesture made me smile. I really did love that man.

Roman headed up the stairs to the bathroom, as the three of us walked into the living room, forming our habitual circle on the rug seated in a cross-legged position. We waited a moment once we were seated. Exchanging nervous glances; Kaya had the sheet of paper with our list situated in front of her. Though we already knew she wouldn't be using it - Mom would know already what we'd written there. After a few moments of this, we took a deep breath together and closed our eyes. Within seconds we were each deep in meditation, the time and practice making it more than simple to simply fall into the exercise, despite the fullness of the day.

"Stupid girl can't get over her mother's one mistake. Millennia later, she still reacts the same way." We heard Mom's voice complain before she appeared. Her dress was a deep green, and it wasn't the only thing different this time. Her face was not even pretending to be serene, or emotionless, as it had been in almost every other meeting any of us had had with her. It was filled with pain, her eyes brimmed with it, dark circles beneath them and a frown etched around her mouth. Her shoulders hunched ever so slightly as if she'd been carrying a great burden. "It is time that I gave you all some answers. The answers I have longed to give you, but could not, and I am sorry for that." She paused a moment before continuing. "Your relationship to Ashlin is one that, as its creator, I am not able to tell you. For reasons that I will never be able to reveal, it is a relationship that, for lifetime upon lifetime, you will have to figure out for yourselves, no matter how disastrous that may prove." She closed her eyes as if she were trying to stop herself from doing or saying something.

"To begin, Ashlin is the first of my children; the eldest. As the eldest, she was given more gifts than any other; a mistake I did not realize at first. It was not until she had lived her first three lifetimes that I came to see that I had given her too much, but by then it was too late to change her. At that time, and for reasons I will not reveal, I created the three of you. You are the second eldest. Yes, you are the same age." She smiled then for the first time in her visit. "Between you I split the power that I had given Ashlin, though that was not her name then. You are already aware of what you were each given. I then turned you out into the world, hoping that I had perhaps gotten it right this time." She frowned again. "I wish I could say I had, but I can't. The rest of my children I then divided even more minuscule, so that none of them

were too distinguished in their gifts, yet still capable of extraordinary things."
She paused, looking pensive.

"Ashlin never forgave me for the rest of you." She said after a short
while. "She has always been jealous. Unable to share power with others. A
consequence I suppose of always having so much. She is incapable of being
happy with what she has as the eldest and most powerful. Creating her as
such was my one great mistake." We saw tears well in her eyes now, though
she quickly closed them tight in an effort to stop them. "She's been punishing
me for millennia for that mistake. Global Warming isn't entirely what people
think it is. It's not a new phenomenon. It is ancient; building and building
over the centuries. It is her punishment for me, and every one of her lifetimes
she pushes it further, and further with the intent that it will someday destroy
me, and all the rest of you. Even if it destroys her, too." This time we saw the
tear escape down her cheek. She paused for a while this time; took the time,
it seemed, to control the tears. Her body was rigidly still with emotion we'd
never seen in her before, and in my case had only felt.

"I can't tell you exactly what her gifts are, only that she is more than
simply the three of you combined. Something I see that you, Lisbeth, have
already realized. It would appear that she has also already informed you of the
ban I created when I became aware of her vendetta against you and myself. I
can confirm it then: you may not intentionally, or unintentionally, kill another
of your bothers or sisters, or their soul mate. I do not mean that you cannot be
killed, simply that it cannot be done by one of your own." Her eyes became
more serious than sad. "No matter what you do to me, I will love all of you
until the end of time. I am your mother, no matter who your human family
might be, and that bond is stronger than anything else that I might feel."

"That said, I must impress one thing upon you. If you want to preserve
this earth and all things living that inhabit it, then Ashlin and Nikolous must
be stopped." She stopped to take a deep calming breath before continuing.
"They have become, over the centuries, the antithesis of what I originally
created them to be. Ashlin in particular is becoming more and more ruthless
in her tactics. I'm sure you noticed, Lisbeth, when you spoke with her. Things
were not quite right." She sighed. "I wish that were able to tell you something
more definitive than that, but I cannot. What I can tell you, however, is
something equally important though of a different origin." She smiled.

"When I created you, I did not intend you to live among humans only to
battle your sibling. In fact all of you were created with a very different intent.
You were to be my Peace Keepers. The intermediaries between humans and
the earth they inhabit. Lisbeth, yours might seem more obvious now than
the others as my music intermediary. You could either help or hinder humans
in their relations with the weather or the other animals you share me with

through your musical gift. I did not originally give you the gift of storm manipulation, only that of hearing the music within them. It can now be seen that Ashlin's actions have forced my hand, changing that fact without my knowledge.

"Thomas, yours is the calmest of the three gifts, and perhaps you think it is the least important. Never let yourself believe that. Your ability to converse with my green children, the plants, will forever prove useful, even in a concrete city. Then of course there is that green thumb of yours that has been saving endangered species of those children for centuries on end. I can't tell you what change will happen with your gift, and even if I knew I wouldn't be able to.

"That is the same for you Kaya, my dear. Though your gift is already incredibly powerful, as Tom has been saving my green children, you have been protecting my non-human children from the very beginning. You have prevented many an extinction, as you already know. Whether it be in your cooking or in your healing, never forget who you are. Modern society might force you to hide, but do not let it stifle you. You will find there are more ways than you think there are to help, even in the twenty-first century.

"I must go now, my children." She paused for a moment, her expression much warmer than when she'd arrived. It was as if her speech had released something in her, at least momentarily, and she was at ease again for at least this brief while. "Do not forget what I have told you. Keep your eyes and ears and minds open every day and every night. Dream freely, live freely and do so together: as Children of the Earth. My children. My Peace Keepers."

None of us spoke as we opened our eyes and came out of the meditation. The room was silent except for the sound of running water from Roman in the shower upstairs. We sat unmoving in the circle and soaked up the silence, staring at the carpet, lost in thought. It was as if we'd been re-awakened; our gifts new to us even after nearly three years of living with them. There was so much to think about, to absorb and try to accept. The sunlight faded as we sat trance-like, and eventually even the shower water stopped flowing. Still we sat. Lost in thought; lost in a world that, until three years ago, hadn't existed, and now we were lost in it.

We sat like this for what felt longer than it was, before we looked at each other, first one of us and then the other looking around at the other two, and exchanged looks that held more meaning than any word could have. There was no need to speak; we understood each other. The gist of that understanding being: so be it.

And so we begin again.

Made in the USA
Lexington, KY
28 November 2011